THE Next PHASE OF LIFE

A NOVEL

Dear Reader:

Out of all of the letters that I have written to be placed in front of titles that I publish thus far, this one brings me the most pleasure since the author, Charmaine R. Parker, is my older biological sister. We come from a family of writers—stemming from our parents—and this novel is long overdue. As the Publishing Director of Strebor Books since 2001, Charmaine has been an integral part of developing our stable of authors. She has been their sounding board, shoulder to lean on, and supporter throughout the entire process of bringing their books to life.

In *The Next Phase of Life*, Tai has recently turned forty and she is dealing what every woman deals with at that age—particularly the ones who are not married and who have yet to have children. She and her friends have to deal with the realization that roughly half of their expected life span is over. But instead of settling down and acting like they are too old to have a good time, they opt for the polar opposite and have the time of their lives.

When Tai's long-lost sister, Trista, contacts her on Facebook after decades of separation, Tai is excited about reconnecting with her slightly younger sister. Even though they both are committed to bonding with each other, they have grown up in completely different situations, which serves as the catalyst for drama, confusion, and eventually revelation. *The Next Phase of Life* is a book about friendship, love, and facing immortality with style.

As always, thanks for the support shown to the Strebor Books International family. We appreciate the love. For more information on our titles, please visit www.zanestore.com and you can find me on my personal website: www.eroticanoir.com. You can also join my online social network at www.planetzane.org.

Blessings,

Zane

Zane
Publisher
Strebor Books
www.simonsays.com/streborbooks

ZANE PRESENTS

THE Next PHASE OF LIFE

A NOVEL

CHARMAINE R. PARKER

STREBOR BOOKS

NEW YORK LONDON TORONTO SYDNEY

Strebor Books
P.O. Box 6505
Largo, MD 20792
http://www.streborbooks.com

© 2011 by Charmaine R. Parker

ISBN 978-1-59309-372-3
ISBN 978-1-4516-0806-9 (ebook)
LCCN 2010916639

First Strebor Books trade paperback edition July 2011

Cover design: www.mariondesigns.com
Cover photograph: © Keith Saunders/Marion Designs

10 9 8 7 6 5 4 3 2 1

Manufactured in the United States of America

For information regarding special discounts for bulk purchases, please contact Simon & Schuster Special Sales at 1-866-506-1949 or business@simonandschuster.com

The Simon & Schuster Speakers Bureau can bring authors to your live event. For more information or to book an event, contact the Simon & Schuster Speakers Bureau at 1-866-248-3049 or visit our website at www.simonspeakers.com.

DEDICATION

To my parents, James and Elizabeth, for emphasizing the importance of education and exposure; for being positive role models; for demonstrating the true meaning of family and friends. Your love is endless. I love you for being you.

To my husband, Ricardo, thank you for your love and support.

To my daughter, Jazmin, you are truly a blessing. I am proud of your accomplishments. Continue to strive and your dreams will become a reality.

To my sister, Zane, who would've thought when you asked me to edit the manuscript for *Addicted* that it would become a No. 1 bestseller? Or that a decade later, you'd evolve into a nationally bestselling author of twenty-five-plus books? Congratulations on your success.

To my sister, Carlita, a superwoman who mirrors many lifestyles as a wife and mother of four who has a full-time career.

To my brother, Deotis, may you rest in peace.

ACKNOWLEDGMENTS

I'd like to thank God for providing me with good health, mind and spirit. Through You all things are possible.

To daughter Tangela and your daughter, Savannah, hugs and kisses.

To Aunt Rose, you are truly the epitome of someone with an incredibly giving nature. Your kindness is appreciated. You have been blessed to live ninety-three years young. May you continue to experience great health.

To Aunt Margaret, you are a wonderful aunt and mother. You and Aunt Rose represent North Carolina royally: kind hearts and good cookin'. My memories will always be cherished.

To Grandma Cardella, rest in peace. You were such a positive influence for all of your grandchildren. You were the pillar of the community and we loved you dearly. Despite your blindness for decades, you showed that you could be strong without sight. How you could make cakes and braid my hair and tend to all of your plants was amazing.

To all of my grandparents, you were special.

To my in-laws, Richard and Pearl, thank you for treating me as your own. To brother-in-laws, David P. and Jerry.

To my brother-in-law, David M.

To Sharon, since age thirteen, we have called each other "bestest" friend (you say I created that word). Although the distance keeps us apart, the bond continues. Your sisters, Lisa and Gail, are like my sisters and we all grew up as family. To your brothers, Gabe (rest in peace), Bruce and Khris.

To my "girls" ("Hey, girl"), Rhonda and Lena, we've celebrated years of camaraderie after meeting in elementary school. We've come a long way and I've enjoyed every minute of our friendship. We share a unique bond.

To my friends (there are so many; please forgive me if I didn't include you as it was not intentional), Donna, Susan, Mamie, Sheila, Cheryl, Teri, Tomi, George, Rico, Joyce, Yvette, Patricia, Maria, Pamela, Ardith, Deb, Noelle, Ola, Sandra, Eddie, Sheree, Bobby, Dwayne, Kirsten, Lee, LaRee, Vicki, Reggie and Sharon J. Denise D., may you rest in peace, girl.

To my L.A. friends, Joyce and Curtis, China, Carolyn, Ruth, Diane and Sharon.

To my nieces and nephews, Andre R (you were like a son during childhood; thanks for being like a brother to Jazmin), Elizabeth, Jaxon, Jewell (rest in peace), Arianna, Ashley, David, Aliya, Andre J, Jonathan, Nicolas, Zachary, Malik, Greg, Stephanie, Brandon, Danielle, Aaron and Audrey.

To my godson, Brian, and his brothers, Adam and Nicolas.

To all of my extended Sherrill family. To George K for starting the reunion, and his wife, Mary.

To cousins Percy, Franklin and Alan, you are truly like brothers. Carl, you are a gem. Fidelina and Terry, Ronita, Debbie, Beverly and Nick, Francesca, James (rest in peace), Gloria Jean, Janet, Karen, Tomi, Derek, Shirl and Ed, Jackie, Tamu and Dean, Isha, Zakiya, Rashida, Sunday, Kwesi, Dana, Jimmy, Mercedes, Melinda, Stephanie, Gregory and many more. To the "younger cousins," Trey, Bo, Alex, Brittany, Benza, Karlan, Dean, Ray-Ray, and all of the others too numerous to name.

To all of my extended Roberts family. Lewis (you left us in D.C. to return to N.C.), Erica (much success on your new Asali Yoga Studio in Harlem), Sheilah Vance (congratulations on your success as an author and publisher: the Elevator Group; it's running in the family.) Dennis, great connecting with you.

To my "new" family, on the Parker and Brooks sides. Aunt Pat, you always remember the special occasions. You do too, Aunt Mary.

To Aunt Barbara Ford, you are full of advice and wisdom.

To Aunt Olivia, you were a joy. You always said I'd someday write my own book. I always remember your words about life: "If you ain't put nothin' in it, you ain't gonna get nothin' out of it." I can hear you laughing now.

To Uncles T, Carl and Cecil, thanks for your kindness. To aunts Jennie and Cle.

To my sisters' close friends, Pamela C., Destiny, Pam, Cornelia, Dawn, Sharon P., Wanda, Debbie, Dionne, Tinera and Charisse.

To the Strebor authors. As publishing director of Strebor Books, I have enjoyed working with you. Welcome to the family. Allison Hobbs, Rique Johnson, Dywane D. Birch, J. Marie Darden and William Fredrick Cooper; I appreciate your friendship. New and veteran authors Suzetta Perkins, Lee Hayes, Harold L. Turley II, David Rivera, Jr., Marsha D. Jenkins-Sanders, Rodney Lofton, Michelle Janine Robinson, Sonsyrea Tate, Che Parker, Dante Moore, Curtis Bunn, Earl Sewell, Oasis, Timothy Michael Carson, Thomas Slater, L.E. Newell, B.W. Read and J. Leon Pridgen II. There are so many of you and the list keeps growing.

To Keith Saunders, your talent is appreciated. Thank you for your photography and design of our covers for Strebor. You are awesome. To Deb Schuler, thank you for your efficiency. You are the ultimate layout designer. It has been a pleasure working with you both. I value our rapport as friends as well as business associates. Strebor is blessed to have connected with such professionals.

To my friends from the journalism world, Toni, Denise, Cheryl, Sunni, Richard, Ita, L'Taundra, Michael and Chris. Keep on writing.

To my dear friend David Mills (HBO's *The Corner, Treme*), you were a talented writer and your memory will linger forever. We know you're enjoying P-Funk heaven.

To fellow authors, I've met many of you through the years at Book Expo America and book festivals. Congratulations on your works.

To the HBCUs, particularly my Howard U. alumni; the North Carolina Central University crew (the fun continues); and Spelman, my sisters' former home. A special shout-out to Morgan State University.

To book clubs for showing your support to authors and appreciation for the written word.

Pleasure 'n' paradise

Tai glanced at the nightstand clock: It was close to midnight. Eager to escape, she gingerly arose from the soft satiny sheets, peeping at her bedmate who was in a deep slumber. *I'm on this beautiful island and it's way too early for me to turn in*, she thought.

There was little time to worry about hooking up pieces for a sensual outfit; it would be quicker to grab a dress—one of her hot numbers. She pulled a fire-red jersey wrap sundress out of the closet and quietly headed for the bathroom. She analyzed the persona reflected in the mirror. Here she was in St. Maarten and confined in a hotel room with a grumpy ex-boyfriend. *Boring* wasn't the word for Vince; he was the king of Lazyville. After they'd had a rendezvous—a quickie—he had done the usual: drifted to sleep in record time.

Tai had buzzed him a few months ago on the relationship rebound. He immediately had agreed to take her to the tropical retreat. She wasn't looking for love; only a travel escort.

She was still recuperating from the grave disappointment of a no-show. Tai had celebrated her fortieth birthday with a big bash when her longtime beau, Austin, decided to pull a disappearing act. After envisioning them as a standout couple on her grand night, when all eyes would be on them, he was nowhere to be found. Tai was forced to celebrate her four decades solo. She had spent months planning the party of 200 invited guests at the

Grand Hyatt in downtown Washington, D.C. Valé, her fashion designer friend, had created a black and gold, form-fitting, one-shoulder dress to show off her curves that she had managed to maintain at her milestone age. Tai was proud that she had held on to her youthful figure and had no problems flaunting it.

Throughout the evening, her guests had continuously inquired about Austin. The duo had been joined at the hip like two peas in a pod. Now, on her special night, he was ghost. Maybe her occasional comments about turning forty being synonymous with marriage had scared Austin. After all, so many brothers shied away from the ring on the finger. However, Tai felt assurance that Austin was ready to settle down after their five-year relationship. She now presumed *commitment* wasn't in his vocabulary when it came to a walk down the aisle.

Despite her constant calls, emails and texts, Austin had failed to respond; she snipped her sweating-a-guy behavior. At forty, she shouldn't chase after any man! Who the hell did he think he was anyway? The chocolate-skinned, baldheaded and dapper attorney was rolling in the looks and intellectual department. But the disappearance proved that he lacked dignity and respect when it came to their relationship. Pulling out on her with no explanation was surely immature. *Oh, well, it's his loss*, she thought. *Moving on…despite the pain and ongoing heartache. Can't let this man continue to play ping-pong with my emotions.*

Tai reached for the washcloth and freshened up, ensuring that the water ran lightly. She slipped into the little halter dress that lifted her 40-Ds and accentuated her curves. She dabbled on foundation and applied eye shadow and mascara, then searched her makeup kit for her favorite lip gloss. She sprayed on Halle Berry Reveal perfume and then turned to get a full-length view in the mirror on the bathroom door. She slipped into her black strappy heel sandals. The red dress complemented her honey complexion; she was pleased with her late-night look.

Tai peeped into their luxurious suite and Vince was like a statue. He had shifted slightly but not enough to awaken. *Boy, I must've put a whammy on him*, she thought. *He's sixty, but damn, he should have a little bit more stamina.*

Tai had dated Vince briefly when she was in her early thirties. Her associates, not her close friends, had considered her a gold digger. But she refuted, saying that she was attracted to Vince despite the age difference; it wasn't for his wallet. Yes, he was wealthy, a surgeon with a mansion in Beverly Hills and the ultimate bachelor. His sprawling spread was a fabulous six-bedroom resort with an indoor and outdoor pool, tennis court and a full gym. It was a fitness guru's paradise and Tai ensured that she took advantage of the amenities. She and Vince would work out on the weights and treadmill and then she'd whip up health-conscious meals in his huge gourmet kitchen.

Tai had met Vince during one of her business trips to L.A. when she was a marketing representative. The two became travel companions and their getaways were mainly on the West Coast: from bed and breakfast inns in Santa Barbara to shopping in Carmel to views of the Golden Gate Bridge in San Francisco. When Tai desired to escape to the islands after Austin's disappearance, she had thought of Vince. Now she was in St. Maarten at the fabulous Sonesta Maho Beach Hotel and he was snoozing in sync with the sounds of the flat-screen TV.

She tiptoed across the room and opened the door, being careful to close it securely behind her. She strutted to the elevator; feeling uplifted and ready for whatever was in store. When the doors opened, she stepped inside and headed to the lobby. The outdoor café beckoned.

Tai spotted a barstool where she sashayed toward and pulled it up to the bar. Scoping out the scene, she noticed that tonight's crowd was thin. It didn't matter; she was simply trying to chill and forget about the whole Austin saga. Sure, she was forty and eager now to find a "Mr. Right," if one existed, but meanwhile, she was in paradise.

"Hey, sweetie, what can I get you?" the charming bartender asked, flashing a Cheshire cat grin.

"I'll take a pomegranate martini. Please make it stiff."

"You bet."

The sounds of Maysa blared through the speakers. Tai loved neo-soul music; it always placed her in an upbeat mood. She absorbed the atmosphere on this moonlit night. A slight breeze was comforting and offered relief from the steamy sunshine that had blanketed the small island during the day.

It was Tai's first visit to the island known for being Dutch on one side and French on the other. Earlier that day, she and Vince had driven their rented Jeep throughout the countryside. They had heard about a nude beach on the French side where they stopped to take in the sights. Of course there were visitors who had no qualms about showing their bodies; no matter their shape or form. Vince had encouraged Tai to shed her swimsuit and join the others, but she wasn't following the old adage: "When in Rome do as the Romans do."

SINGLES AND COUPLES WERE SCATTERED THROUGHOUT THE COCK-tail lounge featuring brilliant shades of turquoise, mango and fuchsia. The bright colors generated a feel of tropical living and created a lively ambience. Tai was enjoying the fruity flavor of her martini and was ready to order a second one. She stopped in her tracks when she locked eyes on a handsome islander. He commanded attention as his smooth cocoa complexion glistened under the low lights. His black button-down shirt showed off his well-chiseled chest. When he caught her look, Tai quickly turned her attention back to the bar scenery. She was slightly embarrassed but also pleased he had noticed.

"Hello, lovely, you sure are wearing that dress. It's on fi-yah." Tai jumped slightly as she was startled. The mystery man had made his way to the bar and was now overlooking her shoulder. "Hope I didn't scare you."

Tai turned and offered a sexy smile. "Oh, no...thanks for the compliment. I think you saw me checking you out."

"I did. What's your name?"

"Tai. And yours?"

"Carlton," he responded, rolling the "Carl" with his accent. Tai was admiring his full physique now that he was positioned close. "Care if I join you?"

"Please..."

Carlton sat on the barstool next to her. "What would you like to drink?"

"Well, I just finished a pomegranate martini." Tai made eye contact and edged closer. "But now I'd like a Sex on the Beach," she said slowly and teasingly.

"Hmmm...cool," Carlton responded. "Eric, the lady wants a Sex on the Beach. And I'll take Hennessy and Coke," he told the bartender.

"Got it. Will make it *real* sexy."

"Where are you from? Here alone?" Carlton inquired.

"I'm from D.C. and yes, I'm alone...for the moment."

Carlton raised his eyebrows in curiosity but he dared not barrage her with more questions.

Tai had never tasted the cocktail, but tonight she thought it was fitting. The name itself conjured up images of how her body was feeling; she was starting to heat up down south. She squirmed on her stool as she crossed her legs.

She sure looks luscious in that red dress, Carlton thought. His mind drifted to Coco Brown and the Phat Cat Players… *Caressing you so close… Sundress…*

"This is delicious. Wow, I've never tried it but was always curious." Tai was enjoying her newly discovered Sex on the Beach. She was relieved to have met Carlton as she didn't want to spend her last night "alone." She didn't mind being restless; just not lying in bed next to a knocked-out lover with a TV watching *him*.

"What do you do on the island? It's such a beautiful place. I can't imagine working here. I'd be stretched out on the sand, laid back and soaking up the scenery."

"Actually, I'm in law enforcement. I'm a cop." Carlton cleared his throat. "Mostly undercover." He stared into her eyes. "But we like to let our hair down, too."

Tai grinned and twirled her stool to face him. "Oh, I'd better behave." She smiled and took the last sip of her drink. Her mellow mood blended with the light jazz. Carlton recognized she was relaxed, and he didn't want the night to end.

"Let's take a walk," he suggested.

"Why not? That sounds cool. It's such a pretty night," Tai agreed.

Carlton helped her from the barstool, admiring her vision of beauty. Now he really could check out the dress he was singing about in his head.

TAI'S AND CARLTON'S SHADOWS DANCED ALONG THE SOFT SAND as they strolled barefoot. The waves of the turquoise sea played their own melody, offering a romantic breeze. They continued to a secluded sandy spot hidden below a cliff overlooking the moonlit landscape.

Wow, now this is what I call paradise, Tai thought, then exhaled.

Tai dropped her sandals and her tiny shoulder bag as Carlton embraced her tightly. They kissed ferociously and groped each other with intensity. Peeling off their clothes, they discovered irresistible passion. Their nude bodies meshed as they lowered to the sand. And the moon radiated a magical love potion.

Listen and lunch

"Hey, girl." Nevada plopped down at the table and sighed. "This better be good. I was working on a new case when I got your text."

"Well, it's all good. I like sharing the crazy stuff. Thanks for stopping by." Tai always invited her best friends for lunch whenever it was time for girl talk. Actually, it was a couple of days early before their monthly lunchtime hookup. She was anxious to share her latest news.

Nevada, a journalist who had lost her newspaper job during the recession, had launched a detective agency, Sleuths on Us. She had received accolades as a star reporter who had won numerous awards, including one for breaking a community case. A local pastor had been brought down on pedophile charges as a result of her clever investigative work. A church member had sent her a letter at her newspaper describing the pastor's past life in South Carolina. He'd been investigated for molesting boys in his church there; and then he had relocated to Maryland. He had befriended three male teens that he later invited to stay at his home. They were all from troubled backgrounds and their parents had welcomed the idea of them living with a "concerned" and "caring" man of the pulpit. Nevada's instincts and journalism legwork had landed the pastor in jail.

A waitress approached. Her exhausted expression looked as if she'd been on skates for eight hours. It was only midday and she was scheduled until closing.

"Hello, I'm Mia. Do you ladies know what you want to order? Drinks maybe?"

"I'll take a glass of Chardonnay, please." Tai picked up the menu and flipped through the pages. "I'll need a few minutes. We have a friend on the way."

"Glass of Merlot for me." Nevada looked at the entrance. "Wonder where Candace is? She's always late."

"Got it. You should know the deal. Shopping, of course."

"Of course..."

Although Candace was the classic shopaholic by nature, she also was employed as a fashion merchandiser for Blitz, a chain of stores on the East Coast. She had graduated from Pratt Institute and was quickly recognized as one of the leading fashion representatives in the field.

Nevada glanced through the menu. It was her first time at Desiree, and it was rare that she could take time for a casual lunch on a weekday. But she always made it a point to appear for their monthly lunches. She was always hustling and chasing behind men for women with trust issues. From silver-haired wives in forty-year marriages to widows checking out new prospects to young newlyweds on rocky roads, Nevada's spy business was on the case. She rarely had time for a breather.

"Finally, I made it. Sorry I'm late. You know me; I had to check out the sales. Tai, why you always pick one of these downtown restaurants? You know I can't stay away from the stores." Candace sighed as she took a seat, dropping her multicolored bags on the hardwood floor. "It's on fire out there today. Whew."

Candace was geared for the sweltering heat in her Marc Jacobs orange-and-lemon sundress and Mario Valentino sandals. She exuded a model image each time she stepped out of her two-level Northwest condo. She looked like she had stepped off the pages of *Essence* magazine. From each hair in place to her glowing caramel skin to her pedicured feet of commercial quality, she ensured she was immaculate whenever she appeared. She was never caught without the serious hook-up, even if she were simply heading to the grocery store. *Hey, you never know who you might meet* was her philosophy. Candace was forever on the prowl for her man of the month. She switched men like most people changed clothes.

"I'm so excited I found all these bargains," she stated, full of her usual pizzazz. Candace reached down and pulled out a teal shirt and held it up, and then a pair of pewter-colored designer flats. Next she flashed a necklace and earrings she'd bought from a street vendor. "Love it." Candace looked at Tai. "So what brings us here?"

"Excuse me, what would you like to drink?" The waitress set the glasses of wine on the table and then turned her attention back to Candace.

"I'll take wine also. Riesling is fine. Thanks."

"Let's go ahead and order. I've got to get back to the office. I'll take the blackened salmon Caesar salad," Tai said.

"The chicken and dumplings for me," Nevada added, suddenly deciding to divert from her thirty-day diet. She needed some comfort food and wasn't feeling the light stuff. Her size-fourteen figure was always undergoing punishment.

"Hmmm…what do I have a taste for…" Candace perused the menu. "What about the shrimp linguine?"

"It's one of my recommendations. I'll be right back with your drink."

"As I was saying, how was Saint Maarten? I bet it was the bomb. You look well-rested. You needed that R and R, as hard as you work," Candace assured Tai.

Tai sipped her Chardonnay. "Girl, it *was* spectacular. We had a great time. The beach was gorgeous and so was the hotel. It was the ideal spot. Even gambled a little something-something." Tai laughed. "No luck there. Then we went to Cheri's to hang out and right up your alley, we shopped in Philipsburg. Talking about bargains. Check out my bracelet." Tai jangled her gold treasure. "But, hey, on the last night, well, it was…*wild*. I got restless hanging in the hotel room so I left to go to the lobby bar. Outside in the breeze—"

"You…alone? Can't believe you went to the bar by yourself," Candace interrupted.

"I did that night. I couldn't stay in that room any longer. It was so sweet of Vince to agree to take me to the islands. I needed to get away, so he cancelled a week of appointments with his patients." Tai sighed and sipped her wine. "Of course Vince didn't know I'd asked him because of that no-good Austin pulling that vanishing act. Vince was fun and not as stiff as he can be sometimes." She laughed. "He always did pick the best travel spots. He's a class act.

"But, girl, the last night was heaven. I met a local guy at the bar, ordered me a Sex on the Beach and before I knew it, I was *on* the beach." Candace's eyes lit up. "And got me some of that rod right there on the sand," Tai whispered like it was the best-kept secret on the planet.

"Oooo, no way…now that's my kinda girl." Candace giggled, commending her act. "You know me—crazy. I like 'em wild. Plus, this is like déjà vu…reminds me of Aruba." Candace had been a contestant on *Wild Isle*, a reality TV show where ten women had vied to hook up with five men. She'd enjoyed the six-week stint on Aruba until she was eliminated during the final episode. Her fondest memory was a hot tub scene where she and Marshall, a body builder from Texas, had poured champagne all over their bodies, then licked it off each other. They had fed each other chocolate-covered strawberries and then tongue-kissed until dawn.

"So how did you get away with that? Vince didn't question you? Weren't you nervous he'd find out?" Nevada shot off the questions; it was the journalist in her.

"Girl, he was knocked out when I left the room *and* when I returned. I was in heaven and so was he. My island man had a buff body; the bomb diggity." Tai laughed and savored the memory. "He was luscious. Mmm-hmm. I suppose I'll never see him again; only in my dreams…"

"Wow, he must've been hot, hot, *hot*." Candace's imagination was running rampant.

"Tell me about it. *Hot* wasn't the word."

Mia returned with their dishes. "Can I get you ladies anything else?"

"No, thanks," Tai spoke for the group, then returned to her hot topic. "Well, do you think it was cool? It wasn't like me these days. I've slowed my roll; don't care for the quickies too much. But I guess meaningless sex is okay now and then," she surmised. "I'm ready to connect with a new man, though…in a meaningful relationship."

"You and me both."

"You're always ready, Candace. You and your manhunts."

Candace took pride in her adventurous dates. "Actually, I have a date tonight. I met him today while I was checking out the shoe sale at Aldo. He's a salesman. I bet he has a foot fetish." Candace smiled mischievously. "I told him I like to have fun, so he's taking me to a comedy club. He wouldn't tell me which one so that'll be a surprise."

"You move fast. I'll be buried in my notes and going over my pics." Nevada pushed a heaping spoonful of dumplings into her mouth. "I'm working on a case with a widow, or at least, an *alleged* widow. Seems like movie material; she's not so sure her hubby is dead. Thinks he may have faked his death or something."

"That does sound like straight out of Lifetime. At least it's interesting. Why does she believe her husband is alive?" Candace scooped up linguine and twirled it around her fork.

"We all know that women have gut instincts, Candace," Nevada replied. "If a woman can sense when her man is cheating, surely she has a sixth sense about whether or not he's still walking the earth."

"Good point," Tai said, taking a bite of her food. "Sounds like an exciting case, Nevada. But, please, whatever you do, be careful."

Nevada giggled. "Now Tai, you know that if I'm nothing else, I'm careful. I'm going to crack this case though; no matter what."

Tai grinned at Nevada, realizing how determined her friend was to always get her way in life. If there was anyone who could find the missing man, it was Nevada.

"Let's eat up before it gets cold," Nevada suggested. "Besides, if we don't finish soon, Candace is going to spot a man and chase him out of the restaurant."

Candace rolled her eyes at Nevada. "Whatever, tramp."

The women all laughed and then enjoyed the rest of their meal.

Strictly business

"Good morning. Next Phase of Life. How may I help you?"
Noni answered from the posh fifteenth-floor office. "Thank
you. I'll transfer you to an employment specialist."

Tai walked briskly past the receptionist's area. Mondays were
always the busiest day of the week. Her black Christian Dior
pantsuit with crisp white collared shirt was complemented by
cheetah print pumps. "Do I have any emergencies?"

"No, not today. We have a lot of people calling in response to
the ad in yesterday's *Post*." Next Phase of Life was picking up
momentum since Tai had started the employment agency two
years ago. After graduating from the University of Southern
California with an MBA, she had returned to her hometown
brimming with ambition. She had aspired to become an entrepreneur in a few years. She had achieved her goal after a frugal
lifestyle of eating at home, maintaining her wardrobe and cutting
back on the nightlife. She had managed to pad her bank account
and amass a decent savings.

Tai took pride in screening her candidates that she accepted
and later sent on interviews. Felicia Brown was her right-hand
manager who ran a tight ship at the office, but also a confidante.
Often Tai shared stories about her personal life but sometimes
was selective about which ones. Felicia was fifty-something and
had grown up in Tai's neighborhood in upper Northwest. They

were old-school acquaintances and Felicia was more like a big sister to whom Tai could consult when she needed an ear. Felicia was always on the up and up with an ongoing positive outlook.

Tai entered her executive suite that offered a sweeping view of downtown D.C. She marveled at the scene of the Washington Monument and Capitol from her L-shaped corner office that exposed the city from various angles. She smiled as she thought about her island rendezvous. Kicked back in her chair, she turned on her desktop iPod and tuned in to Kem's latest single. She swiveled to gaze out the window and soak up the sunshine. Her office was in warm, calming colors of rust and cream. She was startled from her distant thoughts by a knock on her door.

"Come in." Tai turned to face the door. Felicia entered and closed the door behind her. Dressed in bold shades of green and blue, she was pumped up on this Monday. She walked over and sat in the overstuffed chair facing Tai's desk.

"Good morning. Did Noni tell you how the phones have been ringing like crazy? Absolutely everyone wants that modeling assistant position. It's different from our usual inventory, so I can understand. Also we've gotten a lot of calls about the cruise concierge. Who wouldn't want to travel the world? I'm excited about filling these jobs."

"Yes, Noni told me it's been busy. That's great. I'm sure we'll get some good candidates."

"So, how was your trip? You deserved a vacation, finally."

"It was relaxing. Beautiful place," Tai responded bittersweet.

"I was starting to get concerned about you, so I'm glad you got away. You gotta take care of yourself—mentally and physically. Sometimes it gets stressful but you know Noni and I support you a hundred percent." Felicia insisted, "You get your check-ups… but you were due for a head break, too. Austin not showing up for your party was a major blow."

"Right. Tell me about it…"

"Well, hang in there. We've got your back."

"Yeah, I appreciate it. I had lunch with Candace and Nevada last week." Tai tried to shake off her somber mood but was having a hard time focusing on her day's work.

"You're lucky to still be with your girls; that's a good thing. I miss my best friends from high school. They all moved away. I've connected with them on Facebook but I'd love to see them. I'm glad to have met you 'cause, as you see, I don't mix and mingle with too many sistahs. Too much drama if they're the wrong ones."

"You're right about that. I've been fortunate to maintain these friendships for so long."

Tai had met Candace at a high school dance when she was a senior and Candace was a sophomore. They both had been attracted to Trent Jamison, the all-star athletic specimen who had all the girls feening for him. They almost had come to blows but had realized it wasn't worth it; he wasn't interested in either one of them. He'd broken both of their egos when he'd left the dance that night with another chick. They'd been close friends ever since.

Nevada was working as a writer when she was assigned to do a feature story on young talents in the D.C. area. Tai had dabbled for a while in acting and had landed the leading role in the musical *Fame* at the Lincoln Theater. Tai's gifted voice soared as she lifted the roof with her soprano notes and nightly standing ovations. She performed for a year until the show closed and moved to Broadway. She elected not to accept the offer to continue with the show as she didn't want to leave her then-boyfriend, Torian, and head to New York. Reflecting on this opportunity twenty years later, she regretted that she had held Torian on a pedestal, placing her wayward ex before her career.

"Yes, we've been tight a long time. Sometimes it gets rough

and you need your girls. You need to have fun. It's hard for a woman these days; a lot of competition for jobs *and* men. But I believe in bonding. Maybe I should plan a ladies night soon. You'd better make sure you make it. And bring a friend." Tai rose from her desk.

"Sounds like a plan."

Her thoughts raced throughout her head as her creative juices stirred. She wanted to guarantee a fun evening. "Hey, let's make it a seventies party." She sat down, pulled out her notebook and started jotting ideas. In another life, she'd be an event planner.

4

The big throwback

T he strawberry incense permeated throughout the den lit by colorful votive candles strategically placed on the mantle. Magazines with reminiscent covers decorated the glass coffee table: *Essence* issues featuring Lisa Bonet and Vanessa Williams; '70s *Right On!* with The Jackson Five; and *Ebony* graced with the historically black college campus queens. Tai treasured her extensive magazine collection and had selected a mix to represent the mood of the evening.

Tonight, Tai's first level of her three-thousand-square-foot home in upper Northwest would be transformed into a '70s and '80s haven. Glass beads dangled from atop the entryway of the kitchen. A massive, multicolored neon peace symbol hung from the ceiling. Black light posters were plastered on the walls of her cozy den including those of Jimi Hendrix; a psychedelic maze; and her favorite: a chart of Zodiac sex positions. Tai had managed a collection of knick-knacks from her childhood era, many of which were thrift-store and Internet finds.

In her huge gourmet kitchen with stainless steel appliances and granite countertops, recessed lighting glowed upon black-and-white framed photos of film and stage goddesses Pam Grier, Lola Falana and Vonetta McGee. Tai had prepared a scrumptious-looking smorgasbord of her favorite dishes: Buffalo wings, spinach and cheese pastries, ground turkey meatballs, deviled eggs and shrimp puffs. Her best pound cake and peach cobbler also graced the counter. Tai was known for her baked goods and often received dessert requests from friends and neighbors during the holiday seasons. Baking was a hobby and she took pride in every savory moment.

Tai leaned on the kitchen counter island and took in her surroundings. The atmosphere oozed retro and she hoped that her guests would immerse themselves in her shindig. They would start arriving in about an hour. She'd made a conscious effort to invite friends and acquaintances whom had come of age during both eras. Despite her wish to find a replacement for Austin, her main focus lately was to bond with her girlfriends. Life was too short and women could always use an escape. She considered such nights as the optimum way to de-stress.

Tai headed upstairs to her bedroom. Her master suite was her oasis where she spent most of her time. Besides the kitchen, she rarely used other rooms except when she was entertaining. After stepping into the shower in her brilliant yellow master bathroom, she lightly scrubbed her body with oatmeal-almond exfoliator, followed by a lavender and chamomile wash to open up her senses and relax her mind. It would be a long night and she was excited that the ladies would be rolling in any moment. After drying off, she lotioned with a lavender-scented solution. She'd already picked out her outfit and had laid it across her king-sized bed. She pulled on a yellow and green, tie-dyed, long-sleeved midriff top and tied it. She was still able to flaunt her abs. Then she stepped into a pair of jean capris and black tie-up boots. Tai returned to the bathroom where she brushed on soft-yellow eye shadow and rouge on her cheeks. She put on large gold hoop earrings and then a wig with Afro puffs. Gazing at herself in the mirror, she smiled in satisfaction. She looked like she had stepped off the set of a blaxploitation movie. *Superfly* and *Shaft* had been her favorites; not to mention the fine-ass actors Ron O'Neal and Richard Roundtree. Tai reflected on her former crushes and how their good looks and the soundtracks were the highlights of the films.

"Girl, you did your thing. It feels like old school, for real." Nevada flaunted her bellbottoms layered with a dashiki. A black wood fist chain dangled from her neck. Red, black and green earrings complemented her straight-out-of-the-Black-Panther-era look. She recalled reading such novels as *Manchild in the Promised Land* and *Soul on Ice*. Her father, an African-American studies professor and blues musician in Chicago, maintained an enormous library. In high school, she would seek refuge in her home's basement and peruse his bookshelves for what later would be viewed as culture classics.

Candace was such a fashionista and bling artist. She made her grand entrance in a *Soul Train* image wearing an Afro wig, halter top, choker and twirled in a mini skirt to show off her toned thighs. Black knee-high patent leather boots completed her ensemble. "Where's Don Cornelius? Let's get this party started!"

Cori, her older sister, followed behind her wearing a black polyester jumpsuit with flared legs. A thick gold chain graced her neck and a large gold bangle adorned her wrist.

Sierra showcased her '70s flair in a snakeskin top, black bell-bottoms and platform shoes.

Felicia, who had been a teen during the '70s, was styled in a peasant dress and tie-up sandals. Multiple beaded necklaces hung over the scoop neckline.

"Ladies, here are the strawberry daiquiris. Let's toast to Ladies

Night." Tai circled the room and filled all the glasses. "Cheers!"

Ramsey Lewis' "Sun Goddess" blared from the iPod, followed by War's "All Day Music." Tai figured she'd start the flashback night with jazz and mellow music that reminded her of tuning in to WHUR-FM, Howard University's radio station. Back in the day, one could always discover the latest cool-jazz sounds.

"Oh, that's my song!" Cori was ecstatic. "That was the all-time cooling-out, chill-outside-on-the-blanket moment," she said of Maze and Frankie Beverley's "Happy Feelings." "Wasn't life so peaceful and laid-back then? Not all this crap we have to deal with now."

"No, I tell you what I thought was the best kick-back-and-relax song: 'Everybody Loves the Sunshine.' Roy Ayers." *Just bees and things and flowers*, Felicia sang and bopped her head. "You could sit back and groove with your dark shades." She laughed.

They sat comfy style on large fluffy pillows and munched on popcorn—not the microwave version but the old-style Jolly Time that you pop on the stove.

"I tell you one thing. We don't have album covers anymore and these CD covers can't compete. I lovvveeeddd the Ohio Players. Their covers were the best. What about *Honey* with the sister licking a spoonful of honey? Or the one with the bald-headed sister with the chain necklace?" Felicia reminisced.

"Right, and the guy positioned behind her with the dog collar. It was called *Ecstasy*. That was hot," Cori chimed in.

"And then *Fire*; the woman's wearing the firefighter helmet and holding the hose. They were ahead of their time. Erotic album covers. Now that I look back, I was young so I didn't realize the covers were provocative. I just thought they were *hot*." Tai sipped her drink.

"I'll drink to that." Felicia downed her drink; she wasn't fazed about the elegant glass or sipping in ladylike fashion. "Some of us," she cleared her throat, "old-timers remember the cover with the best-looking brothas of all time."

"Which one was that?" Cori laid down the coffee table book that she had been flipping through.

"Black Ivory! *Don't Turn Around!* Those brothas were phine, phine, *phine*. They all had the huge Afros and the one in the center had the most gorgeous eyes. Who were they anyway? Where'd they come from? They disappeared," Felicia gushed. "*Don't turn around 'cause nothing in the past will change,*" she sang. "I loved the falsetto on that song."

"And Isaac Hayes…that chocolate specimen with the bald head. And speaking of voices, his deep tone was soooo sexy. Mmm-hmmm." Felicia licked her lips.

"And, girl, what about slow draggin'?" Cori leapt to her feet and started grinding and gyrating her hips seductively. "I think that was a D.C. thing. Guys would wrap their arms around you, pull you tight and grind and grind. And sometimes, if you were lucky like me," she giggled, "they'd take you all the way to the floor." She laughed as she demonstrated by squatting to the floor as she continued to rotate her lower body and maintain her balance. "I always seemed to be the one to get those!"

"Right and it was bad for me because I didn't have a perm then, so my hair would be soaking wet and flopped by the time I left the party," Felicia added. "I don't know why I wasted my time worrying about doing my hair before I got there." She tossed her hand. "That was a joke."

"Even if you did have a perm, it would go flat. All that body heat working overtime," Cori agreed.

"Yeah, the good old blue lights in the basement," Nevada recalled adoringly. "If you liked someone, you could sneak off to the corner and grind and feel up on each other. Nobody cared."

"Speaking of corner, my favorite slow-drag record, and yes, *record* 'cause that's what the deejay was playing, was 'Stay in My Corner.' I thought the Dells would never stop saying, 'Stay,' and the song went on forever. But that was okay by me 'cause I was lovin' my bump and grind." Cori laughed.

"Mine was the Isleys' "Girl, You're All I Need." Another song that seemed like it would never end. And if you were slow dragging with a guy you liked, you didn't *want* it to end." Nevada reminisced about the popular ballads of the time.

"Or 'Love on a Two-Way Street.' The Moments," Sierra added.

"'Me and Mrs. Jones.' Billy Paul," Tai offered. "Better yet, Earth Wind and Fire. Philip Bailey could handle those high notes."

"The music was *so* tight. There were real musicians and real singers. You never forget those voices. They could sangggg," Cori noted. She was a true fan of the music era that summarized her youth. "Go even further back. 'Going in Circles.' Friends of Distinction."

Cori shared a story about how she and a friend had ventured off during a mountain hike in middle school. It was during a weekend retreat and they became separated from the group. Hours later, they were discovered by school personnel. However, the entire time they were lost, her newfound friend laughed about the situation, while she was nervous and on edge. The hit "Going in Circles" was on a jukebox in the mountain lodge and the two played the song continuously. They remained the best of friends.

"And ladies, getting back to the slow draggin', don't let them get a hard-on! You could really feel it since you were grinding," Felicia added.

"My older sister used to dance on *Teenarama*. You young-uns wouldn't remember that, but D.C. had its own TV dance show," Nevada informed. "I was little, and back in those days, we only had black-and-white TV. I remember the plaid skirts and sling-back shoes and pin-up hairdos."

Sierra looked at Cori. "Your house was the party house! We had some throwdown parties up on the hill." She laughed. "Remember the time your mom came home and cussed everyone out and shut down the party. That was hysterical."

"Yep, we always had the parties."

"Yeah, girl, and what about the day parties? Now those were coollll." Sierra reminisced about how she and friends would some-times skip high school and attend a party at someone's home. They all prayed that no one's parents would show up or find out.

"The concerts were cool, too. The old Capital Centre was the place. Then the free concerts on the Mall. Human Kindness Day with Stevie Wonder," Cori reflected.

"Yeah, but then one time it wasn't so kind. Folks starting tram-pling and then I saw someone hit a guy on the head with a bottle. That was crazy!" Sierra recalled.

"You were right about that. It got out of hand. But speaking of concerts, I know you remember how your mom used to get us tickets to all the shows. Lowe's Palace downtown. The Delfonics. Harold Melvin and the Blue Notes. We screamed our heads off, lost our voices and barreled to the stage to bombard them. They had the dance steps *and* the voices. Those were the days!" Cori relished the memories.

"We had a ton of clubs here in the eighties and nineties. The hangout was Mark IV, then RSVP, then definitely the Foxtrappe," Tai noted.

"Black Tahiti, LA Café, Cornerstone," Nevada added.

"But the hangout was Tiffany downtown. I miss that one.

Everybody was up in that meat market. And the Ibex, girl, we used to swear by that place. The male strippers were off the chain. I remember when my sister got married, my other sister and I went there to find a dancer for her bachelorette party. Folks are still talking about him twenty years later!" Sierra fanned herself from memories of the dancer's steamy, flip-you-up-down-and-around performance.

"Well, the Classics stayed open forever… It was also the cock-watch spot. Those dancers made me lose my panties," Nevada stated.

"Yeah, '*Panties.*' Tell them how you lost your panties, for real," Tai suggested.

Nevada laughed and sipped her drink. "You never let me live down that story. …One night I hung out with this brother I had met through a mutual friend. We hooked up and did a little somethin'-somethin' and when I got home I didn't have my panties!" She roared. "I guess I left them at his place. Now how I did that in the dead of winter and didn't freeze up there, I don't know."

"Girl, one time I had this boyfriend and I'm not sure how I ended up doing his laundry at my apartment…this was years ago…but when I was pulling his clothes out the dryer, there was a pair of panties! Of course, he acted like he didn't know whose they were…Yeah, right." Tai smiled.

"I know you almost died; how mean," Cori suggested.

"I'm sure he intentionally planted them. He ended up being an asshole. He had an ex-girlfriend—maybe they belonged to her—who was insane. Although I think he was a psycho, too," Tai continued. "She was like a fatal attraction. One time we were riding in his car in his neighborhood and she started chasing us like a madwoman. He was turning corners and rolling through stop signs running from this hussy. Then another time, we were actually lying in the bed in his place and she comes into the bedroom. You can imagine the shocked look I had on my face! Apparently, they had lived together and she still had a key to his place. Now that was *scareee*.

"Funny thing is she never said a word to me. She was crunking out on him. Weird…then she left suddenly…"

"Now that's how fools end up getting hurt! Good thing she wasn't violent," Nevada interjected.

"But she was crazy and so was he. I should have known something wasn't right about him. After we made love the first time, he came back and asked me to sleep with his best friend. That sucker! So that obviously meant he wasn't feeling anything special for me; if he wanted to share. Then again, maybe I can understand; this stuff must have been the bomb," Tai teased.

"Those panties in the dirty clothes was a trip. You never know what you might find. Tai and Candace, you heard this story before." Nevada turned to the others. "I kicked my ex-husband to the curb after I found a roll of film in his dresser. My curiosity was killing me so I took it to get developed. Nowadays everything's digital so you can delete whatever you want from the memory cards. But hey, check this out. There were photos of him having sex with a woman in the woods! Now that's some freaky shit. I couldn't believe it. He should've hidden that film better than that. Point is, seek and ye shall find."

"Maybe that's where you started your detective skills!" Tai noted.

"Well, since we're sharing these wild stories…I had come home on vacation and went to this club here in D.C. I was living in Miami then," Sierra stated. "Like you said, so many of the clubs were popular. I can't remember the name, but I think it was in the Adams-Morgan area. Anyway, this guy asked me to dance that night. We didn't talk; only danced. He was looking good so I don't know why I didn't hit on him.

"Then a few days later, I flew back home to Miami. I was at the airport waiting on my luggage. I look up and see the same guy that I had danced with at the club. Now what's the chance of that happening? We were on the *same* plane. We introduced ourselves and of course, we thought it was meant for us to meet again. Now at the club we didn't even say more than hi. So, at the airport we exchanged numbers and promised to stay in touch. He was in the service and was based hours away. He was cute, about six-four and seemed like a sweet guy. Since he was so far, we talked a lot, ran up our long distance bills. Then he finally returned to visit me in Miami.

"Girl, I put on my best lingerie. Then I slipped my Luther CD in the boombox. I was so, so ready for this fine-ass brother. His body was like that.

"But, hey, when he pulled his Johnson out, I almost gagged and passed out. I must've looked like I wanted to choke. I thought, *that's going inside me*?! No way! It was humongous; must've been thirteen inches. I'm not sure if he picked up my expression but I ended up taking it in like a champ…I won't lie, it wasn't the most comfortable, but I hung in there. Whew!"

"Yeah, I had one of them Brontosauruses, too. Loved it, loved it. He was my big ole' chocolate Tootsie Roll pop. I licked it all night long," Candace shared.

Laughter permeated the room. "There is such a thing as *too* big," Cori suggested.

"Right! He told me about some woman who had no problem handling it. She must've had a gigantic twat," Sierra teased.

"Y'all are crazyyyy!" Nevada screamed.

"I've been telling you to come to ladies night. We always have a blast," Tai noted.

"Right. I needed to get out. When I left home, Ryan was stretched out on the recliner watching ESPN. If I'd stayed, I would've had a date with Lifetime."

"I always have dinner dates with Lifetime Movie Network; my favorite," Cori admitted. "Tai, you said we were going to watch some movies tonight, too."

"I'll have to go dig them out later. I didn't get a chance to find them. Let's eat. I fixed a bunch of food."

"You don't have to tell me twice." Nevada wandered toward the kitchen. Others followed to dig into Tai's treats, then returned to the den.

"You've been kinda quiet, girl, and we know you have some stories," Nevada told Candace.

"I'm a late-seventies, eighties chick myself," Candace responded. "We were disco divas." She started twirling around. "Donna Summer was the queen."

"My favorites were 'Boogie Nights' and 'Boogie Oogie Oogie.'"

"Then it was Prince, oh, yeah, and Rick James' Super Freak."

"I used to see Rick at the clubs. He was hanging out like everyday people in L.A. And back then stars didn't always have an entourage," Cori stated. "Osko's was the rage on the West Coast; and Studio 54 was the place to be in New York. The good old disco days. I had an opportunity to experience both clubs."

"'Le Freak' by Chic was my favorite song," Candace shared.

"Yeah, you a chic freak, all right," Tai teased.

"Well-deserved—clothes and men are my *thang*," Candace admitted.

"Okay, Candace, tell us about the Grand Caymans," Nevada urged.

Candace preferred men with unusual tastes and professions and Nevada was aware of many of her adventures. "Well, ladies, and Nevada, you and Tai know this story… I was dating this guy who was president of the Black Scuba Diving Club. His name was Tony and he was also a diving instructor. He invited me to go to the Grand Cayman Islands. They say that's the best place in the world to scuba dive in the crystal clear waters."

"Yeah, I actually snorkeled there on a cruise stop a couple of years ago. Took a chance seeing those stingrays. You couldn't help but think about the guy who was killed by a stingray," Sierra interjected. "But they seemed so tamed, domesticated like you were invisible to them."

"Didn't see any stingrays 'cause I didn't even get off the boat. I was trying to look my best, so I wasn't *thinking* about getting this hair wet." Candace brushed her curls to the side and smiled. "Ladies, this man was fine in that black scuba diving suit. Hmmmm-mmm. When he emerged from that water, he didn't take off his suit. We were on a rented yacht, so we laid right there on the deck and made love, honey. Right there in his suit and all!"

"No, way…what did that feel like? That wet and sticky up against your body?" Sierra inquired.

"Right, did I hear 'wet and sticky'? Did any of you ever hear about folks who are into latex? That's what it reminded me of. Later, he took it all off and we made love again on the deck under the moon."

"Rock the Boat," Nevada teased.

"Yeah, who sang that one?" Candace tried to recall the artist. *"Our love is like a ship on the ocean…"*

"The Hues Corporation," Tai responded.

"Right. I knew the name wasn't that easy. Wonder why a business name?" Candace asked.

"Speaking of names and flashbacks, what about how the brothas went by three names? Think hard. Who was one of the finest actors back in the day? Hint, he had a beautiful wife," Nevada asked.

"Dunno," Candace responded.

"Remember Leon Isaac Kennedy? Married to Jayne Kennedy."

"Oh, yeah, he was fine," Cori noted. "I tell you who I was in love with: Mario Van Peebles, Melvin's son. That movie, *Sweet Sweetback's Baadasssss Song*, brings back memories."

"*She's Gotta Have It* was my flick. Spike Lee set it off with his independent film in black and white. Just loved it!" Candace shared emphatically. "He was set for success."

"Okay, if we're going to keep talking about movies, then I'd better show my DVDs after all. What about *Car Wash* and *Cooley High*? Okay with you ladies?"

Tai headed up the stairs to retrieve the movies. The mellow flow of her '70s night would continue with an all-night filmathon.

Hot and bothered

5

The July midday sun was blazing and the temperature had climbed to a blistering ninety degrees. The forecast had cautioned residents of the D.C. area, known for its humid summers, to stay inside as the "Code Orange" air would be unhealthy. Tai had heeded the warning, although she enjoyed hanging out on Saturdays in summer; particularly the evenings when she'd frequent outdoor cafes and live-jazz lounges.

Tai had prepared a salmon Caesar salad and a fruit medley of grapes, strawberries and cantaloupe. Her lunch would be a welcomed treat as she'd had an exhausting week. A slew of new clients had contacted the Next Phase seeking mid-summer hires; many were seeking high-schoolers and college students. Her business was flourishing; it was the only African-American-owned employment agency in the city.

Tai took pride in her flower gardens. Her home, situated on a corner lot, was enveloped by flowers. Marigolds, geraniums and petunias lined her front walkway and her backyard deck featured plants in bright, ceramic pots. Her passion for outdoor entertaining led her to host cookouts. Neighbors would get a whiff of the barbecued chicken, grilled shrimp and turkey burgers she'd prepare on her deck.

After finishing her lunch in her den overlooking the backyard, she glanced out the window. Her landscaper, Marco, was the consummate custodian of her blooming sanctuary. He had arrived for his regular monthly visit and was planting perennials. Tai took a deep breath and did a double-take.

Marco, apparently finding the heat unbearable, had stripped off his white tee and stood wiping his forehead. The sun glistened on his mocha chest, showing off his abs and bulky pectorals.

Wow, he must stay in the gym when he's not digging in somebody's yard, Tai thought. As the sweat dripped from his chest, she imagined gripping on to this hunk of a man. *Oops, no, not the landscaper...not my type. Plus, I wonder how old he is; looks like a baby.* However, her alter ego was luring her mind in another direction. She arose from the sofa and sauntered to the huge floor mirror in the hall. She adjusted the tie-back on her lime-green halter and mischievously rolled up her jean shorts to reveal more of her thighs.

Tai opened the French doors to her deck off the den and stepped outside. Looking over the balcony, she called in a faux innocent tone, "Hi, Marco, looks like you could use something cold to drink. Why don't you take a break and come inside?"

Marco looked up hesitantly, slightly embarrassed that he had been caught bare-chested. This was the first time that Tai had invited him inside her home. He had always been curious to see her taste beyond the foyer; he'd figured that it was exquisite if it paralleled the outdoors of her home. He had worked as a landscaper for five years and had maintained her yard for two. Marco agreed, thinking he could use a respite from the roasting heat. He picked up his T-shirt and pulled it over his head. He had given Tai a picture show she couldn't release from her mind.

Marco mounted the steps and entered the den from the deck.

"Please, have a seat." Tai motioned for him to sit. She picked up her remote and clicked on the forty-two-inch, flat-screen TV. "Be right back."

Tai later returned with a tray of homemade strawberry lemonade and freshly baked brownies. She set the tray on the coffee table and then sat on the sofa. Directing her attention to the TV, she channel-surfed before stopping at a baseball game; the Nationals were playing the Braves. "You a fan?" she asked.

"Definitely. What made you think I liked baseball?"

"Only a guess." She reached over to pour two glasses of lemonade and handed him one.

Marco sipped. "This is really good. Just right; not too sour and not too sweet."

"Thanks. I love to create my own drinks...and bake. Try a brownie."

Marco took a bite. "Hmmm, this is great."

"Glad you like it." Tai felt awkward making conversation with Marco. She'd never thought twice about him, other than paying him for his gardening services. "How long have you been with ...?"

Marco smiled to himself. All of his customers thought that he was the landscape worker; he was actually an entrepreneur and owned Clean Cut Gardening. He liked to keep it that way; let them believe that he was an employee. He had already now broken his policy of not socializing with his customers. He was kicked back, sipping lemonade and munching on brownies... all a no-no in his book. However, it gave him an opportunity to marvel over his client's interior design skills: her complementary wall colors, sleek upscale furniture and eclectic style of art.

"I started with Clean Cut about five years ago. When I was a kid, I earned money in the summer cutting grass. My dad kept lawnmowers in our garage and kept my brother and me busy in the neighborhood. So I've been working outdoors a long time. Eventually, I taught myself more about landscaping and later, horticulture. I love working with my hands."

I bet you do.

"Well, you do a great job around here." Tai paused. "What do you do when you're not outside?" Tai fished to see if Marco were married. He wasn't wearing a ring but she was aware that many men in his line of work didn't when working with tools. "I imagine you and your—"

"I'm alone; no wife, no kids." Marco finished her thoughts.

"Oh, I see…" She was pleased, but managed a demure expression.

"I'd better get back on the grind. Thanks, I enjoyed that," Marco said as he rose to return to his gardening tasks. He turned to walk out the patio door.

Tai checked out his jeans from the rear. *He's got swag, too. What have I been missing? Must've had my mind* and *eyes in a fog.* She smiled mischievously. *But next time I'll be ready for Mr. Marco. He'll be the gardener and I'll be the hoe.*

6

First time's the charm

Jill Scott's "It's Golden" filled the space in her master suite. *Yes, life will be golden this evening,* Tai thought. After much convincing, she finally had succeeded in getting Marco to accept her dinner invitation. After a luxurious, relaxing bath, she opened the door of her walk-in closet to find the right dress to reel him in.

Hmmm, maybe this will work. She stepped into a black, strapless floor-length dress. It was enough to tease but not reveal too much.

Coolly, she descended the stairs to check on the feast she'd prepared. Baked rosemary chicken, garlic mashed potatoes, marinated carrots and a spinach salad. She'd even baked homemade wheat rolls; something she hadn't done in years. Her favorite carrot cake with cream cheese icing sat on the counter. She remembered how he had enjoyed her brownies. Two bottles of her favorite Chardonnay were chilling in the fridge. Her mission was to impress Marco. *Good cooking may be the key to his soul,* she thought.

Marco would be arriving shortly so she decided to set up her Hidden Beach jazz CDs in the changer. She dimmed the lights in her dining room and kitchen before setting the table and lighting candles.

Her cell phone rang and she looked at the caller ID. "Candace, what does she want?" she said out loud. She answered, "Hey, girl, what's up?"

"Hey, girl, nothing much. Going on a hot date tonight."

Tai laughed. "Okay, 'date' is your middle name. Who is it? Someone new?"

"Girl, you know I love me some men. Variety is what's happening. Yeah, his name is Jordan. He's a ventriloquist."

"Say what? A ventriloquist. Girl, you sure do pick them, don't you?"

"Well, we go way back. I used to turn him down all the time when he asked me out. So I thought I'd try him out for once. I don't have to tell you that I like them wild and crazy. Adventurous."

"You'll have to tell me how it turns out. Where you going?"

"Some party at a hotel."

"Good. I'm glad you're going to a public place."

"You bet. You're like a big sis, so you always tell me to be cool…and safe. What are you doing tonight?"

"Girl, I have me a 'hot date,' too."

"Who—"

"I'll never tell." Tai laughed. "No, I'm kidding. Let's say it's someone I've known for a while, too, but never thought about before now. My landscaper, Marco."

"Hmmm…did you cook him one of your meals?"

"Yes, girl, I plan to lay it on him." She laughed.

"Well, enjoy!"

"You, too. We'll talk later." She hung up the phone.

Tai shimmied into the den and fluffed up the pillows on her sofa when her doorbell rang. She headed to the hallway mirror to check out her look again before answering the door.

"Hi, Marco." Tai beamed as she checked out this hunk of a man; all 175 pounds at five-feet-eleven. He was impeccably dressed in a navy rayon silk shirt and pleated slacks with gator shoes. His freshly shaved mocha skin glistened and his almond-shaped eyes were to die for. She stepped aside for him to enter.

"Come on into the den. I thought we'd have some wine."

"Cool with me." Marco sat on the sofa and listened to the music. It was Will Smith's "Summertime." "You know I like this song; anything about the summer."

"It's pretty tonight. Would you rather go on the deck?"

"Sure." Marco stood and Tai handed him the wineglasses while she grabbed the bottle. They settled at her patio table and chairs. Marco popped the cork and poured the wine.

"I didn't think you were ever going to say yes to dinner," Tai informed. "Are you always so tough?"

"Hey, it's not that. I just do my job, I guess. It's rare for me to connect like this with my customers. " Marco sipped his wine.

"I cooked a special dinner for you…in case this is your first… and last one here." She looked embarrassed. "Sorry, I didn't mean to say that. I shouldn't be judging you."

"No problem."

"Marco, what do you like to do for fun?"

"I love to travel, especially to the Caribbean. I've been to Europe a few times, too. Actually, I go with the fellas to play golf; I'm in a group. We play in Myrtle Beach; sometimes Vegas or Miami. We move the tournaments around. Since my business is best during the summer months, I have to limit my time away."

"I hear you. I like going to exotic places. Jazz clubs. My girl-friends and I get together for lunch at least once a month. You have to find *me* time, so I make sure I do."

"I've never asked, but what kind of work do you do?"

"I own an employment agency. It's called the Next Phase of Life, downtown. I've had it for five years. I help folks get jobs; and that's not always easy during this recession. But so many are out of work, it keeps us on our toes. Business is steady."

"I bet."

TAI AND MARCO HAD FINISHED THEIR DINNER IN THE DINING
room and were now on their second bottle of wine.

"Cheers." Tai touched his glass to a toast. She finally had enough
nerve to bring up her curiosity about his age. "Marco, again I'm
not being funny or anything, but how old are you?"

"Thirty-two...and?"

"Oh, nothing." *It looks like I'll be a cougar. Growl.* "Thirty-two
and a triple threat: good-looking, nice body and personality plus."

"Thanks...you mind me asking *your* age?"

Tai smiled. "Ladies should never tell, but it's all good. I just
turned forty. This was my big one." Her expression suddenly
turned sour after her experience of being stood up by Austin
permeated her thoughts. Seemed like she'd never get the ordeal
out of her mind.

"You okay?"

"Yes, I'm fine," she responded absently. "I'm blessed to be
forty."

"Definitely." *She's wearing that dress in the body of a twenty-year-
old. Wonder why she seems so lonely. Own business, own house...but
that does intimidate some of the brothers. Too independent.*

Tai's thoughts drifted through a time machine as she recalled
how, at one point in her life, she never would have looked twice
at dating a man ten years her junior. Forever desiring her white-
collar dream partner, she also would have overlooked anyone not
in a suit-and-tie image. She had tested the waters with Marco
and was overwhelmed with how well they had connected on a
mental level. Despite being a good fit in body language, his intel-
ligence and maturity demonstrated that age was simply a number.

7

Remember me...?

A whistling teakettle blasted its siren from the stove, awakening Tai who had dozed off quickly on her comfy den sofa. Sprawled paperwork covered the pillows and table. Her late-night plans to catch up on Next Phase office details would be more of a challenge; she realized her bed was calling her, too. She yawned and stretched, then headed to fix her tea. She needed caffeine so she'd ignore the Chai and chamomile tonight, which would relax her too much.

Tai returned to the sofa and stared at the manila folders and notepads. *Forget this; I'm not feeling this biz stuff.* She reached on the end table and picked up her laptop. *I need to catch up on my Facebook, too.* It had been weeks since she had been online; at least on her personal page. Felicia was responsible for checking and updating the business page. She logged in and spotted that she had twelve new messages.

One was from Candace. *Hey, girl. Looking forward to our next luncheon. Lots to dish. How was your hot date with the landscaper?*

Tai responded: *You are crazy! Did the ventriloquist work his puppet magic on you? See you soon.*

Candace was a Facebook queen; when she wasn't streaming through stores, prowling the streets or pecking online, she was all over the site.

Tai scrolled through her messages and one in particular jumped off the screen. *Trista. Could it be…* ? She opened the message to read it and did a double-take, blinking to widen her eyes.

Hey, big sis. It's been a longgg time. I've been searching for ya for years. Thanks to FB, I found ya. Pls contact me.

Tai was amazed at the message. She thought she was dreaming but realized that it was a reality. It was her younger sister, her only sibling, who had reached out to her on Facebook.

Tai, then twelve, was separated from Trista, age ten, after being raised in Salisbury, N.C., a town about thirty miles from Charlotte. Their parents, John and Diana Wilson, had died in a murder-suicide. When the sisters stepped off the school bus, their small brick house along a rural strip was cordoned off and police surrounded the field. They were blocked from entering their home and a neighbor quickly scooped them aside, then took the girls to her home. Miss Laine fought back tears as she attempted to comfort them by offering them some fresh-brewed iced tea and fruit. Tai and Trista were loaded with questions and Miss Laine eluded them by changing the subject. She was patiently awaiting a police officer-psychologist to arrive. It would be his duty to explain to the young girls what had happened. It would be an awful account to describe to the girls whom she had grown to adore since birth. Often she played the grandmotherly role when the Wilsons had plans and needed a sitter.

They were active members in the community and well-respected citizens known for their hospitality and philanthropy in Rowan County. John was the vice principal of a high school and his wife was a schoolteacher in a middle school. Both educators, they had met at Winston-Salem State University, formerly a teachers college, and had married shortly thereafter. John had attended North Carolina A&T where he had received his master's in education.

While Salisbury wasn't exactly Mayberry, it was small enough that word traveled fast and the rumor mill was active. Miss Laine had heard through the clothesline circuit that Diana had an ongoing relationship with the principal of the school where she taught. Of course, he and John had traveled in the same circles.

Once John had discovered the affair, he had announced he would move out and leave the girls with Diana. However, he had determined that he would handle it another way. If he couldn't have Diana, then no one else could either; including the girls. He had arrived home at lunchtime after learning that Diana had taken a midday break; she had taught science classes in the morning and afternoon. He had pulled out his shotgun that he stashed in the shed and shot Diana, then blasted his own chest.

Residents who had gathered on Apple Lane were stunned to see a huge gathering as the result of a tragedy; a rare sight in the rural community.

It was near the end of the school year. Harriet Turner, Diana's mother and the girls' grandmother, lived in Washington, D.C., where she had relocated from the South to work in the federal government. Her husband, Dennis, had died of a heart attack shortly after their move north. Harriet was devastated to discover her daughter's murder at the hands of the man she had grown to adore. When she had heard about the alleged affair, she had realized that something had gone sour in their marriage. She had found it difficult to fathom how he could have transformed into a stone-cold killer.

Harriet, the closest relative, had to make a decision about her granddaughters. Her small apartment in Northwest and her modest salary would force her to choose only one of the two to take under her wing. Tai was the oldest and she favored her because she was extremely bright, affectionate and had a warm and outgoing demeanor. She would experiment to see how life evolved with Tai; if it went smoothly, perhaps she would take in Trista as well. Miss Laine had been fond of Trista, whom she found to be shy and more of an observer than a talker.

After the double funeral service in North Carolina, Harriet had visited with Miss Laine. They had discussed the future of the girls and agreed that Miss Laine would care for Trista while Harriet would take Tai to the city. After all, Miss Laine was like family; and when the names of possible caretakers were pondered, it was determined that Miss Laine was the best choice. She lived alone, was retired, and could open her heart and home to a child. She had no children of her own and was already familiar with Trista from babysitting. She believed in the saying: *It takes a village to raise a child.*

Tai relived the memories of her parents' dreadful fate and her longtime separation from her sister. They were recollections that she stored in the deep well of her psyche; only to emerge occasionally. When she initially had moved to D.C. with Grandma Harriet, she had regular visits with a child therapist. Harriet sacrificed her income to ensure that Tai would be in the best mental state. Tai wondered why she had been chosen to live with their grandmother in D.C. and not Trista. The Wilson sisters had never been close, even when they had lived in their family home. Opposite in personality, Tai never could determine what Trista was thinking. She was quiet and showed little emotion. She loved her sister, deep in her heart, but there was something she couldn't pinpoint...

What a surprise, a shock, Tai thought as she looked at her sister's profile photo. *Trista Wilson,* she repeated. *That's her...aged by twenty-eight years. I can't believe it.* She had never searched for her on the Internet.

Tai typed a message: *Sure, Sis. How can I reach you? We should talk and not online.* Tai then realized that Trista was not online. She would await her response.

Guess I'll get some sleep. Don't think I can focus on work after this awakening… Tai set the laptop on the table, sipped her tea and headed toward the stairs. She hoped that she would be able to catch some Z's. Stunned, it was already like she was in dreamland.

8

Talk is cheap

Candace approached the brownstone and climbed the steps to ring the doorbell. She observed her surroundings. It was a pristine neighborhood block with floral beds and manicured lawns.

She and Jordan had been on several dates and she was eager to see the home of a ventriloquist. Their conversations had been limited. The comedy club didn't allow for much talk with all the howls and roars. Then dinner was so noisy that they could barely hear each other. Candace was looking forward to checking him out in a non-public place. She peeped inside the window, but it was hard to determine the décor. Waiting patiently, she wondered why he hadn't answered the door. She had arrived promptly at 8 p.m. as he had suggested.

Before she could ring the doorbell again, Jordan opened the door wide and motioned for her to enter.

"Hi, Candace. Sorry it took me a minute to answer," he apologized.

"No problem. Lovely neighborhood." Candace looked throughout the living room. "House, too."

"Thanks."

The bronze leather sofa was accented by burgundy pillows. An animal print throw rug sat beneath a trunk coffee table. Large, tall plants stood guard from each corner and lamps with animal print shades adorned the end tables. Art pieces by old-school artist Ernie Barnes highlighted the room, including the one made famous from Marvin Gaye's *I Want You* album cover.

"Have a seat." Jordan directed her to the sofa. She sat and dropped her tote bag and purse on the table. He then sat beside her. "I like your outfit."

"Oh, thanks." Candace blushed. Her fuchsia wrap dress and gold necklace were blinging.

"Did you bring what I asked?"

"Sure did." She pointed to her tote bag and smiled.

"Great. Can I offer you something to drink? I know you said you and your sister were going to dinner earlier."

"Wine is fine, unless you make a mean martini."

"I'll see what's cooking. Be right back." Jordan arose and walked to the rear kitchen.

Candace picked up a magazine and started flipping the pages. He returned with two glasses. She sipped.

"This is good. What type of martini?"

"It's called a Henny Sidecar. Not quite a martini."

"So how long have you lived here?"

"Four years. I got a great deal…it was convenient for me so I can walk to my day job. It's also easy access to Metro. It saves me time and gas since I have to drive to all my evening gigs. In fact, I have a show next weekend. I'd love for you to come. You haven't seen me in action."

"What made you want to do the ventriloquist thing anyway?"

"It was random. I happened to see an ad in a magazine where they were looking to train for carnivals in upstate New York. It piqued my interest so I thought, why not? I've always been an adventurous guy and when I was a kid, my grandfather used to watch the old Howdy Doody show. I also used to try and change my voice. So you had to audition first and I made the cut. Then I was trained in Manhattan. It did take a lot of practice, though."

Candace listened intently and sipped on her drink. Jordan rarely drank but opted for bottled water most of the time. *Maybe he has to keep those luscious lips of his moist at all times, being a ventriloquist.* Candace was attracted to Jordan, who was about six feet, brown skinned with a slim build. He wore his hair in a short Afro, which reminded her of old school. She planned to suggest that he cut it down a little; however, she figured she didn't know him well enough yet. If they were to be an item, she would have to help him in the style area. She was aware that he had to have a touch of crazy in order to work part-time with a puppet pal. She would refrain from judgment though until she became more familiar with his lifestyle.

Jordan scooped up Candace's glass and returned to the kitchen to refresh her drink.

They talked for another hour before Jordan suggested they head upstairs. Candace picked up her bag and purse and followed him up the spiral staircase. Her heels creaked as she ascended the wooden steps. The house must have been built in the '30s, she surmised. It was totally the opposite of her upscale, brand-new condo with modern amenities.

Jordan opened the door to his bedroom and closed it behind him. Candace's eyes roamed the room when she locked on the eyes of Sammy, his puppet. "Wow, that's him?" she asked creepily.

"Yep, that's my buddy; the one and only Sammy you've heard so much about."

Sammy was dressed in a black shirt, black pants and a black-and-white polka dot bowtie. He was sitting upright in a tall, wooden chair. He also wore a short Afro and had huge button eyes with curly eyelashes. He had perfectly curvy-shaped lips that were large and pronounced, overruling his round, cinnamon-colored face. This was definitely a brotha.

"Well, I've never seen…" Candace couldn't find the right words.

"You've seen boy dolls, I'm sure. Just think of Sammy as a large, manly play toy." Jordan cackled. "He won't hurt you. Don't be scurred," he teased.

Candace took a deep breath and looked at Jordan. "I'm not," she lied. Candace thought about how she would have to fake this one. Maybe her mind was playing tricks on her; Sammy didn't look sinister. It was only in her mind, she thought. Jordan was a sweet guy so Sammy was, too. *Hell, why am I thinking like this? He ain't real.*

Candace felt slightly weird and overwhelmed in the room only lit by thick white unscented candles on a dresser. The heavy-cloth, old-fashioned drapery; framed Broadway show posters; and exotic-looking plants added to the mystique. "Where's the bathroom?" she asked.

Jordan, who had sat on the side of his king-sized bed, covered by a dark gray comforter, pointed to the door. "It's down the hall."

Candace sashayed to the doorway and toward the bathroom where she felt more at-ease. The warm peach walls and bright lighting offered comfort; it was a welcome contrast to the dark and gloomy bedroom. *Now, he asked me to bring this outfit so I did. He's really into this game thing. Carnivals? No wonder he wanted me to be a lion tamer.* Candace, who adored adventurous men, eagerly had complied with Jordan's request. He had informed her that he loved to have women dress up in costumes and pretend they were another character. She found this to be creative and fun, so she pulled out an old black leotard from her jazz/tap dancing days, a pair of simple black boots and a gold bowtie. She even had found a whip. She would be a lion tamer all right...or a lioness.

Candace took off her dress and folded it neatly before placing it inside the tote bag. She pulled out the sleeveless leotard and stepped into it; happy that she was still able to fit it like a glove. Then she pulled on the boots; a worn pair that were deep inside of her closet. It was always good to have a pair that you didn't really care about, she had thought. Once she was dressed, she checked out her hair in the mirror. *Maybe I should pin it up a little*, she decided and pulled out bobby pins to create an upsweep. Unfortunately, the small bathroom didn't have a full-length mirror so she couldn't check out from her waist below. She pulled out a bottle of lotion and rubbed it all over her body; she couldn't fathom ashy legs.

She opened the door to head back to the bedroom. It was quiet as a library; she figured that Jordan would at least turn on some music. When she opened the door and dropped her purse and tote bag on the closest chair, she remembered Sammy was across the room. *Yikes, this is weird*, she thought nervously. It was a creepy scene but she decided to act unfazed. After all, she was now in her character. She gazed over to see Jordan lying in bed under the comforter. He had turned on his television to a black-and-white movie. *I should have known he'd like oldies.*

"Hey, where's the lion?" Jordan asked, then laughed. "You look so cool. And you have a whip? All right now."

"Well, I'm trying to play the part, *tiger*," Candace responded sexily. "You got what you asked for." She sashayed, adding extra motion to her hips, as she approached the bed.

"You bet I did. Join me."

Candace pulled down the cover and screamed. "What the fu—?" She jumped back and looked across the room at Sammy, then back in the bed and did a double-take. A female version of Sammy in a black dress with pearls around its neck and bright-red lips was sprawled in the center. It reminded her of a scene straight out of that horror flick *Child's Play* with that crazed doll Chucky. "What's that thing?!" She wheezed. "I know you don't expect me to get in there!"

"Why not, baby? I told you Sammy wouldn't hurt you. And she won't, either. Meet Shelly."

"You are crazy! I'm gettin' the hell outta here!" Candace rushed to the door to pick up her bags.

Jordan jumped out of the bed, dashed around to the other side, and grabbed her arm. "Please, don't go."

Candace jerked it away and looked in his eyes. "Man, you'd better take your freak show and kiss my ass. I mean, I like them freaky but not this *freaky!*"

"Hey, don't you want to put your clothes back on? My neighbors may see you and wonder what's going on."

"No way. Not another minute in this looney bin." Candace grabbed her bags, then trudged down the stairs and out the door.

Candace quickly walked to her car, opened the door and threw her bags onto the seat. She leaned on her headrest and sighed. *What a nightmare.* She was tense and shook up. Then she laughed. *I'm always wanting adventure. Whew. They say be careful what you wish for.*

9

The sisterhood

Tai refreshed her cup of English black tea to help wash down her cinnamon-raisin bagel. Her kitchen table was cluttered with old family photos. The night had been like a déjà vu party with her and the postcard memories; a slideshow of yesteryear. She had spent hours combing through boxes in her storage room. She had acquired the boxes of photos from her grandmother's home after she had passed a few years ago. Many had made the trek from N.C. to D.C. in a U-Haul and hadn't been unearthed since. Tai had reflected on her childhood moments and the cherished times with her parents before their lives were cut short on that fateful day. They had been the picture-perfect family of four. Photos of her and Trista learning how to ride a bike, unwrapping gifts on Christmas morning, and playing in their huge backyard decorated with pear and pecan trees. Vintage photos included her parents posing in their best attire during a dinner dance at the American Legion hall; and sitting in a swing on a great-aunt's porch in Cherokee, N.C. She recalled enjoying visiting relatives there in the mountains and seeing the Native American powwows. She had heard the town was now known for its casino, which was nestled in the gorgeous hills.

Today she would reunite with her long-lost sister, Trista, who had spent years as a foster care child and had lived in three homes since their separation. Trista had lived briefly with Miss Laine, their favorite neighbor, until she passed. It was unfortunate that their grandmother was only able to care for one of them. Tai had been the "lucky" one. Tai remembered that when she first arrived in D.C., she was impressed with the tall monument and historic and government buildings. It was a huge contrast from her small-town life of practically knowing everyone *and* their mama; country stores with outdoor Coke machines; and her favorite tiny cafe with the best French fries and creamy milkshakes.

Tai looked at the wall clock. It was time to head to Union Station to pick up Trista. She was arriving on the 4:15 p.m. Amtrak train from North Cackey-Lackey. She hoped her train would be on time, but if it was late, she would browse the shops in the station.

She was anxious and excited to see Trista—her darling, little sister who was known for her quietness. Trista had always looked up to her and depended on her guidance. It seemed like time had not changed as Trista had reached out again. She had informed Tai that she was weary of her lifestyle and wanted a change of scenery. Trista had worked odd jobs after high school as a wait-ress at various restaurants. Retail clerk was also on her resume. Once Trista discovered that Tai ran an employment business, she figured that she could assist her in finding a job. Tai had agreed that Trista could stay with her for a while until she was able to save enough to rent an apartment. She lived alone and there was ample space for an entire family. Why not let her sister chill with her? She'd be right there to assist her anytime she needed.

It had been decades since she'd seen Trista and they would have to go back in the time machine to catch up to the present. It would be interesting to see her as an adult; all she had were the memories of their childhood. She was sure Trista was just as eager to learn more about her. They were from a small family and Tai wasn't aware of any other known living relatives.

Tai glanced down at the pictures; she welcomed the idea of hugging a family member—it seemed like a century since she'd had the opportunity to bond with blood kin.

UNION STATION WAS BUSTLING WITH TRAVELERS AS THE DOG days of August were in full swing. Families were ensuring they scooped up their last vacation days during summer recess. Tai took the deep escalator from the parking garage to the station entrance near the gates. The arrival board showed the train would be on time. She was an half-hour early so she took a seat in the waiting area. She pulled the latest issue of *Honey* magazine from her purse and leafed through the pages. It was a way to channel her nervous energy.

Tai looked up to see that the Carolinian was approaching the Amtrak station. She and Trista were aware of each other's image from their Facebook photos. Tai also had noted that she would be wearing a purple top and jeans. Trista had informed her she would be wearing jeans, too. "That's all I own," she had said during their call. Tai had figured they would need to go shopping for interview outfits.

Passengers streamed through the doorway and Tai observed each one, enjoying the opportunity to people-watch. She spotted a woman who looked like Trista wearing an orange sleeveless tank top and jeans. She had a buttercream complexion and was of medium build. She pulled a medium-sized suitcase and a tote bag hung from her shoulder.

Tai raised her eyebrows. "Trista?"

"Tai?" Trista slowed the suitcase roll, released the handle and gave Tai a huge hug.

"Wow! I can't believe this." Tai stepped back from the hug and looked Trista over. "Girl, you looking good."

"Thanks...you, too, Sis." She picked up her suitcase handle and stepped aside to allow others to pass. "This is like a dream. D.C....the Nation's Capital. Never been this far north. Just south as far as Orlando."

"Welcome. I'm glad you made it. We've got years to catch up on, Trista. Let's eat."

"I'm starving. That's a long ride. I had some snacks but that didn't last."

Tai grabbed the tote bag off her sister's shoulder and led the way to the front entrance.

"This station is so cool. It's huge, all the stores and restaurants. The Salisbury station is nothing like this one."

"I thought we'd go to B. Smith's."

"B. Smith's?"

"It's here inside the station and owned by B. Smith. She's African American and has her own TV cooking show. She's known for being a chef and an interior decorator. Have you heard of her?"

Trista hesitated. "Oh, yes," she lied.

They walked through the cavernous Union Station with its magnificent architecture and vaulted ceiling. Trista was mesmerized with the spacious station as they headed to the restaurant.

"I'M TANYA. I'LL BE YOUR SERVER TODAY. MAY I HELP YOU?" a waitress asked.

"Yes, I'll take a bottle of Chardonnay."

Trista realized that Tai had not given her the chance to order her own drink. She had presumed that Trista liked wine; however, she was a gin and beer queen and could chug down as much as a heavyweight champion. She was slightly annoyed.

"Okay, I'll be right back," Tanya stated.

Tai ordered the Swamp Thang, a dish featuring shrimp, scallops and crawfish; while Trista couldn't wait to munch on her meatloaf and mashed potatoes.

"Well, I'm excited. Where do we start?"

Trista soaked up her surroundings. "This is fancy. I'm used to small down-home joints 'cause I don't get to the city too much. They've really built up Charlotte, Raleigh, Durham, Greensboro...but I don't get around. A lot of times we didn't go out to eat. Everyone down there knows how to cook so good. Only on special occasions we would go out."

"So you said you worked in restaurants as a waitress. How'd you like that?"

"They were more like cafés. I did pretty good in tips, though. I had a lot of regular customers. My favorite was the Roadster. They had the best deli sandwiches. We were known for our subs and desserts. It was close to the highway so we had a lot of traffic. People passing through."

"Do you think you'd like to work as a waitress again?"

Tanya arrived and placed their entrees on the table. "May I get you anything else?"

"No, thanks, we're good," Tai responded. Tanya poured their wine.

"I don't know about working at one on this scale," Trista scoped out the setting, "but I could try." She admired the white tablecloths, tall windows and elegant feel.

"That's good to know. We'll find you something. You definitely qualify with your experience."

"Do you remember much about us splitting up? My mind is locked on that day when Grandma said you two were leaving me in N.C. but she would try to bring me up here later; once she earned enough money to take care of both of us," Trista recalled as she sampled her dish. "I loved Grandma and couldn't understand why she would leave me behind. Don't get me wrong; I loved N.C. but I wanted to follow you. I resented the idea of being separated from my sister...and my Grandma. I thought it was so mean.

"Then Miss Laine explained it to me; that Grandma loved me with all her heart and she couldn't afford it," Trista continued. "She said that it wasn't that you were the *favorite* but you were the *oldest* and to her, it made sense to pick you." She scowled. "Miss Laine promised that she would love me as Mom and Dad did and that I was a joy to have around. She already had bonded with us as children so our relationship was already solid.

"Miss Laine was a nice lady and I was so hurt when she died. I started thinking about why I was then left alone with no one. That was when I started going to foster care homes." Trista tasted her meatloaf. "This is yummy."

"How was that experience?" Tai inquired and sipped her wine. "Folks in N.C. are so friendly and down-to-earth, I'm sure you were placed with some caring families."

"Yeah, yeah, but I never knew what to expect. Each time—and I was with three families—I always hoped that it would work out. The last one was the best."

"They say, third time's a charm."

"It was a family of six with four children. There was a daughter who was my age and we became really close. I wonder what she's doing now. I lost contact with her after she left for college. I stayed with them until I was able to get my own place." Trista decided to taste the wine and almost cringed at the flavor. It was not her favorite, but she would show politeness.

"It sounds like you had some okay experiences. Now, I was the

same way. Even though I was brought up here, I couldn't understand why I was being taken away. I didn't want to leave you and
I begged Grandma to bring you, too. She told me she would
someday, once her funds were all set and she was established in
her work. Believe me, I never wanted to live apart." Tai sighed.
"So I'm glad we're back together…finally."

"Me, too. I used to go places and I always thought folks were
staring at me. I think I was paranoid. Then I noticed when I'd
show up they'd get quiet all of a sudden so I figured they were
talking about me…or us…or Mom and Dad. That whole murder-
suicide thing was the talk of town…it was full-time on the gossip
circuit. Me, being so young, only ten, I didn't even understand
the whole thing. When I got older, some of the town hens
pulled me aside and broke it down for me. I used to despise
when Miss Laine would drag me to church or to school func-
tions. I felt like everyone was negative. Of course it was sad that
it happened and I was the victim. My dad had blown my mom
away with a twelve-gauge shotgun, and little ol' me was left to
suffer without any parents. Then my only sis was scooped up
and taken up North. Kids also talked about it once I got to
middle school; I don't think they were aware when we were all
in elementary. It was hell dealing with that; it was like a nightmare."

"I'm sure it was. Miss Laine used to write me nice letters and
she used to call Grandma to tell her how you were doing. Then
when she passed, we hardly heard what you were up to." Tai felt
a pang of sadness in retrospect. "We had such a small family that
Grandma used to say the only people down there she was concerned with were you…and Miss Laine."

"Enough of that. The bottom line is that I didn't get to move
to D.C. but hey, I'm here now."

"Right. And it's time for a new start." She motioned for Desiree, who brought the check.

"Sis, we're gonna be okay. We'll make up for lost time. Let's go."

"And Tai, thank you for dinner." Trista forced a smile. "And for letting me camp out with you."

10

Caught in the act

"**S**leuths on Us, may I help you?" Nevada stared at her computer monitor and tapped her pen on her desk. While answering phones in her one-woman operation, she was reading email and jotting notes. She was the ultimate multi-tasker and even though her mind was racing, her fingers were either writing or typing.

Nevada was such a loner with the exception of her sidekicks, Tai and Candace. She had created a shell around her ever since she'd lost her newspaper job. She eagerly would wake up daily with anticipation of an exciting day ahead. She never knew what lay ahead; it was never routine. As a general assignment reporter and later an investigative reporter, Nevada's life had been like an actress' list of movie roles. One morning she would cover the sentencing of a guy who had shot up co-workers at a corporate firm. The following night during single-digit temperatures she would be sitting in a TV network van, invited by a female anchor-woman, to stay warm while they awaited the fate of a hostage situation. There was never a dull moment.

"Hello, this is Mrs. Thompson." Nevada immediately envisioned the fifty-something woman on the line. "Have you had any luck?"

"No, not yet, Mrs. Thompson. I've got some things going and I promise I'll get back to you as soon as possible. I've done a lot of research and searching and I think I'm getting close."

Nevada attempted to put her at-ease. She had been working on her case for a couple of months. Mrs. Thompson was convinced that her "deceased" husband was, in fact, alive. She'd had a memorial service in a local church in his hometown of Maryland. There had been rumors that he had wanted to split with his wife but didn't have the balls to ask for a divorce from their twenty-five-year marriage. Their two adult children, both daughters, were convinced that their dad was still alive; it was far beyond his makeup to suddenly disappear without a trace. They had encouraged their mom to hire a private detective.

Nevada was considered the stable one in her circle of friends. While she had never married nor had the desire, she believed in maintaining longtime relationships. Ryan worked as a Metropolitan Police officer and part-time as a journalist. He was an editor of an online magazine that covered the sights and sounds of D.C. Both careers worked well with Nevada's lifestyle. Her time was limited, too. The majority of her clients were women and she took pride in helping to "capture" the truth. She was determined she would crush Mrs. Thompson's fear that her husband was dead by proving that he was still alive. Her gut feeling told her that Mr. Bob Thompson had faked his death.

She checked the emails from her five accounts, sat back in her chair and became deep in thought. Her mind zoomed as she read any leads dealing with the particular Thompson case. She reviewed her notes from the latest phone calls and, specifically, from her police officer cohort who had provided some promising tips. Johnson was on street patrol and he usually had the word from the streets. They were former high school classmates who had briefly dated before he'd joined the force. This was unbeknownst to Ryan that his lady had a connection within his department.

She looked at the notes from their conversation and Nevada

had an epiphany. She jumped up from her desk and ran down the stairs from her upper-floor home office. She poured a cup of coffee in her travel mug and headed out of the door. She climbed into her Ford Edge SUV and started proceeding in the direction of downtown.

Nevada cruised along L Street and found a parking space in front of a popular nightspot, Cookies and Crème. She had never checked it out but had heard that the dessert bar had the best cookies and cheesecake in the city. It all sounded good to her ears but not to her stomach as she was determined to stick to her new diet. Up the block was Channels, a club that was rumored to have an undercover prostitution ring. The owners had been under watch for a year and it was likely a matter of time before they were the targets of a sting operation.

Nevada was wearing her usual casual getup with a black button-down shirt, black jeans and black Uggs, which were not the choice for summer but were so comfortable, they would allow her to be swift and able to make quick moves. She eased lower in her seat and put on a pair of shades. Of course this looked odd at this hour of the night: 10:25 p.m. But, hey, she had to be incognito. She loved playing the role of a detective aka spy. It gave her an adrenaline rush when she realized she was close to making a discovery or cracking a case.

Nevada opened her purse and pulled out a recent photo of Mr. Thompson. He was handsome with a copper complexion, defined cheekbones, a paper-thin mustache and a bald head. She was aware that he could have grown out hair by this time. However, his features were distinctive. Unless he'd had plastic surgery, and according to his wife, their bank accounts had dwindled—her reason for thinking he'd disappeared—he would have a hard time altering his face.

She looked at the photo and then checked out the crowd that had gathered. A line had started to form to get into Channels, which was a late-night spot that opened at 11 on weekends. Nevada opened her door, got out and walked to the intersection, offering her a keen view of the patrons. She inconspicuously gazed at each person in line. *This is such a cool job.* She figured she'd stick out like a dinosaur on a city street, but she was aware that many in the line would simply ignore her. They would be anxious to get their dance on.

She noticed a figure now at the beginning of the line who was dressed in a black floor-length sundress with long sleeves. She wore a shoulder-length, jet-black wig and large gold hoop earrings. A gold choker hung from her neck and she carried a small gold clutch. The woman made eye contact with Nevada before turning to go inside the club.

Nevada approached as the woman paid the ten-dollar cover charge. "Excuse me, but is your name Bob?"

The person looked down at her, rolled some head and neck, then frowned. "No, dear, I'm *Bobbi.*" It was a faux high-pitched voice that was full of baritone. "And you are...?" The air was filled with plenty of attitude.

"I'm your wife's private detective, *Mr. Thompson.*"

"Oh...my...God..." The gold clutch dropped to the ground.

11

Those healing hands

Gentle but firm hands kneaded along Tai's back as she lay relaxed across the table. Aromatherapy intoxicated her senses and the peaceful trickling of water from the indoor fountain offered serenity. She peeked across the room to see that Trista also was in a faraway place, eyes closed like she was in a warm tunnel. Tai wondered if her younger sister was in dreamland in Aruba, Negril or Barbados.

Tai had selected her two favorite masseurs at Healing Hands Spa to work their magic on her and her sibling. She thought this would be the ultimate treat and an ideal icebreaker to expose Trista to her world. It wasn't that she thought it surpassed Trista's experiences, but she wanted to share her favorite things. Spa massages were at the top of her list, one of her must-have indulgences. Healing Hands was secluded, off the beaten track and hidden off a main road near an Annapolis, Maryland beach. During her summer massage appointments, she would venture to the sandy shore after her rubdown retreats. However, today she was preparing to shop for her upcoming Labor Day Weekend cookout.

TAI'S ORANGE GINGER AND TRISTA'S HONEY ALMOND FRAGRANCES blended with their soothing emotional state to form two sisters in harmony. Their hour-long massages had come to an end. They were in such a relaxed state; wishing they were Krazy Glue and stuck on the massage tables forever. The two women enveloped themselves in plush, soft terry-cloth robes. Tai provided a hefty tip to Garvin and Roberto, both handsome and model-good looking.

Garvin smiled at one of his favorite clients and her sister, whom he and Roberto had hoped to impress during her first visit.

"How was the massage?" he inquired.

"It was the bomb." Trista appeared in a daze. She'd never felt this much on a cloud like she was on an all-time high minus the drugs.

"Wonderful…" Tai nodded her approval. Garvin and Roberto smiled, opened the door and walked out of the private area.

TAI HEADED WEST ON ROUTE 50 AND LOOKED IN THE REARVIEW mirror to see the Bay Bridge. It was near sundown and she wished she could go the opposite direction and head to Ocean City.

"You're quiet. How'd you like the spa?"

"Like nothin' I've ever experienced. It was cool, real cool. Thanks."

"Sure…listen, I need to get ready for the holiday. I'm having a cookout and I thought this would be a good way for you to meet some people."

"Entertainin' folks is your thing, huh?"

"Every now and then…hey, I figured I may as well enjoy the house."

"I can dig it."

"I got it honestly. Remember, Mom and Dad used to host the get-togethers with the neighbors? Everyone loved Mom's desserts.

Maybe that's how I got so interested in baking and entertaining. You'll get to see how we throw down on this end."

Yeah, right. It'll be my style. I can't wait, she thought sarcastically. "I'm sure it'll be slammin'."

PICNIC TABLES WERE SCATTERED ACROSS THE LAWN WHERE MARCO had created a landscape rivaling that of any gardening magazine page. Black tablecloths with purple centerpieces adorned each table. A string of purple lanterns was looped across the back of the deck. A makeshift bar on the deck was the hangout for Tai's guests. Her neighbor, Dax, a professional bartender, worked his magic on the cocktails. His mango daiquiris and vanilla martinis were treasures that would provide a light buzz and then sneak up on you.

Tai had introduced Trista to her friends and co-workers who were feasting on the deck and in the backyard on her grilled menu of barbecued chicken wings, rosemary potato wedges and carrots, red snapper and corn on the cob. Mini cupcakes and deep-dish apple cobbler would be the evening treat. The sun was starting to set and cool it down, although this Labor Day was mild in temperature compared to recent years.

Candace, who was always fashionably late, had yet to meet Trista. Nevada, the standoffish queen, had reserved her opinion of Trista until she'd had more time to observe; her eyes were like a hawk ready to swoop down on its prey. Tai would think lightly about anyone's view of her sister except those of her girls. Felicia's thoughts would matter mildly as she would be assisting Trista in finding a job.

Tai, Trista and Nevada stood in the kitchen preparing more food for the grill.

"Hey, ladies! What's up?"

All three turned to see Candace in her grand entrance, looking like the epitome of a Barbie doll. Today she was rocking a pair of black shorts to accentuate her toned thighs and legs, making a case that her new gym membership was worthwhile. Her silver halter-top was blinging and blinding. Black tie-up heels showed off her calves.

Tai rinsed off her hands in the sink and dried them, then turned around. "We were wondering if you were going to show, or rather, when…you don't miss a thing."

"You're right about that, girl. Now you know I stopped for gas and a couple of guys were trying to holla at me."

"I guess so; that's a cute hooker outfit." Tai laughed. "Just kidding. I am *loving* it." She turned to Trista, then back to Candace. "Candace, this is my sister, Trista."

"Wow, hey, Trista, welcome to the girls club." She walked over and hugged Trista who reached out to embrace her. "I've heard a lot about you. Tai was so excited when you found her after all these years. Hope you like D.C. so far."

"Yeah, I'm getting used to it. I was glad to get up this way…I needed a change." She glared at Nevada, whom she thought was analyzing her. Nevada had that way about her; she could look through you with her piercing eyes as if she were a psychic peering into the future.

Nevada snapped out of it. "It's always good to hook up with family." Nevada was not close to her own family, which was based in the Chicago area. She had moved to D.C. with her parents as a preteen. They rarely had attended her annual family reunions in Chicago. Her dad had been offered to relocate to D.C. to teach music at Howard University. He would have to leave his longtime gig as a blues musician. He'd played for years at the

Back Door and it was a tough decision. Nevada used to travel with him on the local circuit as a young girl. She often had to spend nights in his dressing room—too young to sit among the drinkers. Her dad, who went by the stage name Rockin' Roderick, was a self-taught harmonica and banjo artist. During those years, Nevada would often feel like an old soul in the 1800s in a Southern jukebox joint, listening to blues while her friends were caught up in the trendy disco scene.

"Where are the men?" Candace looked at Trista and swirled her head. "You gotta excuse me, hon. I'm always on the hunt." She laughed.

Trista offered a faint smile that was forced. "No problem, I gotcha." She immediately had picked up that Candace was a style fanatic with the way she flaunted her hair, clothes and body. She suddenly checked out her own outfit; her lifelong and never-fail T-shirt and jeans. This was her everyday getup. Tai had promised to take her shopping for interview wear.

Candace exited the kitchen and headed for the backyard through the patio deck. "Hmmm, this food looks good," she said, spotting the spread on the buffet table near the grill. She picked up a plate and started serving it. "I'm ready to get my chow on." She shook her hips to upbeat sounds from the iPod. She was ready to get the party started, but guests were eating like they were trapped in the woods without food and it was their last meal.

"What's the deal with her?" Trista asked, motioning her head toward Candace.

"What do you mean?" Tai inquired. "She's cool people."

"She thinks she's all that and a bag of chips, if you ask me."

"Say what? No, you misunderstand her. Candace and I go way back. She likes to have fun and yes, she does talk a lot but it's all good. She lovvvves fashion and her personality fits in with a stylista. In fact, she may be the better person to take you shopping."

"Yeah, she's a trip all right," Nevada added. "But a good trip. Not a bad seed on that apple tree. "

"I know ya'll got a bond and I ain't tryin' to break it, either. I'm only speaking my mind," Trista responded, giving a little attitude.

Tai already had surmised that Candace and Trista might knock heads. Candace was an in-your-face type of woman, while Trista had more of a laid-back demeanor. Both were headstrong and knew what they wanted, when they wanted it and how they were going to get it.

Nevada continued to take mental notes about Trista. She couldn't help being a keen observer as it was required in her line of business. Although she had majored in journalism, she also had longed for a psychology degree. She enjoyed getting into the psyche of an individual. But she was learning how to read people firsthand.

Tai loaded her seasoned wings and veggies on a platter to take to the deck. Nevada and Trista followed suit with trays of freshly prepared food. "Thanks, ladies," Tai said, setting the trays on a table for Dax to grill.

Tai looked around. She was pleased with the turnout for her holiday cookout. It was an ideal way to cap off the summer and to introduce Trista to her circle of friends. "Everyone, make sure you eat and drink up. I don't want any leftovers." Tai figured when dusk arrived, and her guests' tummies were full, the cookout would evolve into a true throwdown.

MARCO SAT IN A CHAISE LOUNGE UNDERNEATH A TREE. HE WAS in his comfort zone surrounded by nature, but he wanted some peace away from the crowd. He had planted himself in this position to cool out. He'd already done his share, helping Tai set up the yard with the tables, chairs and decorations. Tai noticed Marco in the far corner of her yard and walked toward him. She bent over and kissed him briefly.

"Why are you way over here? You tired? Feeling anti-social?" She pulled a chair closer and sat down. "I'm waiting for my next burst of energy. I've been in that kitchen *alllll* day. Guess that's what it takes when you're the hostess."

"At least you have your neighbor, friends and sister helping. What does Trista think about your friends?"

"She likes them okay. Although she's not feeling Candace too much."

"And I know why. That girl runs her mouth. No offense to you, sweetie, but Candace is like a time bomb with a nonstop trigger. Does she ever stop talking and listen?"

Tai frowned. "You'd better…"

"Hey, I'm sorry, Tai. Didn't mean to offend you, or your friends. I'm probably just a little jealous. Our time together is so limited and here you are with a bunch of people."

"That simply means we have to plan our own private date, huh?"

Marco smiled and held her hand, stroking it with his other one. "Yeah, baby, a private one it is."

Tai released his hand and stood. "I'd better get back to make sure it's going smooth. See ya." She strutted across the yard back toward the crowd.

THE SUN HAD DESCENDED AND THE PURPLE LANTERN LIGHTS CAST a soothing glow. The music piping through the speakers had aroused the guests who were now doing the Booty Call line dance on the brick patio. The next tune sparked all the veteran hand dancers to grab partners and twirl and kick their moves. Hand dancing had been a D.C. craze for years. Clubs and lounges had hand dancing nights where old-timers showed off their skills and new timers could display what they had learned from classes. It was definitely a popular pastime unique to D.C. like Steppin' was to Chicago.

A select group of hand dancing aficionados gathered on the patio and had a blast spinning and stepping to hand dancing classics.

DJ Rico and Dr. G then decided to change the groove and switched to go-go, another D.C. home-grown sound. The Godfather of Go-Go, Chuck Brown, belted out "Go-Go Swing" and E.U.'s classic "Da Butt" followed.

Suddenly, everyone formed into a tighter circle and started to cheer a particular dancer. Tai looked down from the deck to see Trista rotating her hips and shaking her booty vulgarly. Then she dropped down to get her eagle on and dropped low again and again. Trista had truly loosened up after downing several martinis. She turned toward her dancing partner, Lewis, from behind, then grabbed his waist and humped him. Trista was turning him out. Tai smiled at her little sister. *She has no shame in her game*, Tai thought. *Now I see how she likes to party.*

Candace had given her own show that night, kicking off her heels so she could be as limber as possible. Now Tai could see that she had cornered Mason Montclair, a marshal arts instructor. She was interested in his bedroom moves and wondering if he could teach her to slam-bam the night away.

Tai shook her head. *That girl never stops.* She looked across the yard at Marco and smiled. *Now that's my baby over there.*

Nevada walked up beside her. "Your party-party finally got

started. I see your sis likes to have a good time. Guess she needed a little somethin'-somethin' to get started."

"This makes me want to have a real house party. Folks don't have many of those like it was back in the day. A good old-fashioned house party. Girl, you know my thing; we ladies need to look out for each other. Always find a way to de-stress in this crazy world and have *fun*."

12
Jumpstart

T rista waited on the platform for the next subway car at the Metro station. She had mixed feelings on this day—her first appearance at her new job as a waitress. The Next Phase of Life had sent her on interviews for several positions and the restaurant was the first to make an offer. She had hoped for a different line of work; she was ready for something new and fresh. She also had become a little too comfortable hanging out at Tai's house, doing whatever she chose on a day-to-day basis. Tai always had a stocked refrigerator and bar, the latest DVDs and all of the cable movie networks.

Tai had asked Candace to take her on a shopping spree and she had selected basic colored outfits for interviews: black and navy slacks and white collared shirts and blazers. She hadn't worn pumps in years since going to church with Miss Laine and she was sure she looked awkward in the new ones. It was all a far cry from her T-shirt and jean-filled suitcase. Thank goodness, she could wear a uniform to her new job. A black short-sleeve shirt, black slacks and flat shoes suited her well.

Candace had taken her to suburban discount stores to meet her budget—not the upscale stores where she often shopped. After all, she was a buyer and aware that you didn't have to spend a fortune to look classy. Candace relished the idea that Tai had confidence in her taste. She had scooped up Trista one Saturday and driven her to several stores. She was unaware that Trista had reservations about her; she hadn't picked up the vibe that Trista thought she was overbearing in her eyes. Trista had gritted at the thought that Candace would be chaperoning her for a day. Her talkativeness had driven Trista out of her mind but she managed to pull through the day without any verbal clashes. She kindly had thanked Candace for her efforts and actually putting extra thought into helping her select clothes. She had to give Candace credit that her stylist skills were on point.

During her years at Pratt Institute, Candace was required to pick out fashions for all of the seasons, prom wear, casual dress, after-five, career/business and club scene. She had made high grades and was at the top of her class. In addition to buying, she had experimented with designs: a prom dress and a two-piece bathing suit. With fifteen years in the fashion industry, Candace was proud of her accomplishments and figured she could go toe-to-toe with any major designer. Despite her stellar reputation as a stylist, Candace spent countless hours on the fashion magazine pages; she could never get too much knowledge on the industry and the hottest trends.

Trista edged closer to the platform to enter the train that had pulled up. She was headed to the Gallery Place stop near the Verizon Center and Chinatown. She was slightly nervous on this first day but figured it would be a breeze once she learned the ropes. She'd had plenty of experience waiting tables. Trista hoped that city customers' tips would measure up and surpass those from the rural areas.

Hopping on the train—Tai had shown her the route on a dry run—she quickly took a seat. There was an interesting mix of passengers aboard the late-morning express; from the man in a business suit and briefcase to the teenage boy wearing iPod head-phones to the young woman who appeared headed to her college campus. It was a stretch from where excitement stemmed from your local bowling alley or church fish fry.

Trista had loved the small-town atmosphere, but had started to believe she was missing out on a part of life that was mandatory for her to experience. Rural life had the same issues of the big city such as drugs and crime; they were only on a smaller scale.

Trista focused on the signs to ensure she would not miss her stop. She definitely wanted to make a good impression and not be late for her first day. *I think I can dig this, riding the train.* Back home, she normally had to depend on a friend or co-worker offering her a ride. She had become weary of her spontaneous efforts to get home. She had a reliable co-worker who picked her up, but often she had to scramble to find a way home after a long day.

After the train pulled into Trista's destination, she stepped off and boarded the escalator to Seventh Street. It was the early days of fall and she pulled her light jacket tighter around her neck to ward off the chill. She then thought maybe she was exaggerating the temperature because she was used to a milder climate in the South. This was not what you would call cold…yet.

Trista arrived at Seacoast restaurant, stopped and looked through the windows, then took a deep breath. *Here goes…* She opened the door, entering the restaurant with an *I'm here and you'd better notice I'm on time* look.

"Hi, I'm looking for Cynthia," she announced to the receptionist. "I'm Trista Wilson."

"Hi, Trista. Yes, she's expecting you. I'm Carena. I'll take you to her." Carena stepped from behind the receptionist's booth to show Trista the back office. It was almost lunchtime, their busiest weekday schedule from eleven-thirty to two. Carena would quickly need to return to her station at the booth.

Once they arrived, Carena introduced Trista to Cynthia, a petite, dark-skinned woman in her early seventies who had worked at the restaurant for forty years. Trista had always heard tales of longtime restaurant employees. They especially were honored once an establishment was closing after fifty years and were quoted in articles. Doug, the manager who had interviewed her, had advised Trista that Cynthia had longevity at Seacoast. *Wow, I can't imagine being at this place until my hair turns completely gray.*

Trista had been instructed that she would shadow Cynthia today. She prayed that she wouldn't fall in love with the menu as she wasn't trying to put on any extra pounds. While working a previous waitress job, she hadn't been able to resist the chocolate cake or the sweet potato pie, so she found out that the goodies were steadily appearing on her hips. This would be a no-no this time around. She was new in this city and needed to ensure she was eye candy.

"Welcome. You're right on time, actually early." Cynthia reached out to shake Trista's hand. "My shift doesn't start for another fifteen. You have any questions?"

"No… I'll have to resist my temptation. I *love* seafood. How do you keep from eating too much around here?" Trista took off her lightweight jacket and hung it on the coat rack in the back.

Cynthia laughed. "I haveta keep my cool. It ain't easy. Honey, the crab cakes are off the chain. I'm sure you've heard about the Chesapeake Bay and how D.C. and Maryland are known for their crab cakes."

"I have heard. My sister made some since I've been here and yes, they make you want to slap your mama," Trista teased.

"You from North Carolina, right? I know you're used to some damn good cookin' down there. That's where a lot of the folks migrated from here, and they brought their family recipes with 'em." Cynthia looked at the wall clock. "Okay, we'd better head out." She opened the door and held it for Trista who followed her to the ladies room so they could wash their hands, then proceed to the dining area.

13

In the rhythm

Tai reviewed her daily agenda at Next Phase of Life. Her new list of prospective clients included a high-tech firm, an assisted-living facility, and a national association of restaurant employees. She and Felicia would review the top candidates for the open positions. She walked to the water cooler and filled a glass, then returned to her desk stacked with manila folders. They would have a private discussion before the major staff meeting.

Felicia approached Tai's office door, saw that it was open and then entered.

"Good morning, Tai. How's it going?" She was her usual bubbly self and flashed her sparkling smile.

"Hello, lady, I'm well. It looks like we have potential to fill these positions. The last time this one company advertised, they had twenty-five applicants. This time, they had a hundred and fifty. It shows how the job market is these days." Tai sipped her water. "They want us to help do the screening."

"You're right. It keeps us busy anyway. And that's a good thing." Felicia plopped down on the cushiony oversized chair in the corner. She picked up the latest *Essence* magazine and flipped through the pages. "Business is business…. What's happening on the outside? How's your sister working out? By the way, your cookout was fun. Thanks for inviting me."

"No problem. Glad you enjoyed it." Tai was pleased her cookout was a hit. "Trista's doing okay. Thanks again for helping to find her job. She seems to like it; no complaints. She's been getting great tips. As far as off the job, I think she's a little bored. She goes to work and comes home and that's pretty much her week. Unless I take her someplace. We've done the spa thing; a few restaurants. But I think she's ready for something else."

Felicia closed the magazine and placed it on the table. "What about a club?" She stood and walked toward Tai's desk. "She's young, so I'm sure she'd appreciate the club thing. It's okay once in a while."

"Girl, yes, you see how she got down at the cookout. She's a show-stopper. Lil' Sis *loves* to dance."

"Let's all go to a club."

"You're right. You always help me think," Tai complimented. "It's mainly been jazz clubs for me, but I like to get out to *da club* every now and then, too. I'm not looking for a man this time," she teased. "You know how we do."

Felicia smiled. "Righttt. I ain't looking for nobody, either. Jayson and I have been hanging tight lately. Of course, we only met a month ago. Sorry it wasn't in time to bring him to the cookout." She turned her head toward the door, checking to see if anyone was nearby, then back at Tai. "Girl, he knows how to lay that pipe," she whispered.

"Well, that's a good thing."

"How's Marco? You rarely say much about him."

"Marco's wonderful. He's what I needed in my life." Tai did not offer any details. She would share her personal life with Felicia, but preferred to talk away from the office. Tai stood and looked out of the window. "I'm starting to realize, though, that with Trista around, I'm spending less and less time with him. He seems to be understanding, but a lot of times men keep everything inside. So I'm really not sure what's on his mind."

"Sis isn't blocking, is she?"

Tai laughed. "No, not blocking in that way. There's plenty of action." Tai turned and looked at Felicia. "Before she came here, of course I had more private time…alone…or with Marco. Now I'm splitting time between the two. I'm sure she'll soon start meeting her own friends, and maybe she'll meet a nice guy."

"Like I said, let's go to the club."

"Okay, I'll check with Candace and Nevada. The more of us, the better. We're due for another ladies night."

THE SUN WAS SETTING AT SNAIL-LIKE SPEED AND OFFERING A burst of brilliant orange. Dreamily, Tai gazed out of the scenic window overlooking the Potomac River. She had zoned out briefly, blocking out the chatter of her best friends who had talked incessantly. They had decided to switch up their routine of lunch downtown and have an early dinner at the National Harbor.

Boats docked along the boardwalk and a water taxi rolled out to take riders across the river to Old Town Alexandria. The Harbor in Prince George's County was one of Maryland's latest tourist attractions with its hotels, restaurants and bars. The Gaylord National Hotel was the center of this taste of city life nestled in the suburbs.

Tai, Candace and Nevada had laughed like a chorus of stand-up comediennes, receiving glares from some diners throughout their ruckus. Others were amused that the ladies were in such lively spirits. They were surrounded by an imaginary shield and were in their own storytime world. Rosa Mexicano provided a festive backdrop for the trio's shrills and cackles.

Tai tuned back in to the conversation, realizing that Nevada and Candace had not noticed she had dropped off the radar for a while.

"Girl, I couldn't believe that crazy freak! He must've thought

I was a fool if he really believed I was getting in that bed with a monster-size doll!" Candace roared. "He was outta his mind." Candace shook her head. "Then he had the nerve to have Sammy sitting in the chair looking in our direction. What a creep! I rolled up out of there in a hurry…didn't even bother to change my clothes!"

Nevada took a bite of her enchiladas. "Now that's a wild story! You sure know how to pick 'em, don't you? No wonder you said we'd have to wait and hear this story in private. I don't blame you for not wanting to share this with the world."

"And you know this!" Candace agreed.

Nevada glanced at Tai, sensing her mind was miles away. "You've been quiet; everything okay?"

"Candace had told me she was going out with a ventriloquist, so I wanted to get the scoop. She was right when she said we needed to wait until we got together." She looked at Candace. "After this one, I've heard it all!" Tai tasted her strawberry Margarita. "Mmmm, this is deee-licious."

"Yeah, girl, he's texted me but I want him to hurry up and lose my number."

"Well, I usually don't have too many stories, not like you two… But remember I was on the hunt for the hubby whose so-called widow thought he may have faked his death," Nevada stated.

Candace and Tai both nodded.

"I'll make this short, but he was living the life as a woman. I found him through some leads and when I did, he was dressed to impressed—not hooker style, but classy; a wig and long black dress—standing in line to get into Cookies and Crème."

Candace gasped. "Girl, for real? Stop, this ain't true."

"Oh yes it is. You should've seen that shocking look, like from a bad horror movie." Nevada reached for her Margarita. "I was just as bad. I would've loved to have seen the look on *my* face."

"So what happened?" Tai asked.

"When I reached Mrs. Thompson, she was stunned. She was suspicious he was alive, but she never would have imagined. Then she was pissed. She had no idea he was a cross-dresser. She said he used to compliment women's fashions in TV ads. And then she realized little things were missing like a particular color of nail polish. Or she'd say to herself, 'I thought I bought a new pair of earrings.' So he was sneaking her stuff right from under her nose."

"Wow." Candace was amazed. "So how did she handle it?"

"Girl, she kicked that bastard out of her will and changed her life insurance. Told him to take his crap and she'd never speak to him again unless it was in divorce court."

"Well, your spy skills are on point once again. Another case solved." Tai smiled proudly at Nevada, then looked at Candace. "We're lucky to have *Detective Nevada* in our corner. She's got our backs in case we ever need her."

"I'll be there; Sleuths On Us."

Nevada molded the conversation to a serious tone. "So Tai, I asked earlier but you ignored me. What's on your mind? You were in another space."

"Oh, I'm fine now. I started wondering if I should have invited Trista to come with us. I feel bad that I excluded her; especially since she was off today."

"No, you're okay. We need to keep our monthly girls' outing as it is...the *three* of us," Candace interjected. "Hey, we go way back and we don't need to break the bond. She's your sister but she doesn't need to be privy to *everythang*."

"I guess you're right. I spend a lot of time with Trista and she knows about us meeting today. I think she's fine."

"And you and Felicia already said we're all going to the club.

I'm sure she'll appreciate us including her. And since she's a dance fiend, she's definitely going to have a ball."

Tai soaked up the Mexican energy and culture in the restaurant. A neon blue tile was complemented by folk art masks. The atmosphere was picking up as more guests had entered since they'd arrived in the late afternoon. Her thoughts drifted to Marco; lately, he'd been on the back burner while she focused on girl time as well as me time. She was now in need of Marco time. She would plan a whirlwind evening of passion and pleasure.

14

Keeping the beat

B.O.B.'s "Nothin' On You" kicked out of the speakers and brought Candace and Trista to their feet.

"Yes, that's my anthem!" Candace started rocking to the beat. *Beautiful girls all over the world I could be chasing but my time would be wasted.* Tonight she was dolled up in a red-and-black jacquard form-fitting dress by her favorite Asian designer, Sushi. She had pinned her hair up with chopsticks holding her ponytail in place. She wore a dainty bracelet and stud earrings.

Tai, wearing a low-cut, V-neck pink top, paid homage to October as Breast Cancer Awareness Month. A black pencil skirt and black heels completed the look. She spun around on the barstool to check out the thirty-something ladies doing their thing on the dance floor. She would have joined them but her French martini had her chained to the bar.

Nevada and Felicia had decided to dress down and looked crisp and neat in their boot-cut jeans and heeled boots. They also sat at the bar nursing their Cosmopolitans.

Felicia turned to Tai, sitting next to her. "I told you this was a good idea. Get her out of the house."

"She's having a blast."

Tai had heard about the new club Pulse in Northwest. It was a mixed crowd and three levels featured various music. They were on the R&B/hip-hop floor; another one had live jazz and a third had house music. The interior brick walls offered a rustic look and the low recessed lighting changed colors to the beat of the music. The structure featured a huge wraparound bar with a granite countertop and high ceilings. Circular loveseats were dispersed around the room that featured a black and white décor.

Candace and Trista were no longer solo on the dance floor. A tall, dark-skinned man with deep dimples and wearing a navy suit had approached Candace. A younger, stocky man in a rayon shirt displaying his cut arms was coolly keeping up the beat while Trista made her bold, dramatic moves.

The hardwood floor was packed to the sounds of Rihanna and Drake's "What's My Name."

Tai ordered appetizers at the bar for the five to share. Felicia and Nevada had also been glued to their barstools, but she was certain they'd all eventually hit the dance floor. Trista and Candace returned to their seats at the bar, panting like they could pass out any minute.

Candace glanced in the wall mirror to check that her hair was still in place. "Whew, that was awesome. Brotherman didn't ask me for my number, but it's all good."

"Girl, you are a true playette. The night is young; I'm sure you'll hook one before it's all over," Nevada assured.

"Having a good time?" Tai asked Trista. "You've barely sat down, girl. Party hearty."

"Lovin' it...I need another drink." She motioned to the bartender who walked up to her. "Seagram's gin and orange juice. And a glass of water."

When the bartender returned, Trista sipped her drink and then grabbed a coconut shrimp off the appetizer sampler that also included teriyaki drummettes and mozzarella sticks.

"This club is cool. It's huge; so many folks. Where I'm used to going, I know almost everyone at the club," Trista remarked.

"Glad you like it. I'd heard about Pulse but I'd never been here. There's so many in the D.C. area and I haven't been clubbing in a while. I'm usually wherever there's live jazz," Tai offered.

"Well, don't feel like you had to do me a favor," Trista stated snidely.

Tai looked at her and frowned. *What? Where'd that come from? Has she had one too many drinks?*

They were out to celebrate. Tai glazed over the comment like she was on ice. She refused to let her feathers get ruffled over negativity tonight.

"May I?" A gorgeous hunk of a man reached out in Tai's direction and motioned his head toward the dance floor.

Hmmm, oh, yes. Tai arose from where her body had been attached to reveal her toned legs and curvaceous figure. The smooth effect of the martinis had unleashed her mind and body. She would show this eye candy what she was working with.

15

Brunch on this

The aroma of fresh baked biscuits, turkey bacon, crab-spinach omelettes and home-fried potatoes wafted throughout the house like it was Saturday morning at IHOP. Tangerine-orange juice, English breakfast tea and hot cocoa would complement the meal. Tai delighted in preparing her sister a hot breakfast on the weekends. During the week, it was always a grab-and-go scenario with either a muffin or toast. Trista churned the day at a restaurant; at home, she rarely desired to see a kitchen unless it was to enjoy Tai's cooking.

Tai opened the oven door and pulled out a pan of her home-made wheat biscuits and set it on the granite countertop. She scooped them from the pan onto a platter, then placed them with the other medley of dishes on her center island. *This is a lot of food for only the two of us. But you've got to treat yourself sometimes. I'm sure Trista won't complain.* Tai turned to exit the kitchen to call Trista. She looked up to see her in the doorway.

"Oh, how long have you been standing there?" Tai was startled as Trista had suddenly appeared quietly and as if it were intentional.

"Just got here." Trista inhaled the special meal her sister had prepared. "Wow, you know how to throw down. It looks and smells off the chain. I'm ready to dig in."

"I figured, it's Saturday, so why not?" Tai pulled out two plates from the shelf and handed one to Trista. "What do you want to drink?"

"I'll take the juice."

Tai poured her a tall glass, then prepared a mug of tea for herself and set them on the table decorated with a fall-color motif.

The two sat after serving their heaping plates.

"Hmm, you are a chef," Trista complimented. "I think you need to be with me at the restaurant. I mean, ours is cool and everything, but she can't hold a candle to your cooking."

"So, is the job still going well?"

"Tai, I actually love it. I didn't think I would, seeing that I've been a waitress so many times. The folks are nice and the customers tip well. We get a lot of traffic at lunchtime and on weekends. Mostly downtown workers but on weekends a lot of folks stop in after games or shows at the Verizon Center. Or after the movies around the corner. We get tourists, too, but many repeat customers; especially at lunchtime."

"I'm happy to hear you like it. I told Felicia that she did a good job placing you there."

"Hey, I'm not going anywhere, either. Like I said, at home, I wasn't always feeling the job. Maybe it was where the restaurant was…too quiet. Not enough activity. But here, I'm right in the thick of things. It's a happening scene," Trista gushed and dug into her omelette.

"Have you met anyone? Friends? *Men?*"

"Not really. I mean, some guys have tried to holla at me. 'Hey, Shawtie, can I get your digits?' Stuff like that. I'm not interested. But it's all good. I'm taking it one day at a time. Still getting used to the flava of the city life." She sipped her juice. "Sometimes I miss my homies, but I'll see them again one of these days. They ain't goin' nowhere anytime soon."

"Sounds like you're enjoying your job."

"Yeah, I appreciate old-timers like Miss Cynt—she tells me to call her *Cynthia*...but I can't—she's a sweetheart and she's for real. She tells it like it is. And don't let no customers come up in there tryin' to run a game or being a smart ass; Miss Cynt will go off. My lady is rough...and ready. But I've grown to really like her; guess she kinda reminds me of a mother figure. She's the one I need on my side. The chef and assistant chef are good people, the receptionists are young and friendly, and the other waitresses mind their own business, so I like that. We have waiters but they usually work the nightshift so I can't speak on them too much. But Miss Cynt, she's all that."

"It's a great feeling." Tai contemplated as she sipped her tea. "I never thought I'd have an employment agency. I'd always wanted to be an entrepreneur but maybe a restaurant...modeling agency...store, any business. I'm glad that I was able to help you after all the years that have passed. Now that's worth living for."

Tai and Trista sat on the high-back stainless steel chairs. They were stuffed to the max. It would be a challenge for them to rise up and start moving.

"Tell you what, you did all this good cookin', so I'm gonna clean the kitchen."

"No, you don't have to. I've got it."

"Listen, Sis, I'm not around that much, so you'd better jump on the offer."

"Okay, I'm not going to argue; you see I can hardly move. I really shouldn't stuff myself like that"—Tai rubbed her stomach—"but I deserved every drop." She smiled.

Tai stretched and rolled over to look at the clock. It was 3:42 p.m. She had drifted off to sleep watching Lifetime. She knew it was a no-no to lie down after eating like she had missed meals for a week. She should have pulled out her mat and engaged in some floor exercises. Instead, she had turned on her flatscreen and curled up on top of her bed. Saturdays usually found her either bursting with energy or dragging from exhaustion.

Tai headed to the bathroom to pat her eyes with cold water. She thought about a quick light meal she could prepare to balance the defensive linebacker's breakfast that morning. She walked toward the stairs and stopped in her tracks. She turned toward Trista's room and leaned her ear to the door. Tai could hear Trista softly moaning. *I wonder what's going on in there.* She gently rapped on the door. "Trista?"

"Go away…I wanna be alone."

Tai looked dumbfounded and debated whether to open the door. She sighed and then turned the doorknob. Trista was sitting in the darkness on her bed with the shades drawn. It was close to dusk and normally, at minimum, she would have had on her bedside lamp. "What's wrong? What are you upset about?"

"I told you I wanna be alone. I don't need you messing in my business."

"I'm only here to help. Do you want to talk about it, whatever is bothering you?" Tai did not wait for a response but sat in the chair opposite the bed. "Okay, Sis, talk to me. We're family," Tai insisted.

"Look, if you don't get outta here…I swear, I'll—"

"You'll what?"

"I won't speak to you again, that's what."

Wow, this chick is mean…is she PMSing? Or is this the new Trista?

"I opened up my house to you. I was willing to share my world, my home, my friends, and this is what I get? I'm used to being here alone, so you should be aware that I wouldn't want you sitting around here sulking." Bewildered, Tai shrugged and left the room.

Trista's expressions of excitement that morning about her waitress job were now diminished to feelings of despair. She could not explain her sudden change in mood. Her afternoon had included flashbacks of her previous lifestyle and childhood memories. She could feel the onset of an anxiety attack as her nervousness about ensuring her hidden past was at stake. Tai was a caring sister who had taken her under her wing, providing a comfortable space, sharing her time and finances, and opening doors to her work and friendship world. She wasn't feeling the idolized life; it was intruding on her comfort zone.

Since her three months with Tai, Trista had realized that they were as opposite as Beauty and the Beast. Her seesaw personality was starting to surface frequently. She had tried to suppress her irrational moods but found them difficult to temper at times. Some days it was grueling to witness Tai's *I've-got-everything-I-could-ever-want* attitude. She was at the top of the ladder while Trista believed she was on the bottom rung. It would be an uphill challenge to reach her peak on Tai's planet.

She arose from her slouched position and crept to the door. She pulled it open slightly to see if Tai was nearby. She thought about apologizing but then thought to refrain. She wasn't in any mood to get into a deep discussion about her moping. She closed the door, walked to her bed and stretched across the top. She plopped her head on her oversized pillow and stared ahead. *Maybe Tai will be back to check on me. If she does, I'll tell her I'm sorry for being so rotten. She doesn't understand how I get into this funk. Sometimes I don't get it, either.*

16

Do drop in

The blustery chill breezed through the glass door of Seacoast. Trista brought three glasses of hot chocolate and set them on the table. She picked up the check and Tai's credit card. Tai, Candace and Nevada had just completed seafood linguine, a crab cake platter and blackened tuna. They were preparing to hit the cold during this Christmas season. A round of steamy drinks would help warm them for the frostiness ahead.

It was their first time visiting Trista at her job; they had made a surprise stop at Seacoast and were pleased to see she had skills, providing top service and deserving a top tip. They had observed her spinning on her heels to wait on customers from a tiny, elegant woman with silver hair to a group of hefty guys who looked like Redskins tryouts. Trista resonated with confidence and satisfaction; she appeared to love being in her element.

"I enjoyed the food. We'll have to make this one of our stops for our ladies lunch." Candace sipped her cocoa.

"Trista was right about the crab cakes. I'm glad we came through; I think Trista appreciated it, too." Tai leaned back in her chair and checked her phone. No calls or texts from Marco. She had placed it in her purse so not to be disturbed during dinner. She wondered what would be the ideal holiday gift for him; they had now been together for five months. She was still getting to know him and his taste.

"Thanks for the treat." Nevada finished the last drop in her mug. "I've got the next one."

"You're welcome."

"Definitely thanks," Candace agreed.

The saturation of downtown with Christmas lights captured the holiday season. Residents quickly ducked in and out of doors to avoid the bitter cold and look for gifts from the numerous specialty stores. Others strolled to soak in the festive atmosphere. Tai favored her tradition of making at least one visit to the area during Christmastime. This year included a stop at Trista's place, located in the heart of the action.

Visions of her grandmother window-shopping downtown in-filtrated her mind. She would have Tai in tow as they perused the aisles at the old Lansburgh and Woodward & Lothrop department stores; both now a mere memory as they had permanently shut their doors. Her favorite pastime had been peering into the candy counter window on the first floor and sweating the chocolate peanut clusters. Her grandmother always would order a pound for the two of them to share. Candy counters in department stores were a thing of the past. Tai had especially enjoyed the store windows with the animated figures in motion. They would stroll along the sidewalks and observe the tiny characters prominently on display. Afterward, they would wrap up even tighter and head to Sixteenth Street to walk along the paths of the Christmas trees. A decorated tree from each state would grace the area in front of the White House; fifty in total plus the national Christmas tree.

"Well, are you ladies ready to hit the stores?" Tai asked.

"Ready when you are." Nevada stood to retrieve her coat.

"Now you don't have to ask me. Shopping is my middle name and 'sale' is imprinted on my forehead." Candace laughed and wrapped her scarf around her neck, then pulled on her coat.

Tai slipped into her jacket and then headed to the back to look for Trista. "We wanted you to join us, but I didn't know you had to work late."

"Thanks for stopping in. You see this place stays busy."

"And you are doing great handling it, too. I can see how you keep in shape. Whew."

"Right. I rarely get a break except the one I'm scheduled to get." Trista handed Tai back her card. "I was getting ready to bring it to you."

"No problem. I wanted to see you alone anyway. You take care." She hugged Trista. "See you tonight. Be safe."

"Bet."

Tai walked back to the front of the restaurant and the three stepped out into the chilly air.

17

'Tis the season

Tai darted throughout and spritzed the first floor with a seductive scent. Candace had schooled her about fragrances and how each one produced various moods. She was ensuring that this one spelled s-e-x. Her iPod was loaded to continuous play of romantic ballads.

The Christmas tree was lit and the pine aroma wafted throughout the den. It stood guard next to the fireplace that was heating up the room to a toasty temperature. The bottle of champagne in the metal bucket was chilled to perfection. It was a season to celebrate the occasion, but it also had been six months since Marco had entered her life. He was the king on her throne any day. Sometimes being independent could hurt a sistah and one needed to keep that in mind. It didn't mean one couldn't be empowered or show strength, but men loved women who could also get weak in the knees and be humble.

Tai sashayed, feeling sexily clad underneath her flowing dress. She couldn't wait to show off her new Victoria's Secret ensemble. She had saturated her body with Calvin Klein's Euphoria and lotion. Her open-toe black stilettos displayed her freshly pedicured toes polished in Lincoln Park at Midnight. Marco was a foot soldier so she knew he would adore her twinkies.

Blackstreet's "Joy" pumped through the speakers and Tai twirled to the harmonious ballad. When the doorbell rang, she straightened her dress, smoothing it out and adjusting the shoulder strap.

She slowly opened the door and her mouth grew into a wide grin. She batted her eyelashes—*this mascara works*—and puckered her lips to kiss Marco's.

"Hi, baby," Tai said seductively, "you are right on time." She motioned for him to enter. "It's cold out so I've got a fire going to keep us nice and warm."

"Hi. It feels great in here."

Tai led him into the den, emphasizing the motion of her hips.

"Let me take your coat," she said, reaching for the wool black trench.

Marco held up his hand and removed his scarf and gloves. "I got this, thanks." He unbuttoned his coat and Tai melted.

The hunk was completely in the nude.

Tai gasped. *Naughty but nice.* "I can't believe you…" She giggled, then tossed her head and shook it. "But you sure are sexy. I won't ever put anything past you."

Marco quietly removed his coat and laid it on the chair. He pulled Tai toward him and slowly grinded her. "And what are you hiding?" He pulled down the shoulder of her dress and Tai shimmied out of it as it dropped to the floor.

"I knew you had something special for the occasion."

Tai stepped back to show her red bra and thong set, her hips protruding as she twirled around to tease his Pride.

"Hmmph, hmmph, hmmm." Marco licked his lips. He reached out and gently eased Tai onto the rug just in front of the fireplace. She stretched out on her back with her heels in place on the carpet. Marco lay beside her and lightly kissed her neck. He then reached over and trailed her body, placing more light pecks on her chest, her nipples and navel before reaching her moist patch. He opened her lips and inserted his tongue while enjoying her peach nectar. He swirled and swirled until Tai let out a soft moan.

Tai slightly opened her eyes and admired Marco's physique. His Pride was now engorged and the imaginary taste infiltrated her mind. Marco squatted over her, knees on each side. Tai eagerly stroked his member and licked gently as she savored the moment. His cologne was working overtime, creating excitement in her wet patch and tantalizing her nostrils. She feverishly picked up the pace as she grew more intense with her sucking. Marco attempted to be resilient but as time passed he was uncertain he could maintain control. He reached over on the chair and pulled his coat to the floor. He dug into the pocket until his found his man cover. Tai glanced over and released him. He quickly placed on the condom and mounted her, gently sliding into her womanhood. He started with smooth thrusts before gradually increasing with more intensity. Tai rotated her hips to each thrust and kicked her stilettos in the air and closed her legs snugly around his back. She pressed tightly to grip him. They continued until the ultimate climax. Sweat and scents mixed as they immersed in sexual bliss.

TAI AND MARCO SAT ON THE RUG IN FRONT OF THE FIRE, WHICH had died down considerably before Marco had piled on more logs from the deck. They had showered together before returning to the fireside for champagne and dessert. Donny Hathaway's "This Christmas" helped set the mood.

Marco popped the cork and poured the liquid into two champagne glasses. He handed Tai a glass, picked up his and pecked her lips. He raised his glass as Tai did hers.

"To us. Happy holidays, baby."

"To us. Happy holidays to you, too. What a way to bring in the New Year. We're only a week early, but oh well…"

Marco sipped his champagne.

Tai brought the glass to her lips. *Cheers. This young man is not only a fantastic lover, but he's up on the mental thing, too. He knows how to please a lady…*

She set down her glass and pulled her sheer top over her head and laid it on the rug. She gently took Marco's glass from his hand and placed it on the coffee table. "I'm ready for Round Two." She smiled seductively.

18

Forty-one and flirty

Tai couldn't believe that her birthday had rolled around again. She had desired to have a creative event to celebrate No. 41. Hell, last year was a bust after she'd planned a grand party only for Austin to pull a no-show. Despite it being a year and having found her new love for Marco, she still couldn't squash the experience. She was burning that Austin had embarrassed her in such a way in front of her friends.

This year, she wouldn't go for an extravagant ball like she was a queen—designer attire on an imaginary red carpet and all the hoopla. She would bring in her birthday on a simple scale. Ladies night with the '70s and '80s theme had been a splash, so she decided another chick night would be in order. She would invite the same crew for a repeat.

CANDACE KICKED OFF HER HEELS AND PLOPPED ON THE SOFA. "Girl, this better be the bomb. Not to say your birthday isn't important"—she fanned herself—"but I had a hot, hot date. This man is phine with a capital P!"

Nevada suggested, "Aren't they all? At least, according to you."

"Honey, you are simply jealous!"

"I have my boo and he's waiting for me at home, just as he always does," Nevada defended herself. "So patiently and he understands I've gotta have my own space. Sometimes it's ladies only. I need the reprieve, to get away and be with my peeps. Ryan will be there *whenever* I get home."

"Yep, and one of these days, you're going to walk in and he'll be outta there," Candace rebutted teasingly.

"Well, for now he's addicted to his TV and his cell…and his laptop."

"And you forgot to mention sports. They all love the hoops, and the touchdowns, and the home runs," Tai added.

"ESPN junkies. What I don't get is why do all the sports have to be on at the same time? Pro and college football; pro and college basketball; baseball; golf tournaments. Everything is overlapping. Why not one sport at a time?" Nevada asked.

"Honey, *I* get it. I realize I may as well learn about the games because it's all so important to them." Candace curled her legs up on the sofa. "This new honey, he's a *ladies* man. He is so smooth and gentlemanly. His pockets are lined—"

"What is he? Let me guess…a…" Ideas rolled through Nevada's mind.

"No, girl, he's got a normal career. He's a photographer, but he used to live in the Midwest and he was a storm chaser! He used to get paid for his videos."

"I don't know how you do it. You sure know how to find 'em."

"Hey, they gravitate toward *me*. I must have my radar running for the strange and stranger." Candace laughed.

Tai entered the den from upstairs. "Sorry, I had to change. I've been running around here all day. Thank you for coming. I'm waiting on Cori and…"

"My sis is always running behind. You should know that," Candace stated. "Cori thought she'd beat me here but I showed her that I can be on time, too. She should be here shortly."

"Well, before the others get here, what's up? What's new?" Tai inquired.

"Same old, same old for me," Nevada stated.

"Like I was saying, this new guy, Brendan, is such a good catch. He is truly for the ladies. He won me over from the get-go," Candace admitted. "I met him at this launch party for Emanuel Ungaro. They have a new haute couture line for women. You should see the dresses. I'm dying to get me one of those bad pieces. Step out in a crowd and everyone will notice. Ungaro's known for saying, 'I dress mistresses, not wives.' I just love him!

"Brendan's from Florida so he was complaining about the cold weather, so he wanted me to stop by his hotel room at the Ritz-Carlton. I told him that D.C. winters are actually mild compared to most places," Candace continued. "I was definitely going to heat him up. Take him back down south." She smirked. "But duty calls. I had to be here for my girl." She looked at Tai. "I wouldn'tve missed it for the world. So let's get this party started!"

Tai brought out serving platters of fried spring rolls, fresh stir-fry veggies and jasmine rice. Candace and Nevada served their small plates and drank their usual helpings of wine. Tai joined them as they sat on the floor around the coffee table.

"This is simple but delicious. You need to open your own restaurant or start a catering business." Nevada savored a roll and dipped it in teriyaki sauce.

"Thanks." Tai offered second helpings but they both refused. She looked at her watch. "I hope Cori and Sierra get here soon."

She made her way to the kitchen with the empty platter. Nevada stacked the plates and followed Tai.

"You said there would be a surprise. And I'm dying to find out. You know the deal with me." Nevada was anxious.

"Yes, Miss Detective, but this time you'll have to wait."

After Cori and Sierra arrived, Tai was relieved. Everyone needed to be there by midnight.

TAI'S WINE COLLECTION HAD GIVEN ALL A BOOST. THEY'D PROBABLY need to crash at her place tonight. No drinking behind the wheel. Thinking ahead, all had come equipped with their pj's and overnight gear. Tai had a stash of blankets and pillows and was prepared to open her home until dawn. She wouldn't have to worry about disturbing Trista who was working the overnight shift at the restaurant.

"You have the best stories!" Candace turned toward her sister, Cori. "Guess I was too young for you to share with me back in the day!"

"You ain't heard nothin' yet." Cori laughed, then sipped from her wineglass. "Do you remember my friend Tara?" she asked Candace.

"I remember her...she was always cussin' and grouchy. She had a hard edge. You'd never think those words would escape her mouth by looking at her. But she was smooth."

"Yep, that was her. My girl. She'd take three hours to get ready to go out with us. Probably an hour on her hair, an hour on her makeup, then an hour on whatever she was wearing. We really had to have patience to hang with her."

"She was always dressed to the tee, though. She looked like she made a point to be neat every time she stepped out." Candace smiled. "I'm the same way, so can't blame that she was. Whatever happened to her anyway?"

"That's a good question," Cori responded. "I lost contact with her. At times she was a little strange and then we ended up growing apart." She continued, "Well, there was this guy named Rocky that we knew. He was a mutual friend. I used to sleep with him sometimes; nothing serious. Just one of my bedmates. We had a weird attraction.

"His family lived in Philly, so one time he invited both of us to go there with him. It was a special event that weekend. So, we said cool and the three of us rode up in his hoopty.

"Girl, we were chilling out at this apartment, drinking and having fun. She was always so evil and complaining and mumbling. But girl, whenever she was around him, she was *soooo* not her. She was like, '*Rocky…Rocky…,*' rubbing on his head and trying to talk all sexy and girlie-like. Kissing up to him, basically. Not like her usual hard, cussing-like-a-sailor mouth.

"Well, we all got blasted—remember we had taken a road trip to Philly with him—and next thing you know, we were in a threesome," Cori continued. "I was pissed because I wanted him to *myself.* We were used to doing our thing, and I didn't like sharing him with Tara. They had never hooked up; at least not that I know of.

"We then ended up in the shower, all three of us…and we were grooving and both of us were washing and lathering him. I couldn't stand it! So I pulled off the showerhead and sprayed her hair!" Cori laughed menacingly. "I said to myself, *Biatch. Now take that! You always worried about your hair. Now stay away from my man!*"

"That was mean, Cori," Candace chastised her sister. "But that is funny as hell." *I sure wouldn't want no hussy messing up this hair.*

The other ladies roared with infectious laughter.

"You lying! Now that's a crazy one! Remind me to never like the same man as you!" Nevada joked but was quite serious.

"Did you stay friends with her when you came back to D.C.?" Tai asked.

"Hell yeah. We were still cool. She was livid with me for a while. We did ride back in silence for the most part. It was a crazy feeling. But yeah, we smoothed things out and started talking and hanging out again…a few months later."

Tai looked at Nevada. "Remember one of my favorite stories… and I always think about this incident. That bartender that I hooked up with. He was a good-looking brother. I'm sure he made good tips at that club…it was called…the…"

"Red Room," Nevada recalled. "Oh, yeah, I remember."

"Ladies, I went to his place," Tai continued. "I just knew I was going to have a hell of a night with this man. But look, we never even got down. He had the *ugliest* feet in America. I couldn't get past them so I got turned off.

"When I was telling Nevada about the whole thing, and that I couldn't look at his feet, she looked at me and said, 'Well, what about his piece?'" Tai dropped her head and laughed. "She was so serious when she asked, too."

"Yeah, I was like, ugly feet, but how was he looking in that other department?" Nevada stated. "You thought I was wild for asking you that. Girl, we had some wild times."

"And that's why it's a good thing to have our ladies nights. We can share our stories." Tai arose and walked toward the kitchen. She looked back in the den. "More Mojitos coming up!"

The surprise of the night, a freaky trio of handsome brothas, stood in their birthday suits in the center of the den. Each was the flavor of the month. Rod, a tall, chocolate hunk, displayed his extra-long shaft covered in a cheetah case. Reel, the sandy-brown stallion, had an extra-long tongue. Rope, who had a chiseled body wrapped with thick string, was geared to capture the ladies with his sado-macho skills.

Rope started gyrating to Babyface's "Whip Appeal." He pulled Cori toward him and lured her to the corner of the room. He whipped out a pair of handcuffs and placed them behind Cori's back, cuffing her to the sturdy chair. Rope scooped low and grinded on top of her, giving her a lap dance. He twisted and grinded, facing her before turning his back to her and providing a rear view of the perfect ass.

Cori's face lit up like a Christmas tree as she restrained from looking embarrassed but loving every minute of this private show. The others looked on in amazement as Rope sat on Cori's lap, faced her, bent his body backward onto the floor and locked his heels into the back of the chair. Then he smoothly flipped his legs over his head and stretched his heels into the floor before drawing them underneath his body. *Wow, I've only seen this with the contortionists at the UniverSoul Circus. This man's got skills. I'd love to see what he's working with under the sheets*, Cori thought. *I'd love to hire him for my own exclusive show…*

Reel sleekly eyed Candace and Tai before setting his eyes on Nevada. Perched upright on the sofa, she was praying that she wouldn't be part of the act. After all, she was the observer, not the participant. Her watchful eye was always roaming, trying to ensure that she never missed a beat. Reel approached Nevada with a sexy swagger and halted in front of her. He stuck out his tongue and licked his lips.

Wow, I've never seen a tongue that long! Nevada squirmed and realized she was the next "victim" of this fantastic freak show.

Reel gently touched her shoulder and eased her to lower herself on the sofa. He placed her legs horizontally across it, then fell to his knees. He released his tongue and started teasing her with soft kisses, then progressed to distinct laps on her neck. Boyz II Men's "I'll Make Love to You" provided the ideal background.

He flipped her over and seductively pushed her top upward. He sweetly flickered his tongue on the back of her neck, on her shoulders and down her back. Nevada melted like a Hershey's Kiss. Reel's wet kisses were tender and tantalizing. She imagined herself being licked and lapped for a full day by this gorgeous man with the lizard tongue.

Candace watched Reel lusciously lick up and down Nevada and envied the ecstasy. She sat cross-legged and secretly hoped that Reel would entice her, especially when the mix-tape CD segued to Maxwell's "Pretty Wings." *That's my favorite song*, Candace thought.

After the ultimate lickdown, Reel stood up and smiled as he maneuvered his way to Candace. Nevada lay satiated in another world. She so needed this diversion; her new detective cases were both intriguing and challenging. She'd awaited an opportunity like this; to relax and ease her mind. She didn't realize a handsome specimen would be the one to satisfy her every desire.

Candace grinned from ear to ear. *This Daddy Longtongue is here to please me.* With legs crossed, she kicked her thigh-high black suede boots in and out as she anticipated Reel's next move. *Baby, do me, do your thing…*Maxwell continued to croon. Reel kneeled before her and gripped her boot. *Oooo, what a nice grip.* He slowly and seductively pulled the boot forward until it was completely off her foot. He removed her sheer knee-high, textured sock to reveal her freshly polished toes in Give Me Moor color. Her smooth foot shone from Candace rubbing it thoroughly with moisturizing lotion for extra-dry skin. She wiggled her toes. *Thank goodness, I used some spray so my feet smell like I've just stepped out of the shower. And they ain't ashy!*

Reel massaged her foot, taking Candace into euphoria. She was a sucker for a foot massage. Any man who rubbed her feet, especially with peppermint oil, was tops on her list. It was simply blissful. Reel propped Candace's right leg up over her left thigh. He positioned himself on the floor directly in front of her and continued to massage her leg, foot and toes. "Nice color."

Hmm-mmm. "Thank you." Candace blushed and smiled.

"You're welcome. Nice feet, too."

"I try." Candace wiggled her toes.

Reel stroked the top and bottom of her foot, then massaged each toe. His tongue protruded and he licked her toes, then sucked each one while moaning, expressing the pleasure derived from his foot feast. Normally, he would lick a woman from head to literally toe. He always had to check out the feet first before lavishing them.

Candace became engrossed in a fantasy featuring her in the role of the Queen of Sheba and Reel as her personal foot masseur. She imagined being back on the reality TV set of *Wild Isle* and trapped on the private island with Reel. He would stroke and suck her feet continuously until she requested a break, which would be *never*.

Reel lapped her toes until the scene transformed to the final leg of the show: Rod. He stood in the center of the room and grinded to Usher's "There Goes My Baby."

He has the most beautiful ass I've ever seen. Tai figured she would be the finale as others had already been blessed with a seductive treat. Last was not always the least. With Sisqo's "Thong Song," Rod picked up the tempo with twirling and turning as he teased. He had been a much sought-after dancer who had gained a reputation throughout the D.C./Maryland and Virginia area, better known as the DMV. His "rod" had garnered him the nickname because of his length…had to be a thirteen. He hurled his body around to reveal toned thighs and a beefed-up chest. His "rod" worked overtime as it swung with each beat; the cheetah shaft cover was mesmerizing. Rod smiled incessantly as he was aware that his swift moves were adored by the ladies. He was truly known as a dick tease, literally.

"Work it, baby!" Candace roared. She jumped up to join Rod in this seductive show. "You got *skills*, so I know you've been around the block."

Cori cheered on, "You got that right, Sis. Do the damn thing!"

Rod intensified his movements, now teasing the crew with his gyrations, rolls and thrusts.

"Dollar bills, ladies!" Candace shouted. She whipped out one from her purse and placed it in Rod's G-string.

He moved closer. "Honey, I'mma attack you." He enveloped her with a lap dance.

"Oh, please do!" Candace bravely groped his rod. "What a pipe!" She fell back to let the other ladies enjoy the visual.

Rod eased up from Candace's lap, still shaking his gigantic cane and pulled Tai up toward him. He embraced her and grinded with full force. It reminded Tai of her old school days when she would dance snugly with a hormone-blazing guy at a blue-lights-in-the-basement party. Rod had no inhibitions and he loved having his monster tool on display. When the chorus kicked in again, Rod suddenly lifted Tai into his arms and spun her around to the hip-hop beat. Tai realized the 3 R's were there to please, but they were definitely more than she had bargained for. What better way to celebrate her forty-first birthday…

When the song slowed, so did Rod. He had placed Tai on her feet and she later sat back down to observe the show. Now Reel and Rope had joined Rod in the center of the room. They pumped to the sounds of their theme song: They brought all of the ladies to their feet and Tai's house was now the scene of a humpfest.

The 3 R's pulled the ladies close and grinded and humped and rocked till the break of dawn. When the women were all spent, the 3 R's took turns feeding them chocolate strawberries. The indulgence would only rejuvenate them for part two of this ecstasy experience.

This puts a new meaning on the 3 R's, Tai thought. *No reading, 'riting or 'rithmetic with this trio. They know how to school you, all right, and I'll take lessons anytime.*

19

Jungle gym

Tai peered out of the window of her fifteenth-floor office. The bumper-to-bumper traffic and pedestrians created a maze of evening-rush hour activity. She attempted to re-energize from a hectic day at the Next Phase: three meetings and budget planning for the new year had caused her to feel brain-dead. Her body was equally drained.

It was her fifth scheduled session with her personal trainer, Hasan, and she was in no mood to do the slightest workout. Her mind wandered to stretching out in bed, curling up and munching on her favorite potato chips or cashews. She'd had a light lunch of a tossed salad with carrots, raisins and sunflower seeds. Tai particularly planned to cut back on calories and had been faithful. Occasionally, she would have a setback and end up splurging on snacks. As her thoughts trailed, she tried to come up with an excuse to skip tonight's workout. She picked up her cell to call and cancel.

No, I'd better go. It was only the start of her resolution to remain fit by dieting and exercise. She had always been committed to maintaining but in recent years, she discovered she needed an extra push. Signing up with a trainer would force her to stick to a regimen. She had enjoyed her first session last week with Hasan. When she'd arrived home, her hot tub of water and Jacuzzi were calling her name. It had been a chore to make it to the office the next morning.

Tonight would be a stress-reliever after her and Marco's first dog-and-cat fight—a simple disagreement that had transformed into a heated argument. Tai had felt disrespected when Marco's ex-girlfriend had called him while he was at her place. He'd answered the call, apparently because she was blowing up his cell with calls and text messages before he finally picked up. He demanded that she lose his number. Marco thought Tai was upstairs taking a bath (she'd only run the water), but she returned downstairs to get her novel she'd left in the den. She had over-heard him and had become enraged. He left after she refused to let him explain and apologize. Tai later decided that she had overreacted and called to apologize. She figured it had been silly to give him such a hard time; after all, it wasn't his fault that he had a woman still feenin' for him. He was a total package: per-sonality, looks, and he was packing in the right places. It was understandable how the woman would be clinging on, hoping to never let go...permanently.

Now that she had forgiven the incident, she couldn't wait until the weekend. Valentine's Day would be an opportunity to rekindle their romance on a much better note. Their little getaway to Massanutten would provide plenty of ambience in the mountains where they could be cozy and cuddle up in their private cabin. She had attempted to find a resort in the Poconos, but they were all booked. The weather this time of year was uncertain but she'd heard that no snow was in the forecast. Tai would make up for her spoiled behavior.

TAI PLACED HER BAGS ON THE BENCH AND OPENED HER GYM LOCKER. Then she glanced in the mirror. Her sleeveless tank top showed off her well-toned arms. She wore loose-fitting black sweats with a tie waist. She was prepared to be comfy. She pulled back her hair and pinned it up to rest atop her head. Sweating would be part of the routine, but her hair didn't have to look like a mop afterward. She looked at the clock. Her session would start in thirty minutes. She would warm up by doing light routines and be ready when it was time to work out vigorously. She spritzed on a mist of vanilla musk and took a deep breath. Despite her exhaustion, she would play a mind game and pretend she was exuberant and gung-ho for the intense workout ahead.

Tai's new rule was to eat before 8 p.m. Her plan would occasionally allow her to nibble on appetizers or snacks, but she would refrain from heavy meals. She enjoyed cooking, so this was at the top of her mission-*not*-accomplished list. After leaving the office, she had stopped at her favorite diner and ordered a light dinner before heading to the gym.

Ten-pound weights in hand, she stood in front of the mirror and started lifting one hand at a time. The tricep curls had been working overtime as she was noticeably firming and toning her arms. She posed in position and did lunges with both legs, then marched in place.

It was 8:05 p.m. Tai had gazed at the clock to see that Hasan was late. She continued with her warm-up after climbing on the treadmill. She would start out slow as the faster speed would be during her training session. As she took small, short strides on the machine, she looked out of the floor-to-ceiling window and watched passersby on the street. It was unlike Hasan not to be on time. The gym area was sparse with only two other patrons who were winding up their routines. Tai felt uneasy as she didn't want to be left alone and decided she'd leave, too, if Hasan didn't show. She stared out the window, then suddenly noticed a reflection in the glass. Hasan was standing behind her. She gradually slowed and shut off the treadmill, then turned around.

"Hi, I thought maybe you had forgotten about me." Tai sighed. "I was warming up to get ready."

"Yes, I'm sorry I'm a little late. I had a phone call that I needed to wrap up. I couldn't seem to get away. I apologize."

"It's cool. It gave me some extra time. I've had a stressful day, actually week, and needed to work some of this drama off my mind."

"Sorry to hear about the tension. We'll do a full workout to eliminate your pain." He turned to walk toward the weights.

"Let me show you. This is the newest add-on to your routine. I want you to practice this at home." He moved up close behind her like a sandwich and overlooking her shoulder, he demonstrated how he wanted her to do lifts.

Then he lay on the carpet to show Tai the sit-ups, push-ups and leg lifts. He arose. "Now, you do it: first sit-ups…"

Tai stretched on the floor and did reps. Then she sat up and whipped her legs around and lay facedown. She lifted her body and did a repetition of push-ups. *I never thought I could do these.* She was determined to prove to Hasan that she was focused and capable and could perform like she was a celebrity superstar with her private trainer.

The two gym patrons had headed for the locker room and were now leaving the facility. "Good night," they said in unison.

"Good night, see you next week." Hasan looked at them as they exited the self-lock door. Guests had a special card to gain entry after closing time. Hasan was scheduled to close out tonight. He had pulled a ten-hour shift and was beat down; however, he was proud that he had signed up five members today. There was an in-house competition for Employee of the Month and it was based on the number of new guests. To date, he was leading. Hasan had a charismatic nature that matched his well-defined body. His piercing eyes looked through you as if he could read inside your mind. Even a shy church mouse would find him appealing.

After her round of push-ups, Tai sat Indian-style to catch her breath and take a moment to regroup. Next Hasan asked her to lie flat for her leg lift routine. Tai complied with his request and repeated the steps.

Tai was invigorated after her workout. She was ecstatic that she was sticking to her guns about keeping up with her annual resolutions. Usually by February they were dropped off her radar. They were never any fun and were tough for her to maintain. So far she was successful with the workouts.

She debated on whether to take a shower before leaving the gym. After all, it was chilly outdoors and she would put herself at risk once she stepped outside. *Oh, well, I can't take this yucky feeling…too sweaty for me. I don't think Hasan will mind. He said he had some paperwork to do so I think it's cool.* She took out her duffel bag from the locker and pulled out her body wash, clean lingerie, and towel and headed to the stall. After the quick shower, she dressed in a one-piece jumpsuit and threw on her Nikes. She put on her coat and grabbed her purse and duffel bag. Tai remembered that she was to call Trista before leaving. She wanted to ensure she had made it home safely on Metro or if she needed a ride home since she was also downtown late. Trista's shift was to be over tonight at 9:30; it was now 9:15. Usually when Trista had a late shift and if it coincided with her training session, she would swing by the restaurant and pick her up.

Tai stopped and pulled out her iPhone to call Trista. Her phone was dead and her charger was in the car. She had mistakenly left it on as she usually shut it down to save power. She walked toward the gym's main office.

"Hey, do you mind if I use the land line? My cell died and I need to call my sister. Figured I'd call before I left out of here. I might have to pick her up from her job."

"Sure, Tai. Help yourself." Hasan pointed to the phone on the desk where he sat leafing through papers.

Tai picked up the receiver and dialed Trista's cell. There was no answer. She hung up and called again. Still no answer. *Hmmm, I hope she's okay. That's strange for her not to pick up. I would send a text, but I guess she took the subway.*

Hasan looked up from his paperwork. "Didn't reach her?"

"Right, she didn't answer. Guess I'd better get going."

Hasan stood and walked from behind his desk. "Not before we finish some business."

"What's up? I'm paid up through the end of the month, right?"

He approached her with a sly grin. "Most definitely. You're good." He gently removed the duffel bag from her hand and then released the purse from her shoulder. He placed both on the desk.

"Maybe you should take off your coat. There's no rush."

"I—" Tai reached to pick up her bags off the desk; he softly but firmly gripped her arm.

"Nice coat but perhaps you can rest it on the chair." He walked behind her and draped it off of her shoulders before removing it. He laid it on the chair.

"Listen, Hasan, I'm not sure what's gotten in to you, but I'm—"

Ignoring her comment, he continued to undress Tai by unzipping her jumpsuit and pulling it down to reveal her curvaceous figure. *I knew she was holding. What a banging body. I've been undressing her with my eyes and now I see the real deal.*

"Really, Hasan, you know I've gotta go. I have an early day and I need to get out of here." Tai tried to resist his charm but the Idris Elba lookalike was working her libido. She could feel the moistness stirring and that was her weak spot. She was tempted as if it were a million-dollar check dangling before her and daring her to give in. Hasan walked toward the door, closed it and then dimmed the light switch.

Tai turned around as he walked back toward her. She was in her lingerie. *I must look sexy in my Nikes, yeah, right.* "It's hard to resist—"

He placed his finger on her lips to quiet her, then suddenly kissed her deeply as he embraced her around the waist. "Now it's time for the real workout," he stated seductively. He removed his sweats and his wife beater. Hasan wrapped his arms around her waist, lifting her and carrying her across the room. He mounted her on a high table and planted kisses on her neck.

Tai gave into temptation and wrapped her legs around his back as she sat up and he stood before her. He was ready to disrobe his throbbing member but realized that Tai was shaking her head. "I've got a coat. Girl, you're going to make me wait." He walked to the coat rack and reached inside his coat and pulled a condom out of his wallet. He returned to the table. Tai was the epitome of a feline waiting to attack. She squirmed and rolled her eyes upward, anticipating a euphoric experience. A personal trainer was definitely in dynamite physical condition; this one was eye candy to boot and she was sure that stamina was in his vocabulary.

Hasan lowered his boxers and kicked them off on the floor. He placed on his condom, positioned himself and slowly entered her wetbox. Starting with slow motion, he pushed and thrust as Tai became tender and moist. The steady and smooth rhythm continued as Tai grabbed hold of his neck as she threw her head back in ecstasy. She whimpered, then bit her lip as she felt an explosion ready to erupt. She didn't want to cum prematurely before her trainer was exasperated. He had been persistent about her staying for this late-night rendezvous. She loved the diversion from the straight-laced image she had to portray at the office.

This was her private time to be spontaneous and get satisfied on a whim. She lived for moments like this…and of course, her ladies nights, another opportunity to unleash her every desire.

Hasan pounded her as if it were the last piece of pussy he'd ever be granted. Tai enjoyed the continuous pumping and again resisted cumming. She wanted it to be as one.

"Oh, baby, baby, yeah, this is so goooood. Sooooo gooood. You're going to make me…explode…this is hmmm-hmmm. Yeah, yeah… Yeahhhhh."

Hasan lay atop Tai. He lightly kissed her neck and then her lips. Tai had cum in sync with him and she lay there with a smile. *Now that's what I call a workout. Shame on me…but next week can't come any sooner.*

HASAN ESCORTED TAI TO THE FRONT DOOR WHERE SHE TURNED around to face him. He pecked her lips before opening the door.

"See you Thursday." Tai smiled demurely.

"Bet." Hasan closed the door and looked out the window to ensure she was safe inside her car. He headed back to the office. He put the papers in a neat stack and would be back on task in the morning. Reclining in the chair, he relished his rendezvous with Tai. Since she'd started as a client, he'd found her attractive, but he had refrained from making any moves. Usually, like the old cliché, he didn't mix business with pleasure. Tai was an exception.

20

Mountains and moods

Marco eased down the hill in his F-150, careful not to slide into any of the cars that were stranded on the side of the road. Climbing down this mountain would take a lot of skill. A foot of snow had invaded their romantic Valentine's Day escapade. It was a welcome sight as they drank wine into the wee hours and embraced by the fireplace. It had been soothing to watch the snow blanket the resort during a lovers' weekend, creating a spectacular winter wonderland.

Tai had adored being locked in with Marco. Her feelings were becoming stronger as they were connecting in mind and body. Every time they had a getaway she realized that she could survive simply by his presence. He pleased her so profoundly one-on-one that she didn't desire any outside elements. He alone was total satisfaction.

As he maneuvered his way through the snow to reach the base of the mountain, Tai's thoughts drifted to five nights ago. It had been pure passion at the gym. While she had enjoyed the evening, she had been haunted by her unfaithfulness. No, she and Marco weren't married, but she was always one who believed in commitment. On the flip side, she didn't see anything wrong with an occasional *slam-bam-thank-you-ma'am* hookup. Those one-night stands could do a girl good. It was when you started to develop feelings that you put your emotional state at-risk. While she was in love with Marco, she realized she may have been in lust with Hasan. Tai had thought perhaps she wouldn't return for her future training sessions, but Hasan had succeeded in getting her into a groove. She had observed some of the other trainers at the gym and considered him the optimum; he was also the manager. For now, she'd stick to her guns and keep up her resolution to work out routinely.

Marco was truly a sweetheart and had been quite attentive lately. *Maybe he senses something's up. Maybe not. He's trying so hard to make up that whole ex-girlfriend situation. Again, I may have overreacted. Deep down, I must still be harboring bad feelings. I stuck with Austin those five years and never wandered off base. Then he shredded to threads what I thought was the ultimate relationship. He ripped apart my heart with no forewarning. Then came Marco, like a winning-lottery ticket—one in a million chances—a man of any woman's dreams.*

"This snow is a challenge." Marco moved the steering wheel back and forth, skillfully making his way downhill.

"You're doing good. Glad we brought your truck instead of my little baby."

"Right. We would've been stuck like these other cars." Marco referred to vehicles they were passing on their path. He adjusted his shades. "Since we rushed off, you feel like stopping for breakfast?"

"Sure. What about that little country inn down the road? We passed it on the way here. I can eat my healthy stuff there. I heard they've got a low-calorie menu."

"Cool."

Tai eased back in the seat. It would be a two-hour drive home; the scenic route through rural Virginia might be exactly what she needed to regroup. She would attempt to erase the fantastic fling, but the gym workout weighed heavily on her mind.

21

Ties that bind

Tai was getting acclimated to having Trista around, but it seemed that with their busy schedules they'd had little time to connect. They were beginning to bond in a strange sort of way. It was a strain, but she was always the type to give everything her best effort. She had contemplated what they could do to smooth out their relationship.

She figured that a girls' day was in order. It would be the two of them.

Often Tai would catch glimpses of Trista in a daze. Whenever she would inquire about her thoughts, Trista would brush her off and simply disregard her. Tai felt the dishonesty and wasn't sure how to penetrate deeper into Trista's mind. Tai found her to be in her own world. She had hoped that she would develop some close relationships outside of their circle. This would enable her to become more independent. Her long hours at the restaurant kept her fatigued and rarely free for outside activity.

Tai had decided to break the ice—again—and conjured up the ideal day of sisterhood.

Tai and Trista emerged on the enclosed rooftop wraparound lounge. The brilliant rays provided warmth at their table in the revolving restaurant. Storybook views of the downtown landscape featured images of the White House, Washington Monument and Capitol. Other angles revealed the Potomac River, the Smithsonian and Constitution Hall, which Tai noted as the R&B haven for concerts.

After ordering a round of Bellinis, Tai and Trista culled over the brunch menu. They both settled on shrimp salad with mandarin oranges and pecans. They decided to eat light as the signature dessert, key lime pie, had a reputation as the best in the city.

"I thought we'd hang out today. Since we have such busy schedules and you work a lot of nights, I figured we could have some time together. Sorry you had to work overnight on the last ladies night. The Three R's were awesome. You would have loved it. I'll try to see if we can do a *three-peat*."

"I'm sorry I missed it, too. I heard Candace talking about it. Of course, she talks about everything."

"Yeah, that's my girl. She'll never change. In fact, she has something planned for the two of you."

"The two of us?"

"Yes, it's a surprise."

"I don't like surprises."

"Well, I'll never tell." Tai scooped up a spoonful of her pecans and oranges and savored the blend.

"Okay, guess I'll have to wait."

"So, I know you still like your job. I can see you're thorough. You're always on time and have a good attitude. I'm glad that you were a good fit. Felicia always gets compliments about you on the follow-up calls. And that's a good thing. It will be easy to place you the next time around. Many times our employers contact the previous ones for reference."

"I like it all right. The tips are decent and the folks are friendly. If I left, I'd really miss Miss Cynt. She's like my rock. She keeps it real and looks out for me. She's only been there forty years." Trista sipped her Bellini. "These are good. My first time trying one."

"Right. We need to make some of these at home." Tai raised her glass and sipped. "You never talk about North Carolina. Do you miss it at all? This is a big change and you lived there all your life. And it's the opposite for me; it's been years since I've been there. I would like to go back one day."

Trista adjusted in her seat. "Why? What's there for you?"

"It would be great to rekindle my roots. After all, that's where I was born and grew up." Tai gazed out of the window. "It would be hard to revisit the memories of Mom and Dad."

"Listen, you don't want to deal with that," Trista advised. "There's no need in going back. Like I said before, everyone was so negative about the whole thing. It's not a good idea. You wouldn't like it."

"I wouldn't say that…I wonder if the family ever has reunions but we just don't know about them. I feel like I've been shielded from my past."

"We don't have much family there anymore. Not in Salisbury anyway. I heard we have extended family in other parts like Durham and Asheville. I've never met them."

"That's what I mean. You never really know your roots unless you explore." Tai called the waiter's attention by motioning to him. "Maybe I've been hanging around Nevada too much. She's always checking out all angles."

Gary arrived at the table. "Yes, may I help you?"

"More Bellinis, please. Thank you."

"Sure, I'll be right back."

Tai pointed at the window. "See over there. Those buildings are part of the Smithsonian."

"I remember the schools always had field trips here in high school. I was sick when my class came up, so I didn't make it."

"Well, we'll have to plan a museum day, too. That's one thing about Grandma; she believed in culture and used to take me to museums and events all the time." Tai paused. "I'm sorry. I'm not trying to rub that in."

"No problem." Trista frowned.

"Hey, seriously, like I said, we can catch up. That's going to be our next girls' day." Tai sipped her Bellini. "I'll never forget, I used to love to go to parties as a teenager—of course, I love them now, too—and Grandma stopped me one day and said, 'You need to do something cultural for a change.' That really made me think. So that's my motto forever. You need to mix pleasure with education."

"One day, will you take me past the spot where you and Grandma lived? I've never seen the house. That's if it doesn't bring back bad memories."

"Oh, no, only good ones. Sure, we'll drive by one day. Every now and then I swing through the neighborhood. Most of my friends have moved away. Some of their parents still live there." Tai stirred her drink and took a sip. "What are your long-term goals? Where do you see yourself in a year or two?" Tai was hinting at finding out how long Trista was planning to stay at her home. She wasn't trying to rush her away, but she had been used to her privacy. Fortunately, Trista normally worked the evening shift so they rarely were at home together. It wasn't that she minded her presence; sometimes Tai preferred to be alone. She treasured her "me" time, but if anyone were to "invade" her space without her objection, it would be her sister. Tai was all about family.

"I'm digging the waitress thing, but lately I've been thinking about taking some courses. Maybe at UDC."

"I'm all for that. I'd help you with your tuition. Grandma always stressed education. As long as I have Next Phase of Life, you don't have to worry about employment, either." She picked up her glass and encouraged Trista to raise hers. "Cheers," she said as they toasted.

Trista appreciated all that Tai had done for her: opening her home, finding her a job, offering sisterly chats, treating her to restaurants and events. She was trying to find her niche in the city. She enjoyed her waitress life—she had managed to keep the pounds down—and had found the customers interesting. The repeat ones would tip her well. Tai's sister circle was cool but she craved finding her own posse. One better would be to have a hookup like Tai had with Marco. She witnessed that he had absolute adoration for Tai and she admired that quality in him. Trista envisioned that one day she would be in the same scenario.

She relished Tai's efforts to give her a lift in spirit. Today was the perfect example. When Tai could have been relaxing from her stressful week, she was out and about to ensure Trista had a pleasant day.

Trista sensed that Tai was attempting to pick her brain. She realized that she had an invisible shield surrounding her and she was often standoffish. She would shut herself down and avoid opening up to others—even her only sister.

The Bellinis were taking effect and Trista found herself mellowing out. "Sis, I haven't told you how much I appreciate you helping me out. Sometimes it's my nature to be laid-back so I don't talk much, say too much. I'm sure you say I'm hard to figure out. But I really do thank you. I feel like you rescued me. I liked it in Carolina and all, but it was time for me to get out of Dodge. Start a new phase. I was getting so caught up in the same ol' stuff. I needed change.

"Before the Internet, it was hard finding folk. So it was a blessing I could reach out to you." Trista touched her chest. "I mean, I could never thank you enough. You didn't hesitate when I sent you the message and you responded. You didn't have any issues with me coming here. I can imagine some sisters would have said, 'Hell no!' But you said it was no problem."

"Trista, you are all I have. Yeah, we have some relatives out there...somewhere...but we don't know them. So, you're all I've got. It means a lot to me; you mean a lot to me, and I'm glad we're back together."

Gary returned to the table and picked up the empty glasses and plates. "Another round?"

"Oh, no, thanks. But give the bartender props."

"Thanks. Will do. Glad you enjoyed them."

"I'll take two slices of the key lime pie, though. I hear it's the best around."

"Definitely." Gary turned to walk away.

Tai cleared her throat. "Trista, I feel like I'm probing...but you need you a man, honey. I'll be blunt."

"You ain't telling me nothin' I don't know." Trista looked out the window. "Just need to find one out there." She turned to Tai. "You know of one?" she asked sarcastically.

"He's out there, but don't settle for less."

Hmmm, she went from attorney to landscaper...although there's nothing wrong with that picture. Was that settlin' for less? Trista thought. *My man seems like he's time enough for her, though. He's not hardly a slouch and title means nothin'. And their ten-year age gap doesn't mean a thing, either. The guys who try to move up on me seem to be temporary; that's why I don't be bothered. They're looking for that one-time action. No thanks.*

"Oh, I'm sure he's out there," Tai repeated.

"Bet."

"I'm surprised you didn't move here with one waiting in the wings," Tai stated. "The North Carolina brothers seem to be dedicated. They appreciate what they've got. And a lot of them move here to D.C."

"And I wonder why…D.C. used to be known as Chocolate City."

"Yeah, Parliament had an album with that name."

"Back in the day, that's all we heard down our way," Tai noted. "Must've been a lot of competition. The ratio of men to women was off the chain. At least that was the word."

"You're right. I think it's tempered now, but it was a high ratio. But girl, now, no matter where you are, there's a lot of man sharing going on."

"Sho you right."

"I definitely don't want to share Marco." Tai reflected on how she'd kirked on him after discovering his ex had persistently drowned him with texts. "Although you never know who's doing who."

"Well, looks like I don't have to worry about that for a minute. Nothin' cookin' in this kitchen."

"It's just a matter of time, girl."

"I agree. I ain't gonna trip."

Tai paused. "You've never told me about…Dorian." She had recalled the one time Trista had briefly mentioned him. She was aware that Trista was sensitive about the subject but decided to broach it anyway.

"Well, I…"

"If you don't feel comfortable talking about it, that's fine. We were just talking about men, that's all, and man sharing."

Trista was feeling the effects of the Bellinis; she was more cooled out than usual. "Tai, Dorian and I had dated three years. He was a lot to handle and I couldn't deal with his issues anymore."

"You only told me that you split with him right before you came up here. And you were abrupt when I asked you what was going on. So I figured, leave it alone."

"Well, that wasn't exactly the deal. Dorian and I started liking each other in high school. Then he went off to school on a football scholarship. He had it all—the body and the brain. We lost touch after he left for college but then years later, he returned. We hooked up and it was all good. He graduated and got hired in an entry-level position at a distribution plant in Thomasville."

"I've heard of that. Where a lot of our furniture is made."

"Right. Well, before long, he got a promotion. He then got access to the business office and let's say, he couldn't resist the temptation. He was always a math whiz and he ended up working with accounting. His boss really trusted him. Little did he know, Dorian was dipping and dabbling; making those numbers work for *him*. Every time I looked he was dropping deposits in my bank account. I figured he was on the up and up, right? He'd gotten a promotion with a decent raise. As far as I knew, he was bringing home good pay and sharing it all with me.

"At that point, we ended up moving into our own place. Nice little apartment on the outskirts of town. I didn't have any suspicions whatsoever. He was good to me and that's all that mattered. He'd stepped it up with a new car, loaded, rims, sound system, the whole bit. We were living large. No struggles.

"Then one night, we were sitting in the living room. Sheriff's deputies were knocking. Dorian panicked after looking through the peephole. He was acting like a madman; trying to figure out a way to escape. I didn't know what was happening so, me being uninformed, I opened the door and let them in. They had a warrant for his arrest. Found out he'd been embezzling money at the job. I had no idea it was going down like that."

"Sorry to hear. That's sad and for him to be so smart. He channeled it the wrong way. So is he locked up?"

"Yep, he's incarcerated. I really felt bad that he couldn't resist getting involved in that craziness. He had a partner in crime, too; a lady named Hazel. She was older and had been at the company for twenty years. She went down, too, and she's in the slammer."

"You were lucky that you didn't get charged since money was deposited in your account. How did you manage that?"

"They'd been watching him for a long time and knew that I had no knowledge. I guess they were clocking my moves, too. They could see I was going about my business doing my waitress thing." Trista sighed.

"You hang in there with him?"

"It was hard for me but I felt that I had to. He'd delivered all the goods and gave me everything I ever wanted. Clothes, the bling-bling, spending money, all that. Even the love I'd never gotten…" Trista paused. "I mean, the love I *stopped* getting after Mom and Dad were gone, and you and Grandma were outta the picture. I supported him all the way so yes, I was a ride-or-die chick. I didn't turn my back on him, so he can always say I was his rock.

"The folk in the community kept telling me he wasn't any good; that I needed to drop him. But I wanted to stand by my man. I'd go once a month to visit him. Most of the time I went alone; sometimes a friend rode with me."

"So, no contact anymore?"

"I made one last visit the week before I got on the train to come here. It was sad. He felt like he was losing a part of him. By me moving here we wouldn't see each other much, if at all. We've kept our bond despite the lockup. But one day, I may cut it with a clean break." Trista moved her hand as if she were slicing. "At first, he wanted me to make a pact with him. I'm too young to be waiting around. A girl's gotta have fun. And if I meet someone who's cool, that's all right; and if I connect with someone who can break me off a lil' sumpin'-sumpin', that's even better. Hell, I ain't giving up my life 'cause he gave up his."

"And you definitely don't have to." Tai was aware that Trista might abruptly change the subject after rambling about Dorian. She didn't want to lose the momentum, so they could continue with her plans for the day. "Glad we ate light. We've got another date…with the nails shop."

Oh, I really don't care about my nails. They always chip and if they don't, I'll probably bite them anyway.

Tai always kept her nails polished. The colors were a reflection of her mood and whatever she selected would match her spirit.

They arose from the table with their heads spinning from the bartender's Bellinis like the encircling restaurant.

22

Twin win

Candace bustled through the doorway of Tai's office. She pulled off her coat and laid it on the chair in the corner, then walked toward Tai's desk. Her burgundy sweater knit dress was complemented with gray textured hose and black suede boots. A burgundy and gray thin woven scarf was wrapped around her neck. Her look was impeccable and she was trying to squeeze in her last days of winter wear. Spring was blooming only weeks away. She had a whole new wardrobe she wanted to wear before she had to surrender it for the warmer season. Candace had been making frequent trips to New York during her buyer weekends. She also had enrolled in fashion workshops to enhance her credentials and expertise. Fashion was ever-changing and she always ensured she was in the know.

"Girl—"

Candace stopped abruptly in her tracks as Tai put her finger to her lips to indicate for her to be quiet.

"Yes, Ms. Washington, we will do all we can to help your son find a position," Tai assured the caller. "Yes, we have everything we need to get him started and on his way." Tai nodded profusely. "Tomorrow at one o'clock. That's right; he is to see…" She refrained from a huge sigh. "Yes, thank you and have a good evening." Tai hung up.

"Sorry, Candace, now that's what I call a concerned parent. Her son is twenty-eight years old and hasn't found a job in at least a year. We have the right position for him based on his work experience." Tai swiveled in her chair, and then motioned for Candace to sit.

She ignored her as she was too bouncy to be still. "Girl, you have a helluva office space here. I don't get here too often; guess that's why I forget how it's set up." She walked over to the wide window. "Gorgeous view…I wouldn't get a thing done up in this place. Little too comfy for my taste."

"Candace, I don't think you could ever hang on to a job where you were confined to an office space. You'd have to be chained to the desk on lockdown."

"Hmmm, now that sounds like an adventure." Candace laughed as she paced back and forth. "I wouldn't mind that as long as there's a fine man with the key."

"Sounds like something you'd say." Tai walked to her small fridge and pulled out a bottle of water. "Care for one?"

"Sure. I feel like I'm moving too fast."

"Well, what can I do you for? You rarely stop in." Tai sat back on her desk chair.

"Yep, there is a real reason I stopped by, but you know I love you, boo. Can't stay away too long," Candace joked. She looked at Tai slyly and grinned. "You're always talkin' 'bout Trista and how she needs to meet someone of the other gender. Maybe not to walk down the aisle but to hang out with."

"Especially since…" *Never mind. I don't need to share with her about Dorian. None of her business that he's serving time.*

"Especially since what?" Candace repeated.

"Nothing."

"Okay, if you say so." Candace sat down and crossed her legs. "Well, I've got someone for your sis to meet. In fact, there's two of them. Girl, I met the finest eye candy you'd ever want to see. Those M&M's melt in your mouth, honey."

"So, by two, you mean that there are *two* you want her to meet?"

"No, one for me and one for her. They're twins!"

"Twins? That's cool. What are their names?"

"Randall and Robert," Candace responded enthusiastically as if she'd found sunken treasure.

"Where'd you meet them? Or do I need to ask? You are a man magnet."

Candace laughed. "If you wanna call it that. I saw them while I was walking not far from here. They spotted me first and rolled down the window. I gave them my number. At first I was trying to figure out if they were both interested, say, a ménage à trois. Then I thought, hey, I need to hook up Trista."

"So, when's your first date, or I guess, double-date?"

"Once I get the okay from Trista, it's on. Girl, they are, whew, good-lookin'—"

"Candace, looks are fine but they don't make the man." Tai smiled, briefly visualizing both Marco and Hasan, her mystery man. "Although they certainly don't hurt."

"But you know me—they've got to be working it in the style department. I could see inside the car that they were dressed sharp; nice suits."

"What about the shoes? You can have on a boss outfit but then check out what's on the feet. That can say a lot about a person."

"Who you telling? You know I check out the total package. But in this case, I couldn't see that deep into the car."

"What kind of car? Not that that means a thing. Sometimes all the flash means trouble."

"Girl, they were actually lowballing it. Car was modest, nothing serious. I didn't even notice. I was too busy noticing the body wear."

"It's all good. I'm sure Trista will be excited. She's always saying how she never gets but so far with these D.C. men."

"Well, I'm telling you that I got a good vibe from these brothers. They were gentlemanly with their comments and not raunchy. Didn't make me feel like a piece of meat." Candace didn't mind pickup lines, even if they were corny; she just despised lecherous talk. "I told them I had a friend who could join us. If it's a go, I'll probably set up something for this weekend. Why wait? Strike it while it's hot. I wouldn't want to keep them waiting too long." Candace's mind started racing. "I'll plan the night. Maybe go eat and then hang out in Georgetown."

"Sounds like a plan." Tai paused. "You may need to take Trista shopping." She dug into her wallet and handed Candace cash. "Here, please help her find a dress and some shoes."

"Cool. Girlfriend will need to step it up with these guys. They were definitely reeking of expensive cologne and I was checking out the sheen on those suits."

"I hope this works out. If nothing else, Trista will have an opportunity to meet some new friends."

Candace rose up to leave. "And you don't have to worry 'bout baby sis 'cause these men are on the up and up."

"Thanks for thinking of her."

"Oh, sure, I'm always on the lookout. Not being selfish this time. But I'd love to have them both for myself." Candace laughed as she put on her coat. She looked at her watch. "Gotta go, dearie. Nice chattin' with you. Got a date." Candace walked to the door and closed it.

"What? With who—" Tai smiled and shook her head. She was talking to the door. *Date and she's gone in a flash. She'll never change. Candace is* living *her life.*

Tai recalled once when she and Candace were at a house party in a nice condo on the Southwest D.C. waterfront. A friendly man had started a discussion with Candace, then asked her what she liked to do for "fun." Tai broke out in laughter and thought, *You're asking the wrong person. She always has fun. When doesn't she have fun?* Candace had laughed at the inside joke.

The intercom buzzed, interrupting Tai's thoughts.

"Yes, Noni?"

"Ms. Washington is on the line. She wants to know if her son will be going on interviews tomorrow or just in our office."

Tai sighed. *Not her again; I just hung up from her. She needs to let her son grow up. Making all these follow-up calls.* "Noni, please tell Ms. Washington that he is to be here at one o'clock tomorrow. I presume he's going to be dressed his best. I cannot confirm any interviews. Thank you for calling." *If he gets the job, and I'm sure he will, I hope Mom doesn't blow up the phone at the workplace.*

Tai sat on the bed in Trista's room and admired her sister. Trista had shed her Cinderella image and was the picture of beauty. Trista exuded a newfound confidence simply by examining herself in the full-length mirror. Tai had treated her to the salon earlier that day and her hair was striking. Then Tai pulled out her cache of makeup to create her sister's baby doll face. She had enjoyed piling on the foundation, bronzer, eye shadow and mascara to design a luscious look for Trista who commented that she hadn't worn that much makeup since her senior prom.

Trista felt slightly awkward as it also had been years since she'd been in a dress; not since her first date with Dorian when she had attempted to make an impression on him. Her shapely legs were rarely revealed as she kept them hidden under pants and jeans. Tai had complimented her throughout the day, attempting to help her build self-confidence. Tai could not understand why Trista was reluctant to think or dress outside of the box. She needed to abandon the T-shirt and jeans look if she wanted to step it up in the game; at least steer away from the dress-down as the norm.

"I love that dress. Black always works," Tai complimented yet again.

"Thanks. Candace and I went to three stores before she found this one. She really knows her bizness."

"Definitely. I tell her she needs to go on and move to New York or Cali and become a stylist for the stars. Plus, she knows how to save a ton of money."

Trista smoothed out the little black dress, then turned around to view the back, which had a circular opening that offered a teasing display. It was an odd feeling to see her legs in black suede heels. She absolutely despised pantyhose but figured she could bear them for tonight. She'd opted for textured tights. Trista's large gold hoop earrings peeked from beneath her fresh curls. Gold bangles adorned her wrist. She was pleased with what was looking back from the mirror.

Candace had schooled her about the twin brothers; that they appeared to be professional and clean-cut. Candace didn't like to inquire immediately about one's occupation although she craved the adventurous. She sensed that these two didn't have a blah career; there was something different about them that she couldn't pinpoint.

She and Trista had joked that they hadn't decided which one they each would connect with. Perhaps they'd do a coin toss or see whose personalities were a match. Candace didn't have a preference; she would go with the flow. Trista was easy to please; she hadn't had a real date since arriving in D.C. a little more than six months ago.

While they waited for Candace's grand appearance, Tai and Trista toasted with wineglasses to celebrate Trista's hot date night. Trista hoped that the twins would work out. She was feeling ashamed that she had to depend constantly on Tai picking up the tabs and treats. It would be kinda nice to have a man who could wine and dine her on occasion; being treated like a lady would boost her ego. She sensed that Tai was aware she suffered from low self-esteem and that was why she paid so much attention to her every move and emotion.

"This will be different. I've never dated a twin. I can't wait to see if they're as fine as Candace says. Sometimes I think she's looking through coke-bottle glasses. Not! No, actually she has good taste so I'm sure they're hot." Tai sipped her wine. "Girl, you look great. Folks wouldn't recognize you. Hopefully you'll give the casual look a break. Not to be judgmental or anything, but you don't do yourself justice. You conceal your assets, Sis. If you want to hook a brother who's got something going on, then you've got to look the part. I always say, you could be the most ignorant person out there, but be well-dressed and carry yourself a certain way, and no one will ever know unless you open your mouth."

"Hey, hey, sistahs! You can see I'm ready for our double trouble tonight. Alexander Julian." Candace twirled her dress. "And Marc Jacobs." She kicked up her heel. "Chic freak," she teased. "That's me."

"What time will they be here? They're running late and that's a bad sign," Trista noted.

"Oh, give them a break. I'm habitually late. Gotta make sure I'm glammed up to a tee." Candace poured her a glass of Chardonnay. "Hmm…just what I need to kick start. I can't wait to see which one's my date. Sorry, Trista, but if the one I'm with

starts acting on the boring side, honey, we will be making a switch."
She did a round-the-way-girl neck roll and batted her eyes.

"Hey, it won't matter to me. I've lost my little black book for
six months now. All the guys I run up on be calling me a dime-
piece. Well, hell, if I'm a 'ten,' then why can't you hook a sistah up?
They want to play, no pay. I don't have time for that anymore."
Trista looked at Tai. "I appreciate my sister helping me out, but
I can't expect her to take care of me forever."

Trista had been able to offer a small amount as rent to help
Tai's mortgage. Tai loved the grocery store—she'd often drive
to the suburbs to Whole Foods and Wegman's—so Trista rarely
shopped for food. She wasn't a fashion hound so she didn't shop
for clothes, unless she was with Candace; it was usually a special
occasion when she needed a specific outfit. Trista was adjusting
to life in the city and was ready to establish her own life and place;
not depend on Tai.

"Sis, take your time. That's what family is for. No worries," Tai
responded genuinely.

Candace glanced out of the window, contemplating why the twins
had yet to arrive. She was notorious for lateness but it was now
an hour. Her cell phone vibrated. The caller ID read: *Twins*.
"Here they are now, but I didn't see a car drive up." She picked
up the line. "Hi, which one of you is this?"

"It's me, Randall. Candace, we apologize for being late. We're
a few blocks away. Can you and Trista please meet us outside?"

"Excuse me?" Candace was appalled that the so-called gentlemen
weren't planning to ring the bell and greet them at the door.

"Is anyone there besides you two?" Randall turned the BMW
745 onto Tai's street and pulled up in front of her house.

"Just Tai—"

"Please come outside," Randall insisted.

"I wanted you to meet—"

"I don't want to meet…sorry, it's just that we have reservations and because we're running late, we don't want to come in. Okay?"

"Okay," Candace said sourly. "We'll be right out."

"What's wrong?" Tai inquired.

"Randall said they were in a rush and they're late. Sounds like we're going to a nice place for dinner." Candace glanced in the mirror for a once-over. "You ready, Trista?"

Trista took a deep breath. "Yep." She was slightly nervous and didn't understand why, although it was her first blind date. Maybe that was it. *I don't know what to expect. There better be some connection; especially after all this anticipation.*

Tai waited at the door as the two walked out and approached the car. The driver quickly waved his hand but she could barely see him in the dark. She closed the door. She was a little apprehensive but Trista was grown. Candace seemed to be a good judge of character, although she preferred to walk on the wild side. *Too bad they were too rushed to come in*, she thought. *I really wanted to meet them. I also wonder which one will be with Trista.*

Randall walked around the car to open the front door for Candace. She admired his fashion statement: a navy pinstriped Giorgio Armani suit with a pale-yellow tie and black lizard shoes.

"You look nice," he complimented Candace.

"Thanks. So do you. Love your suit."

"Thanks." He returned to the driver's seat.

Robert had gotten out of the passenger side to help Trista inside the backseat on the left side. "I'm Robert and this is my brother, Randall."

"Nice meeting you both."

As Robert closed the door before getting in the backseat on the other side, Trista admired his—*their*—good looks. They appeared

to be identical. Their almond complexions and pencil-thin mous-
taches showed off smooth skin. Under their suits, you could see
physiques that were used to the gym. The five-foot-ten twins were
definitely polished and charismatic. *No wonder Candace took to
them immediately. They have that wow factor. I've never been into the
suit-and-tie crowd, but maybe Robert and I will be a good mix.*

Randall spun the car around and pulled out of the community
before heading south on Sixteenth Street. He turned his head
slightly to talk over his shoulder. "Trista, your sis must be doing
okay for herself; owning a house up here in this area." Randall was
familiar with the Gold Coast, an area of brick homes near Rock
Creek Park known as one of D.C.'s affluent African-American
communities. His deceased uncle Denton once lived in the neighborhood.

"Yes," Trista responded proudly. "Tai has her own employment
agency, the Next Phase of Life. It's downtown."

"And it's thriving," Candace interjected.

"Cool. And what about you?" he asked Trista.

"I'm a waitress."

Robert looked at her with admiration. "Bet you do good on the
tips."

"Not bad. I've only been there five months. In fact, I've only
been in D.C. for six. I'm from North Carolina. Decided to move
here with my sister. So far, it's working out okay." Trista hoped
that life would continue to run smoothly in the Nation's Capital.

"What about you two?" She paused. "I don't usually ask," Candace
lied. "What do you do for a living? It's only been twice, but when
I see you, you're cleaned up nice," she complimented.

"I can say the same for you." Randall smiled. "Well, Robert and
I run a family business. Our parents left us an inheritance and we
opened a couple of neighborhood corner stores. We've had them
a few years. I'd say we're doing okay for ourselves. A lot of stores

are closing in the strip malls with this economy, so I'm glad we put ours on the block in the hood. Folks always need something and can walk to get it. The schoolkids are our biggest customers; they love those snacks. They be lined up after school—sodas, chips and candy. Then of course milk, bread and eggs keep us in business, too. And don't let it snow; we always have to have extra stock."

"And what do you like to do for fun?" Candace inquired.

"We travel a lot…when we get the opportunity."

"I *love* to travel. My job requires me to go to back and forth to New York."

"Right, you told me you were a buyer."

"Yes, fashion's my game. Actually, I'm going to New York next week. It's Fashion Week."

"I've never been to New York," Trista stated. "This is the farthest north I've been so far. Coming from a small Southern town, this was enough of a culture shock. But I'd be down with going to the Big Apple one of these days."

Robert looked at Trista. "You will someday."

Randall peered over at Candace.

"I can see you like surprises. You haven't said where we're going." Candace gazed out of the window. She hadn't paid much attention to Randall's driving.

Randall looked at Robert in the rearview mirror, then smiled at Candace. "No, but relax; it's all good."

Must be a special restaurant or someplace nice, Candace thought.

What's up with these brothers? Why can't they tell us where we're headed? Trista wondered.

RANDALL CONTINUED DOWN SIXTEENTH STREET BEFORE TURNING on Harvard Street toward the Adams-Morgan area—a neighborhood of popular shops and late-night restaurants. The trendy community was known for its eclectic and ethnic mix of residents and businesses.

"I love this area. I guess we're going to a restau—" Candace stopped when Randall turned off the main commercial district and onto a residential street. *Wonder where we're going*, she thought, but decided to remain quiet. Sometimes she figured she talked too much. She wanted to turn around to make eye contact with Trista but refrained. Trista couldn't understand why Candace wasn't being inquisitive; her usual self. Two strange guys and it was her first date since she'd been in D.C. She would've preferred to have known her exact destination.

Randall pulled up in front of a condo complex and then started to search for a parking space. He circled through the neighboring streets until he found a spot. After parking, he hopped out to open the door for Candace; Robert did the same for Trista.

"Well, ladies, we hope you don't mind walking a couple of blocks." Randall put his arm around Candace. "It's a little chilly but not too bad."

"Hey, I'm fine. Thankfully, I have on my comfies." Candace checked out her feet. "I go with the flow." She looked at Trista. "You okay?"

Trista looked at her feet. Her heels were much lower; plus, she was used to walking from the subway to work. "I'm cool, thanks."

Candace's thoughts started to race and she was determined to be quiet about their destination. *I can't imagine, but again I'm the adventurous one. Hope I haven't gotten us into anything crazy. Poor Trista. She was game and trusted my judgment, so hope this proves to be a real double-date.*

As they strolled, Trista admired the character of the buildings. She could tell that some of the older facades had been recently upgraded and would be upscale once inside.

When they reached a building that was part brick and wood, they climbed the stairs. Randall rang the outside buzzer.

"Hey," a male voice responded.

"Hey, man, it's me; Randall with Robert."

When the buzzer sounded, Randall quickly grabbed the door and opened it for the others to enter. They headed for the elevator.

"Where are we?" Candace couldn't bear to be silent anymore.

"At one of my boyz'… We figured you wouldn't mind." Randall looked at Candace as if he could peer through her. "I know you got all dolled-up, but—"

"It's okay," Candace responded, imagining what kind of evening they would experience. *Hanging with the boyz, huh? Not my cup of tea but sometimes you gotta go with the flow.*

The elevator arrived and they stepped in and got off on the tenth floor. Before they arrived at unit 1000, a man peeped out the doorway and looked both ways. As they approached, he did a double-take. "Man, ya'll didn't tell me you were in the company of some fine ladies. What's up with that?"

"Man, we told you we were coming through. You don't have to know all our bizness," advised Robert, who was the quieter one. He motioned for Candace and Trista to step inside the door.

"Hi, lovely, I'm Tyson." He shook Candace's hand, then looked at Trista. "And you are…"

"I'm Trista." She reached out her hand to shake Tyson's.

"I'm Candace."

Tyson took Candace's and Trista's coats and hung them up. "Care for something to drink?"

"Yeah, man, what you got? Ladies first." Randall looked at Candace.

"Hennessy Black, Cristal, Grey Goose, Stoli…"

"Any wine?" Candace inquired. "We'll take wine, please."

"Sure, baby, whatever you want." Tyson headed to a corner bar where he reached on a rack for two wineglasses and then walked into the kitchen. "Fellas, you can help yourself. Ice bucket's full." Randall and Robert walked over to fix their drinks.

Candace motioned for Trista to follow her to a picture window. "Wow, this is a gorgeous view."

Tyson walked over and handed them their wineglasses. "Baby, this is one of the best in the city."

"And it helps to have a corner unit," Candace suggested.

Tyson pointed to the right. "There is the National Zoo and you can see some of Rock Creek Park." Then he directed them to the left. "And over there is the skyline of downtown."

"This is so cool." Trista marveled at the city views.

"Yes, you really do get the cosmopolitan flavor here," Candace chimed in.

Crossing the room to join Randall on the cream sofa, Candace ensured she sashayed toward him. *I'm such a tease*, she thought. Trista followed suit and sat with Robert on a chocolate-colored corduroy loveseat.

After several rounds of Chardonnay and Hennessy Black, Randall spoke up. "We could've gone to a fancy restaurant, but we thought we could do a more private thing. Tyson's cool with it…although we didn't tell him to expect company."

"I'm certainly glad you brought these gorgeous ladies with ya." Tyson kicked back to check out Candace and Trista. "I'm only sorry you didn't make it a triple thang."

Candace giggled nervously. Trista sensed a suspicious relationship between the twins and Tyson. She also thought it was odd for them to get dressed for a night on the town and end up at a buddy's place. It was her first date in the city, so she decided to accept the situation for the moment.

Sensing a sudden apprehension, Randall broke the ice. "Hey, let's order some Chinese. I'm sure you two must be starving by now. You've gotta eat."

"I'll get the menu." Tyson rose and walked in the kitchen.

While sharing carry-out dishes of Kung Pao Shrimp, General Tso's Chicken and Scallops in Black Bean Sauce, Candace played Twenty Questions. She discovered that Robert and Randall had met Tyson when they used to visit their uncle in D.C. during their teen years. They had grown up in Atlanta and spent many summers with family in the North, including Philadelphia and New Jersey. Their parents had owned a tiny local food mart in Atlanta and had taught them the ropes to open their current cornerstore businesses.

The twins were the typical bachelors; neither having been married at age forty-one. Both had children back in Atlanta. Candace didn't pry about the number of children or their ages; she figured she wouldn't pull the 4-1-1 act yet.

"Do you two usually do this double thing? Do women ever mistake one for the other? Do you ever switch and pull a fast one?" Candace rattled off the questions.

"Girl, you don't care what you ask, do you?" Trista interjected. "I bet they do. The only way I could tell maybe is that Robert," she looked at him and smiled, "doesn't talk as much."

"Yeah, I'm kind of low-key. Randall was always the talker. I usually let him do the wheeling and dealing. He's got the gift of gab." He looked at Candace. "Guess you two are a match."

"Looks that way, huh?" She eased closer to Randall on the sofa.

Tyson, despite being dateless, sensed it was moving into a romantic mood and after he refreshed Candace's and Trista's wineglasses, he stepped away and dimmed the lights. Instead of jazz he switched his stereo to some heavy ballads.

Robert led Trista to the balcony and the light breeze was refreshing, although chilly. He wrapped his arms around her and they cuddled, admiring the moonlight and the views. Randall snuggled with Candace as they stretched on the sofa while soaking in the sounds of Sade.

Tyson quietly retreated to his bedroom to allow the couples their private moments. He could call it a night as they could let themselves out. If they decided to crash in his space, that would be fine, too. The twins were like his right-hand men; in fact, he felt like a triplet. Their ties were bound.

23

Ex-capade

Marco leaned back in his recliner and flicked on the remote, then searched for a show or movie to catch his interest. He had prepared dinner for Tai and was eager to discover how she would rate him in the kitchen. After all, he would be graded by an accomplished chef. Tai had mad cooking skills.

He had decided he would give it a try as he was used to living alone and if not dining out, he would attack his fridge for cold cuts or leftovers; or his freezer for microwave meals. Since dating Tai, he'd become spoiled with homemade dishes. He had bought a cookbook touting easy recipes and now the aroma of honey-baked chicken, and a broccoli and cheese casserole wafted throughout the kitchen. He'd picked up a cake from his favorite bakery.

The dining room table was set and he had lit two candles to create the ideal atmosphere to impress Tai. It was only his second attempt to offer her a romantic evening with dinner at his modest Silver Spring home, just beyond the D.C. line in Maryland.

Marco lived simply with basic furnishings. A long black sofa with earth-tone pillows captured his gardening lifestyle. A glass coffee table displayed home and garden magazines. Plants took more ownership than furniture throughout his home.

After years of a bachelor lifestyle, once changing women like he did his laundry, he finally was convinced that he had found his soul mate. He adored Tai: her gorgeous face and body, her amusing personality, her devotion to family and friends, her lifestyle and her brains. It was almost too perfect, he thought. But he never believed that any human should be put on a pedestal. While he never had expressed all of his admiration to Tai, he showed her with his actions. He refused to give her a big ego.

Marco had surprised his own self when Crystal had popped over last weekend. He had sworn to Tai during their mountain getaway that Crystal was history; the ties were severed. He'd assured Tai that their spat due to Crystal blowing up his phone was meaningless. However, Crystal was not an easy one to dismiss from his life. She had arrived about midnight, awakening him after he'd drifted to sleep in his den. Marco had been alarmed when he heard the constant banging on the front door. He figured it must have been an emergency as it was rare to have late uninvited visitors. When he looked into the peephole, he was stunned to see Crystal.

He politely asked her to leave; however, she continued to pound on the door. Respecting his quiet neighborhood, he reluctantly allowed Crystal inside. She was the epitome of a rag doll with her frazzled hair and disheveled clothes; she looked as if she'd crept from an alley. She confided that she'd had sleepless nights and couldn't survive without him in her life. She reeked of alcohol and Marco was concerned that she had driven to his home under the influence. When they had dated, she never appeared "drunk," and could hold her own when it came to drinking. She was one of those women who could drink but never display more than a buzz.

Crystal touched Marco's sensitive spot and instead of telling her to get the hell out, he offered her to sit so they could talk. It had been almost a year since they'd been in a relationship and yet she was still trying to hang on. He knew if he gave in, she would never disappear from his life. It would only encourage her to continue pursuit. Marco was satisfied completely, as a whole, with Tai; nothing was worth risking their bond.

Crystal looked so distressed that he showed compassion by offering her some hot tea, which would help to relax her nerves. Then Crystal feigned exhaustion and begged if she could simply crash on the sofa in the den. Marco agreed as he didn't want her to risk leaving to drive the five-mile distance to her home. After bringing her a pillow and blanket from the upstairs closet, he inquired if she needed anything else and if not, he was heading to bed. He asked her if she left later during the night, to be sure to lock the front door behind her.

MARCO SHOWERED AND RELISHED THE WARM WATER TRICKLING down his body. He'd had a busy day as he had explored the Internet for prospective clients. He also had site visits at some of the new home communities in the D.C. suburbs to see if he could secure contracts. During the winter months, he would always drum up new business to ensure his spring and summer would be viable landscaping seasons. He was both physically and mentally weary. After stepping out of the shower, he grabbed his towel to dry off and wrap around his chiseled physique.

He opened the bathroom door into his single candlelit master bedroom and sat on his king-sized bed.

"Hmmm, hmmm, hmmm, you still looking good."

Marco jumped up to see Crystal standing in the dark corner. "What in the hell?!"

Crystal slowly emerged from the darkness. "You always did like candles." She was completely nude. "I realize I look a mess, but I'm feeling much better now. What about you? After that long shower you took; must've been twenty minutes." She steadily walked toward him. "You thought you could get rid of me that easily, huh?" she teased.

Marco sat back on the bed and eyed Crystal before him. Her body was in fit shape as she consistently watched her diet and exercised. He recalled even when they would vacation, she would insist on finding time to work out. Without the clothes, she was a much better vision. Her hair didn't look any worse than when she arose in the morning.

"Did you miss me as much as I missed you?" Crystal continued her ploy to seduce him. She could sense that he was becoming a little weak. She was known for being aggressive and manipulative; perhaps the reason she was such a successful saleswoman for her thriving high-tech company. She also had become familiar with stretching across the desks of numerous top-level executives. She had created her own *Let's Make a Deal* game: You offer me a contract and I'll deliver the goods—quick, easy and right on time.

"Crystal, I think you'd better go—"

She stood between his legs and when she noticed his eyes locked on her vagina, she gently pushed him backward across the bed. She unwrapped his towel and saw his member was engorged. "All ready and waiting for me, I see." She climbed on top of Marco and teasingly swung her breasts across his face, letting them lightly touch his nose and mouth. *Just a little more dick tease and I've got him now.* She stood on her knees and touched his penis, then started to massage it.

"Crystal, listen, I only let you in because you seemed desperate."

"And now we're finding each other irresistible. You know you want me, Marco. It's been toooooo longgggggg."

She reached down to kiss his lips.

Marco raised her gently as if he would turn her over, then quickly jumped off the bed, grabbing his towel. He rewrapped it around his body. "Crystal, you really must go. I'm sorry."

Crystal was stunned as she sat on the bed. "But, Marco…"

"You've gotta go. I didn't mean for it to go this far."

"Baby, we were just getting ready… And you've got me hot and bothered. That's not fair." Crystal batted her eyes flirtatiously and curled her legs up on the bed.

"Look, I'm not trying to be mean. We haven't been together in almost a year. I'm involved with someone I care about. We no longer have a connection.

"You knocked on my door at midnight and I was kind enough to let you in. I know some brothers who would've turned you away." He sat on the bed beside her. "Please get dressed and go. You're able to drive now and you need to go home." He reached over and gave her a hug, then a peck on the forehead. "Just go."

Sadly, Crystal stood up, looked down and walked to the door. After opening it, she looked back at Marco, walked out and shut the door behind her. She would get dressed downstairs where she'd left her clothes.

Marco turned on the iPod on his nightstand and glanced down at his carpeted floor. He escaped to the sounds of Anthony Hamilton.

Marco had started to tell Tai about his late-night surprise but figured it would make a bad situation worse. She'd already slammed him for the phone calls from Crystal. Lately, she had continued to act distant at times since their Valentine's Day weekend. He couldn't fathom what was on her mind; sometimes Tai could be tight-lipped.

MARCO PICKED UP HIS CELL AND TEXTED TAI:

Looking forward to tonight, sweetie. He expected her to arrive in an hour at seven-thirty.

Me too. Can't wait to taste you and *your special meal,* Tai replied.

TAI NOW HAD EXPERIENCED SEVERAL GYM WORKOUT SESSIONS— of the lovemaking kind—with Hasan. This week's had been the best yet. They had not only polished off the office furniture, but Hasan had lured her to the equipment area. Treadmills, Nautilus machines and weight benches would have new meaning. The two had developed a sex maze in unimaginable positions. It had been an adventure exploring the gym by flashlight. Hasan had pulled out his stash of Patron and glasses from a duffel bag.

Tai started to turn down Marco's dinner invitation; especially since it only had been two days since her amazing night at the gym. She was on a guilt trip. But she knew that Marco had put his heart and soul into preparing her a special meal. Even more difficult was Hasan's invitation to return to the gym tonight afterhours. She was beginning to feel more and more guilty about the rendezvous. Her mind was playing tricks on her and she was toying with the idea that she was developing feelings for Hasan. Then again, it was obviously lust.

She truly loved and adored Marco. And he didn't deserve her occasional cheat nights, she often thought. Marco was her anchor and offered his full support in all of her endeavors. He was proud that she was sticking to her resolution to maintain optimum health by joining the gym—and actually going to work out; not just being a member in the computer system.

Marco had his own home gym where he would spend many days at 4 a.m. lifting weights. Usually he started visiting his clients at 7 a.m., so it had become a ritual to do a half-hour workout before beginning his day. It was cooler in the morning, particularly during the summer months, and he favored working in the early morning during milder temperatures. However, clients like Tai were on his afternoon schedule.

Tai rang the doorbell at Marco's home. She noticed the lights were dim. *Marco always sets the mood right.* She brushed her hair into place; she already had done the makeup check in the lighted car mirror.

Marco opened the door and hugged Tai as she entered.

"Hmm, you smell nice. Look nice, too." Marco sniffed. "You're wearing my favorite."

"Halle Berry. Thanks. What you cook? Smells good."

"You have to wait and see." Marco took her coat and hung it in the closet, then took her hand and led her to the dining room where he had lit jasmine candles that served as an aphrodisiac.

Tai figured she was in for a meal prepared with love followed by endless affection. At least for this moment, and throughout the night, she would erase Hasan from her mind.

Marco pulled out a chair for Tai who took a seat at the mahogany table. He headed to the kitchen to retrieve a bottle of Riesling. Marco was a wine connoisseur and had a cellar built in his basement. His collection included at least a hundred bottles from Moscato to Chardonnay to Pinot Grigio to Merlot and Shiraz. He often visited local wineries as he escaped in the countryside scenery. He was an outdoorsman and beyond the gardening and landscaping projects, he enjoyed skiing and whitewater rafting; neither sport interested Tai. She was truly a citified chick.

Marco returned with the chilled bottle and filled Tai's wineglass, then sat at the other end. He couldn't wait to find out how Tai would critique his cooking.

24

Double dippin'

Randall, Robert, Candace and Trista had developed a bond of friendship. While Candace patiently waited for a love session with Randall, Trista was reserved and cherished the laid-back relationship. Candace had merely experienced a simple kiss. She wanted to ravish Randall and was plotting to one day surprise him with a sudden seduction. She was quizzical why Randall hadn't made any moves—it had been two months.

Their double-dates were always just that—double—and Candace knew that twins were tight-knit but not to this degree. She figured that at some point they would break off separately. They had gone to underground clubs, afterhours spots and friends' houses. Candace presumed that Randall and Robert favored dark-lit places. In fact, they had only seen the twins during evening and nighttime hours.

She barely knew Trista and didn't feel comfortable about displaying her aggressiveness toward Randall. Trista was so chilled out by nature that it aggravated Candace; she didn't want to appear that she was a hound, always at the ready. Tai was her girl, and she'd simply done what she'd been asked: connect Trista with a prospect. But she had her own motivations.

Candace sensed that Trista lacked self-confidence in relationships. However, when she was on the dance floor, there was no stopping her. She would break free from her shell.

Randall and Robert had invited Candace and Trista to ride with them to New York. They were simply going for the day and would leave during the wee hours and return that night. Trista had debated whether they should join the twins; they barely knew them but they seemed positive. They operated their family business with care, and were intelligent and well-groomed. They enjoyed their extravagant lifestyle: tailored suits that made fashion statements and pockets lined with cash.

Candace convinced Trista to ride along with the twins to New York. It would be Trista's first visit and a place where she had longed to go. Trista found it hard to resist despite her reservations to go with two strange guys. She was still becoming acclimated to living in the city and all of its characters. Her dating game in her small hometown had not reached beyond certain limitations. Trista trusted Candace's judgment and decided it would be a win-win situation; Candace would feel special and Trista would experience New York. Tai planned to take her someday for a sisterhood weekend. They would still have the opportunity in the future.

Robert pulled up to the house and waited for Candace and Trista. It was 4 a.m. and they would arrive in New York about 8. It would be just in time to experience all of the sights and sounds on a bright Saturday morning. Once in the car, they headed up Sixteenth Street to Colesville Road to pick up 95 North. They made one stop at the Maryland House rest stop before traveling the New Jersey Turnpike. Hours later, the George Washington Memorial Bridge awaited and the Statue of Liberty beckoned.

New York was familiar grounds for Candace as the fashion

industry demanded regular visits. Trista was in awe of the expansive skyline of towering buildings and skyscrapers. She envisioned the missing Twin Towers.

Trista gazed with awe out of the front window. "Wow, I've never seen so many buildings. I thought D.C. was big."

"Baby, it's an experience." Robert had driven the entire trip, although Randall had offered to share. He and Candace were cuddled on the backseat. Candace had dozed on and off throughout the ride as hip-hop CDs continuously played.

After crossing the bridge into the city, Randall announced they would be dropping off Trista and Candace.

"Where?" Trista inquired.

"Take us to Junior's. Times Square. I'd like some breakfast." Candace sat up groggily. "I need some caffeine to wake me up. Then I've gotta have a slice of cheesecake," Candace added about the original Brooklyn institution renowned for its dessert.

"That's cool." Randall maneuvered his way past Yellow Cabs and a sea of people dressed in various styles and representing a myriad of ethnic groups.

As they continued into Times Square, Trista was mesmerized with the constant rows of shops and restaurants. *Maybe Robert will give me some money so I can shop*, she thought. *If anyone can hook me up in the clothes department, it's Candace.*

When Robert drove by the huge billboards, Trista became engrossed with the enormous city. She was anxious to reach their destination and couldn't wait to explore.

Robert pulled up in front of Junior's. "Well, you ladies enjoy yourselves. We've got some runs to make. If you need us, hit us on the cell. We won't be too far away."

"No worries. This is my second home. I'll initiate Trista and she won't want to leave," Candace responded.

Robert reached in his pocket and pulled out five hundred dollars and handed it to Trista. Her eyes lit up like a Christmas tree.

"Wow...thanks, Robert." She pecked him on the lips as she buried the bills in her purse, then stepped out of the car.

Randall knew he had to follow suit, so he handed Candace a wad of bills. She thanked him and didn't bother to count. She grinned as she was aware it was significant enough to allow her a shopping spree.

"What time will you be back?" Candace quickly jumped out after stashing away the money in her bag. Several drivers honked their horns impatiently.

Randall rolled down the window to respond, yelling loudly over the horns. "Take your time. We're in no hurry. We'll call you."

"Okay, maybe we'll have time for a show." Candace opened the door for Trista to enter the restaurant.

"Hi, welcome, ladies. Two?"

"Yes. May we have a booth, please?" Candace followed the hostess to a corner booth.

"Coffee, ladies?" a waitress inquired.

"Definitely. Thanks." Candace opened the menu.

They both ordered omelettes and French toast.

"Well, what you think?" Candace was eager to hear Trista's opinion.

"I never imagined it to be like this. All the people and stores. I can't wait to shop. I know you know the best spots, too. I could get used to this."

"Yeah, I always love when I have to come up for Fashion Week or to make my buys." She pulled out an *Elle* magazine from her purse. "Actually, I need to see what's in style for the fall." Candace received at least ten fashion magazines each month. She habitually perused the issues in search of the latest trends and designs. In addition to web sites and email lists, she would watch everyday people on the city streets to see what was fashionably appealing. Today, she actually felt underdressed in her Juicy sweatsuit and tennis shoes. However, it was the way to travel in the middle of the night.

"So, were you expecting them to give us some cash?" Trista sipped her coffee.

"Honey, please, yes."

"But that seemed odd to me; they don't even know us like that." Trista was perplexed. "And why did they rush off? Dropped two women in New York alone and disappeared like it was nothin'. They seem cool and everything, but something's not right. I can't put my finger on it."

"Oh, girl, you're sounding like your sister now. She was giving me the blues about us taking this little trip. I come here all the time. It was nice to be chauffeured for a change."

"I hope Tai isn't too worried about us."

"Yeah, I know; she really wasn't feeling us coming here with them."

"She always thought it was strange that they only pick us up in the dark. Even last night, she said she didn't care. She was coming to the car to meet them. I'm sure she was tripping with them having on the dark shades after midnight."

"Right. I wanted to say something, but you know how Randall is so sensitive sometimes. He doesn't like me to ask too many questions. But then when we got on the road, they took those shades off."

"Wonder whose car they're driving? You think it belongs to one of them? I get the feeling they borrowed it."

"Yeah, you know how many *boyz* they seem to have. Always showing up in a different car. They use their apartments, their

cars; you name it. Like I said, I've slowed down on the questions."
She rubbed her fingertips together. "As long as they're keeping
us happy, guess that's what matters."

"Guess you're right."

"I thought we were going to hang with them for the day. But
they must've come here for business or something. Maybe it's
connected to their stores. Dunno." Candace smirked. "Either way,
we're going to enjoy our day. We can go see if we can get half-price
tickets first for a show on Broadway. Then we can hit the stores."

After enjoying their diner experience, Candace and Trista
shopped along Broadway, finding costume jewelry and small
trinkets. In Times Square, they purchased show tickets to a 2 p.m.
matinee. Trista stopped at a street vendor table and purchased a
couple of "I Love New York" souvenirs. Trista was impressed
with the fast pace of walkers who were swiftly able to maneuver
their way through the crowded streets. She'd never seen such a
huge store as Toys "R" Us where they stopped to explore.

They eventually made their way to the famous Macy's where
they found bargains to die for in the department store. Candace
started to take her through the garment district but opted to take
the subway to Fifth Avenue. They could have gone by taxi but
she figured the experience for Trista would be rewarding. Trista
was used to riding the D.C. Metro system, but it was in no comparison to the New York subway ride.

After emerging onto Fifth Avenue, Trista was in awe of the
rows of upscale stores. Gucci, Fendi, Louis Vuitton, Prada, and
Versace only made a dent in the mix.

Priscilla, Queen of the Desert at Broadway's Palace Theater was
thrilling. Replete with a trio of singing divas and drag queens in

wild costumes, the musical was just what Candace's personality craved. As they followed the throng of theatergoers to the lobby, they decided to stand on the side and people-watch.

"That was great! Thanks for thinking of the idea." Trista beamed, enthralled with the dazzling performance. "I can't wait to come back up here."

"Maybe you can come with me on my next fashion excursion. Fashion Week for spring/summer will be in September. That would be great."

Candace's eyes perked when she spotted a prey victim who was well-dressed with smooth skin and a neatly trimmed beard. He appeared to be alone or perhaps he was waiting for someone. *I would be caught here in this sweatsuit instead of my Prada suit. I'd like to catch his attention, but I'm not representing…the real me. But then again, who cares?*

Trista was busy observing the crowd. The experience was amazing as she'd only been to school plays. The dancing in the Broadway show had been especially entertaining. During the performance, she'd visualized herself being on the stage; appearing solo and wooing the crowd. She'd been so engrossed in her daydream that Candace had nudged her when she didn't respond to her whisper. She'd asked her if she thought the dancing was fabulous.

Candace had decided to approach the handsome catch when she noticed another guy, also a piece of candy, walk up to him. He was meticulously dressed in a sweater, tie and khakis and wore designer black-frame glasses. He locked arms with the other man and they smoothly walked out the theater.

Trista spotted the disappointed look on Candace's face. "What's wrong?"

"Oh…nothing." *Guess that wasn't meant for me. I definitely wasn't what he wanted. Shame on me anyway; I'm here with Randall. But a girl's gotta keep her eyes open.*

Candace looked at her watch. It was now 4:45 p.m. She checked her cell to see if Randall had texted her. "Wonder what they're up to? No word yet."

"They said they'd be in touch with us. Looks like we came here with them, but then they went ghost on us. Doubt we'll spend any time with them."

"That's a little strange. I thought that was the whole idea; for us to spend the day in New York. I'm here all the time and if that was the case, we could have come together... without them."

"True dat. Well, where to now? I'm game for whatever." Trista looked up and down Broadway. "Which way?"

"Okay, let's go to Harlem. I'm sure you've heard a lot about it. It's changing though... not like the old days." They headed for the subway and rode the train to the 125th Street station.

They visited ethnic stores, passed the famous Apollo Theatre and made a stop at the Hue-Man Bookstore and Café on Frederick Douglass Boulevard. Candace thought it was important to support the African-American community. She bought Zane's latest novel, *A Three-Piece Meal*, and Trista bought Cairo's *Kitty-Kitty, Bang-Bang*. Then she selected Allison Hobbs' *Put a Ring on It* for Tai. The title attracted her as her older sister was now forty-plus and she'd heard so much about her disappointment with Austin and their five-year relationship. She didn't know if Marco was the marrying kind, although he appeared to be devoted. Candace thought about Nevada and picked up *Love & Justice* by Rique Johnson. She figured the detective love story would be a welcome addition to her massive book collection of suspense and mystery novels.

After making their purchases, the two sat in the café area and ordered a muffin and tea. They discussed their day and how it was about to be dark soon.

Candace's cell vibrated. She looked at the caller ID. It was Randall. She picked up quickly. "Hey, love."

"Hi. You enjoying your day? Where are you?" Randall responded.

"We're in Harlem, at the Hue-Man Bookstore. How 'bout you?" Randall cleared his throat.

"Sorry." Candace remembered that he often was evasive when she asked questions.

"We'll be there to get you in thirty. Look out for us."

"Okay, will do." She hung up, stunned by Randall's abruptness. "They'll be here in a half-hour. I like them and all, but they are some strange dudes."

"Well, look at it this way. At least we got to shop and go to a show." Trista looked at their purchases, now consolidated into two large tote bags. "Tai really didn't want us to come but I'm glad we did anyway. Sometimes she acts overprotective. She forgets I'm a grown woman."

"No, she's just looking out for you. Cori does the same thing with me, but I don't always let her know my *bizness*. Speaking of Tai…"

"Yeah, I guess I should call her. Let her know we're okay. Actually, I'll text."

"Let her know," Candace looked at her watch, "we should be back by ten-thirty or eleven."

"Okay." Trista opened her phone and texted: *Hey Sis, luvin NY. Leaving soon. Back there by eleven latest.*

Tai responded immediately: *Great. Whew. Wondering if you were OK and having good time. Look for you then.*

It was almost dark when the twins pulled up. This time Randall was driving and they both were wearing shades again.

Maybe that's their thing, Candace surmised. *I won't ask again about those damn shades. Whatever...Trista and I enjoyed spending that money.*

Candace and Trista hopped into the backseat with their large totes and Randall pulled off.

"I see you ladies didn't waste no time with the shopping thing." Randall looked through the rearview mirror.

Candace smiled. "No, we didn't. Thanks again for making that happen."

Trista responded, "Yeah, thanks. I enjoyed the trip." She smiled. "We also went to see *Priscilla, Queen of the Desert.* My first real show other than high school. And it was off the chain."

"Glad you enjoyed it." Robert took off his shades and rubbed his eyes before placing them back on.

"What did you do?" Candace slipped out.

Randall started, "Now, what have I told you about—"

Robert grabbed his arm on the steering wheel. "We went to visit family...and some friends."

Candace and Trista looked at each other and shrugged. There would be no more inquiring about how the twins had spent their day.

Robert turned up the radio. But Trista tuned it out and sang her own melody in her head. Jay-Z and Alicia Keys' "Empire State of Mind" was all she could hear at the moment. *Now you're in New York, these streets will make you feel brand new, the lights will inspire you...*

25

When duty calls

Nevada lounged on her sprawling sofa. A small empty bag of barbecue chips and a package of chocolate chip-pecan cookies were on the coffee table—a sign she had strayed yet again from her diet. She had been munching and snacking throughout the afternoon. She had decided to take a break from being on her laptop since the morning. It seemed that when she started working on a new case, she would crave sweets and snacks. Perhaps they provided the boost that she needed.

Her latest case involved a newlywed in her late-twenties who was suspicious that her husband may be a cheater. She had provided his job details, his alleged hangouts and names of associates. Nevada figured this would be an easy task; cheating husbands had become her most popular cases. She thrived on catching them and would get an adrenaline rush when she did. In addition to her detective agency, she was a contributing writer to an online site geared to investigative techniques. To enhance her detective role, Nevada had taken online courses in personality traits and psychological profiles. Sleuths On Us originally had evolved from her desire to assist women.

It was Saturday and she loved tuning in to some of her favorite shows. Lifetime Movie Network and Investigation Discovery were her preferred daytime channels. At night she would watch *Cops* followed by *America's Most Wanted*. Tonight's *Cops* episode focused on cities with the highest crime rate for last year. She witnessed firsthand the lifestyle of a police officer. Being in a relationship with Ryan was enough to be reckoned with. He had been on the Metropolitan Police force for more than twenty years. She thought about him now as he was on the late shift. The police chief had called the weekend one of the city's "All Hands on Deck." He was required to work despite it being his weekend off. Nevada prayed every time Ryan walked out the door.

They were a match as neither had ever desired to have children. They had at least twenty nieces and nephews and several god-children who lived locally.

When *Cops* ended, Nevada grabbed the empty bags and put them into a plastic bag before dropping them in the kitchen trashcan. She didn't want Ryan to find out she'd been cheating from her diet. She had given the façade that she was sticking to it faith-fully. She didn't feel like being reprimanded by him. He was a complete health nut and an avid vegetarian. She rarely cooked because of their opposite food lifestyles, so they were well known in the restaurant circles. Of course, she felt blessed to have the ultimate chef friend, Tai, where she was always welcome to place her feet under the kitchen table.

Nevada returned to the den and sat back on the sofa to watch *AMW*. She treasured the show that had swept so many criminals off the street and into the slammer where they belonged. She intently followed the cases to learn about character personalities and modus operandi. It was a learning tool that also piqued her interest in how real-life situations could develop and culminate. She had studied people and found them fascinating. Her years as a journalist had offered the opportunity to meet all types of char-acters: media personalities, celebrities, politicians, community activists, business owners and everyday residents.

AMW featured a domestic abuse case where an estranged boy-friend had returned from the military and discovered his girlfriend in a new relationship. He had crept up on the couple while they sat on a porch swing, then slain both of them during an ambush. Sadly, the suspect had escaped capture and was on the run. He had been spotted in several states. Before the commercial break, the host announced the next segment. Nevada eased to the edge of the sofa and watched the re-enactment while the host unfolded the turn of events:

There's a fifty-thousand-dollar reward for our next case. Two men have taken Miami by storm with a series of bank robberies. On October 10, 2009, the duo hit the Bank of America Biscayne Bay branch. Then on November 23, 2010, just before Thanksgiving when bankers were busy preparing for the holiday, they robbed the SunTrust branch in Coconut Grove for an undisclosed amount. Most recently they have been linked to at least three robberies in the Washington, D.C. metropolitan area.

Miami-Dade Police need your help in finding these scam artists. Ironically, they are identical twins and have operated the same in both robberies. They are clean-cut, impeccably dressed in business suits and expensive shoes. In fact, they dress identical to throw off customers and tellers. One approaches the teller while the other stands guard at the exit. Often bankers do a double-take to see if they are looking at the same person.

They are known to lure unsuspecting females to assist them in doing their dirty deeds; first by wooing them with wads of cash and buying them jewelry and clothing. Later, after enticing the females, they trick them into being getaway drivers by telling them they'll cut off their monetary supply. Some women have fallen victim to these thugs who appear to be professional gentlemen on the outside while being the slimy creeps that they are.

Two photos appeared on the screen with names, heights and weights.

Take a good look to see if you know Jansen and Jarrod Turner. They are known to frequent nightclubs, preferably dimly lit; smoke fine cigars and dress in high-end apparel. They are high-rollers who have been spotted in South Beach and Las Vegas. The twins are originally from Florida and have family in Miami, New York and in the Washington, D.C. area. They've been on the run for a year and a half. Remember, there is a fifty-thousand-dollar reward leading to the arrest and conviction of Jansen and Jarrod Turner. Authorities from both jurisdictions are on standby for your calls. Dial 1-800-CRIME-TV if you have any leads. Now for our next case…

Nevada fell back on the sofa, held her chest and gasped. "That's Randall and Robert! The twins!" *Oh, no. I hope Candace and Trista are safe. I've got to call Tai, but first AMW.* She grabbed her cell off the end table and called the station where volunteers were accepting calls. Nevada paced back and forth as she described the twins in detail and said she could identify them. She was extremely nervous and upset, but remained calm while providing information. She agreed she would be willing to work with police. Officers representing both Miami, D.C. and New York were at the station. Nevada confirmed that they were in and around the D.C. area.

Unbeknownst to the twins, and Candace and Trista, Nevada had followed the twins one night after they had dropped off the ladies. Her inquisitive nature had caused her to grow suspicious. Tai had informed her that the twins never came to her front door whenever they picked up Candace and Trista.

After contacting *AMW*, Nevada quickly called Tai, who was already a bundle of nerves. She had felt uneasy about Trista and Candace going to New York with the twins. But she later backed off as Trista sometimes accused her of being too motherly and unreasonably worried. Tai answered the cell after the first ring.

"Hi." Tai watched an interesting scene in a TV rerun. She and Candace always caught up on the wives and housewives shows.

"Listen, this is urgent, Tai. Those twins, so-called Randall and Robert, are actually bank robbers known as Jansen and Jarrod. I saw them on *America's Most Wanted*. I've already contacted the station and police—"

Tai jumped up, walked briskly to her living room and peeped outside of her front window. "No way!"

"Yes way! They showed their photos on the show. You know I got a good look at them that night I trailed them to that building."

"Oh, no…and I didn't see them that well inside the car. They were wearing shades."

"Where's Trista? At work? She's got to be careful…"

"Nevada, she and Candace went with them to New York today."

"What? New York? Why the hell did they go there?"

"The twins invited them to go hang out for the day. Trista was excited. She texted me some hours ago to say they'd be back home about ten-thirty or eleven."

"Let me go. I'm calling the police."

"Hurry, please! I guess I'd better not text her back 'cause they could be in danger."

"Right…but we gotta be cool with this. Can't let on that anything's up. Be safe. Text me if you hear more. Bye." Nevada rushed off the call and contacted Metropolitan Police to tip off that Jansen and Jarrod Turner had two females in their company. They were both innocent with no knowledge of the twins' background or that they were wanted fugitives. She provided Tai's home address and noted that the four were en route from New York. Police quickly set up a sting operation to nab the suspects. Undercover officers in unmarked cars were deployed to the scene where they would await arrival of the fugitives.

Nevada was thrilled that she was actually a part of old-fashioned police teamwork. Ryan would be extremely proud of her. She'd be in rare form once he arrived home to find out that she was involved in the bust. She figured he'd already heard that the manhunt was active in D.C. after the nationwide search for the twin bank robbers. She had been instructed that she didn't have to be on the scene, but agitated and eager, she couldn't resist witnessing the takedown. She left her home and rapidly drove off in her SUV heading for Tai's house. She would park but remain inside her vehicle. While Ryan had experienced criminal takedowns on a regular basis, she was eager to see such an encounter.

TAI NERVOUSLY SAT IN HER LIVING ROOM AND CONTINUOUSLY peeped through her sheer curtains. She had lit a candle so not to draw attention to any lighting in the front. *Thank God that Nevada's the true detective that she is. It pays to have friends who always have at least one eye open. I'm so scared for Trista and Candace. I tried to discourage them but I knew that Candace was New York street savvy. I never was feeling those twins. But Candace always falls for the men, no matter what. A man only needs to have it going on in the looks and fashion departments and she's hooked. I pray for their safety and their safe return.* She gazed out of the window again and this time noticed a few cars pulling onto the street. The drivers searched for parking spaces. Since it was Saturday night, some residents had gone out so parking was plentiful. After the three cars parked, no one emerged so Tai presumed they were unmarked police vehicles. *Wonder if Nevada's coming over? She'd better stay low if she does. But she's got street smarts, so I'm sure she'll stay undercover, too. Whew, talking 'bout scared; this is insane. I need a few drinks about now.*

An hour had passed since the police had arrived. *I wish they'd hurry up and get here. I'm afraid to call or text Trista; that wouldn't be smart. I wish I could warn her. But this is where your faith comes into play.* She closed her eyes. *Lord, please bring Trista and Candace home safely. And make sure those two idiot brothers are taken down. I want them* under *the jail!*

Tai checked out the time. It was 11:17 p.m. She presumed that the fugitives were still en route to her home. She couldn't wait to see her sister's face. For once, this experience had made her realize how much she cared for Trista. Nothing had produced this emotion until now. She'd been unselfish by opening up her home, and introducing her friends—her world to Trista. But now she was feeling a true sisterhood bond. Yes, they were opposites but had grown as one; at least in her eyes. She figured herself as the wiser and would totally take blame if there were a violent or tragic outcome. She continued to pray for their safe arrival.

Tai heard the tires of a car approaching. Her street had been silent with the exception of a few neighbors returning home to their driveways. She peered out the window and noticed a car cut off its lights and pull into her driveway. It wasn't the car the twins usually drove but the same one that they'd taken to New York: a black sedan with tinted windows. Tai's heart started racing and she wondered if she should jump up and run for cover. She decided it would be better to stay put and observe the scene. The twins never walked them to the door, so she didn't have to worry about the twins seeing her or sensing something was wrong. The street savvy she did know was to be cool at all times. It would be only a matter of time before the police did their justice.

The twins opened the doors for Trista and Candace who both

grabbed their tote bags from their shopping spree. They hugged and lightly kissed them before getting back inside the car. Trista and Candace headed toward the walkway and continued to the front door. Suddenly, they turned around to see several cars swoop in front of the driveway to block the twins' exit.

Trista and Candace had shocked and puzzled expressions and turned back to see Tai whispering to them to hurry inside the house. They followed suit by dashing up the stairs. Tai quickly closed the door and locked it.

"What's going on?" Candace dropped her bag.

"Yeah, what's happening? Something up in this quiet neighborhood?" Trista chimed in as she placed her bag at the door. "Were those the five-oh pulling in to block them?"

Tai walked to the front window and peeped outside. She motioned for Trista and Candace to sit on the sofa. "Yes, the police. You ain't ready to hear this, but those twins, Randall and Robert, are actually wanted for bank robberies."

Candace jumped up. "What?"

"Girl, they are fugitives from Miami. That's why they were rolling in the cash."

"How you know?"

"Our dear friend Nevada saw them on *America's Most Wanted* tonight. She called the show and tipped off police."

"How did she know what they looked like?"

"I never said because I knew you'd be pissed, but I asked her to trail them that third night you went out. I didn't understand why they never came to my front door when they picked you up. Supposed to be so-called *gentlemen*...Nevada said they'd gotten away with two robberies in Miami and are linked to several here."

The three women looked out to see the twins in handcuffs. Tai was glad the incident had ended peacefully without shootouts and other fanfare she had only witnessed on the screen. She sighed and shook her head, then sat on the sofa. Trista and Candace joined her.

"I can't believe it. This is like a damn dream." Candace leaned back.

"We've really gotta thank Nevada. We owe her our lives. Who knows what could've happened next?" Trista was in a daze.

"I'm thankful that you're safe. I was really blown away when Nevada called me. We'll have to hear the whole story from her."

The three sat stunned on the sofa and soaked up the incidents. They were speechless.

"Where is Nevada anyway?" Candace looked out the window to see the twins in an unmarked car.

"Knowing her, I bet she's out there scoping out the whole scenario," Tai assured.

"You're right. Ms. Sleuth really did her thing this time." Candace was relieved.

After the police cars cruised away and a tow truck removed the twins' car from the driveway, the doorbell rang. It was Nevada.

When Tai opened the door, all of the ladies did a group hug.

"We can't thank you enough." Candace shook her head. "I guess I found the right ones that time."

"Thank you, Nevada. We were lucky we didn't get hurt; all the way to New York and back. Whew. You are one hell of a detective."

"You're welcome, and thanks to *AMW* for airing the show." Nevada accepted the accolades. *Candace, you're always searching for the "right one,"* she thought. Nevada recalled the movie *Looking for Mr. Goodbar* and how the lead character's casual affairs eventually led her to a psychopath. *Hell, you found the wrong eye candy this time, Candace.* "Tai, this may sound crazy at a time like this, but you feel like fixing us some Cosmos?"

"I think I could use something stronger. What about some Long Island Iced Teas?" Tai had already been on a mental drink mission, when she'd first received Nevada's call.

"Now, those will knock us out," Nevada agreed. "Ladies, by the way, those fools weren't Randall and Robert; they were Jansen and Jarrod."

They walked to the den while Tai headed to the kitchen to mix drinks. Nevada placed the CD in the changer. Tai returned with four glasses on a tray.

"I can't believe tonight." Nevada reflected on the drama of the evening. Her thoughts replayed the entire screenplay as the scenes had unfolded like a movie. She savored the moment. Playing detective had made her feel like a heroine from a novel.

26

Mimosas and the morning after

Tai had put her foot into fixing one of her fabulous Sunday brunches. After last night's adventure and ongoing rounds of drinks, Nevada and Candace had decided to spend the night. They had crashed on blankets in her den, their favorite hangout.

As they sat around the table in the eat-in kitchen, they toasted with Mimosas to Nevada's cleverness and observation to help bring down the twins. Their spread included homemade waffles, scrambled eggs with provolone cheese, turkey sausage, grits and a cantaloupe and honeydew salad.

Tai figured it was worth celebrating their rescue and the twins' capture. She was always seeking a reason to utilize her newly renovated kitchen. It was her favorite room in the house and offered a certain coziness.

"Girl, that was deeee-licious." Nevada shook her head in admiration. "You sure know how to work this kitchen. You probably get tired of me saying that, but it's true. You should start your own catering business."

"Maybe someday. I can't get the whole thing out of my mind about those twins."

"Nevada, we can't thank you enough for your help. Randall and Robert, my ass. Jansen and Jarrod were some serious crooks. I can't believe I was ready to drop my panties for that creep...I just knew he was packing. He was packing all right; guns and drugs." Candace sipped her Mimosa. "I was such a fool, falling for him in the first place, and then I pulled in Trista."

"That's okay. You didn't have any idea." Trista reflected on the twins. "The signs were all there; never taking us to their homes—who knows where they lived? Switching out the cars; wearing the dark shades."

"Yeah, they were city slicksters. I'm glad they did drop us off in New York. It sounds like they were doing their thing up there. We could have gotten caught up in that mess or ended up in a ditch somewhere. We were treading on thin ice and didn't have a clue." Candace sighed. "We could've been charged along with those monsters. What you call 'em; wolves in sheep's clothing?"

On the local morning news, the anchorman had described Jansen's and Jarrod's background. He revealed a track record that was a mile long with petty theft expanding to the big-time gangster crimes. The twins were from the Miami suburbs and both had graduated from the University of Florida. They were business majors who had started an import-export company that later became a fledgling operation. To cope with its failure, the two devised an intricate but simple scheme to rob banks. Amid the trendy Miami lifestyle of beach life and palm trees, the twins blended into the backdrop with ease as fashion plates and suave personalities. They were likable and charming; women flocked to their beck and call. Unfortunately, some of their female cohorts were arrested and serving time. In addition to being getaway drivers, they allowed the twins to make huge deposit amounts in their personal bank accounts. The twins had coerced them into opening multiple accounts at various banks. It was likely their mission with Candace and Trista; perhaps to groom them to be accomplices or use them as pawns to gain whatever were their desires. Candace realized perhaps this explained why Jansen had never attempted to get intimate with her; nor Jarrod with Trista. They wanted to impress the women with splurging to net their trust but yet keep them at arm's distance.

Jansen and Jarrod had become drug kingpins and made their living traveling up and down the East Coast. Their New York trip with Candace and Trista was to secure a major deal with a Colombian cartel. The women would have helped to shield them and with their upstanding appearance; they could have thrown off suspicion. When police examined the car, they found a cache of weapons and cocaine buried in a hidden compartment underneath the trunk.

Nevada had listened to the newscast with pride and invisibly had given herself a pat on the back. Ryan had called her once he'd seen her late-night text informing him that she was the source of the capture. She'd also notified him that she would be staying over at Tai's for the night. As for the $50,000 reward, she planned to guard that prize as long as possible. She presumed that eventually he might find out through police chat and if so, so be it. She had maintained the longtime relationship with Ryan; however, it seemed that there was a missing link. Nevada had stopped bringing up the subject of marriage. Whenever she did, Ryan would become irritated. She couldn't help recall what her mother always said: "If you're good enough to sleep with him, then you're good enough for him to marry you."

Although it was the trend now to live together eternally, and have children without marriage, Nevada held on to her old-fashioned values. At forty-three, she was aware that children were likely not in her future. However, marriage was tangible; it was simply that Ryan might not be groom material.

"That's exactly how a lot of women get caught up and locked

up; helping out criminals and then taking the fall," Candace stated. "Guess they were working on us; get us right where they wanted us and then we'd do whatever they wished."

"Well, lesson learned. All that glitters ain't gold." Nevada smiled.

"I'm serious," Tai agreed. Her thoughts raced to her own golden boy, Hasan. She hadn't returned to the gym in a while. Her personal trainer sessions had ended and she debated whether to restart them. It was too much of a temptation; seeing him made her crave his full-body workouts. It was awkward to visit the gym; she would speculate that she would eventually be wrapped in Hasan's arms and around his body. Lately, she realized that she was more focused on Hasan than toning her body—the reason she had joined the gym. She had lost sight of her goal. So far, she had held her secret about Hasan from her girls. *Some things you keep tidy*, Tai thought. But she was now torn. *Should I keep my rendezvous with Hasan who allows me to feel risky? It's an exhilarating experience. Or be true to Marco who has my back? I love him, adore him, but there's no excitement involved. No sneak and cheat effect.*

"Ladies, I've got something to tell you 'bout. It's deep, really," Tai informed.

"Let me get another Mimosa first." Nevada jumped up from the table and poured from the pitcher.

"Why don't we move to the den?" Tai suggested.

"Sure thing." Candace arose from the table as the group settled in the den. "I ate too much and feeling lazy."

"Well, this will get your attention." Tai set her glass on the table. "My gym workouts are really workouts."

"What you mean? You said the trainer was nothin' but the truth." Candace winked. "Fine body, tight ass, abs, chest…"

"Yeah, all that and more. We've been knockin' boots all over that gym."

"Oooo, tell me the dirt." Candace laughed.

"It's not funny. I'm starting to feel bad about it."

"Never feel bad when you're getting your sex on," Candace chided.

"I've fallen deep in love with Marco. He's no longer merely someone I'm dating. We really have a special bond."

"I thought you said that crazy woman was blowing up his phone," Nevada inquired.

"I did, but we got that all straight. It's not his fault. I was pissed about it so I did take it out on him. And Hasan was right there to help me forget about it. I mean, those nights at the gym were smooth. We started out on the office desk…"

"Oh, my…" Candace teased.

"And ended up on the equipment."

Candace leaned forward. "Now tell me about the positions, honey."

"I don't think they're any we haven't tried."

"All right now." Nevada admired Tai's free attitude.

"No, on the serious side, I'm at a point where I don't know what to do. It's lust, of course. He makes me feel so sexy and I love the idea that we're sneaking. It's kind of like our own little dirty secret. So that's fun…but I realize that Marco loves me. He's shown me time and time again. I'm starting to think it's not fair to Marco. Of course, I'd love to continue to have my pumpkin pie and eat it, too. Hasan is all that. But I'd better break it off. I can find another trainer, or maybe I don't need one this time. He's shown me the basics so I can go from here."

"Girl, if that's what you want. But you know me; the more the merrier. I'm always looking for the next one. If it's double or triple at the same time, that's cool with me. I'll date more than one. Variety is a win-win." Candace looked at Trista, who had remained quiet throughout Tai's revelation. "I didn't tell you this, Trista, but remember when we were in the theater and you asked me what was wrong? Girl, I was in New York with Randall and sweating this guy in the lobby...until I realized he was gay. If his date hadn't shown up, I was ready to make my move."

Trista grinned. "Oh, that's why you looked disappointed."

"Right, I don't like turning down any prospects."

Tai reflected again, replaying the gym nights in her mind. It was such a thrill, but her intuition was strong that she should cease the sexfests.

"I've gotta stop. After all those years of being faithful and committed to Austin, and he ended up not giving a damn, I finally believe I have a man who does. And I don't want to take a risk losing him for some booty calls. Forty-one and I've had my fun, and it's time to get serious. After all, that's what I've been waiting for and wishing for. Now, it's right here in my face and I'm playing a game?" Tai took a sip of her Mimosa. "No, ladies, I'm calling it quits. Marco's the man. I'll have to kiss Hasan goodbye."

"Hmmm, girl, you sure? It's been years since you weren't stuck in a relationship with only one guy. You've always been stable— you and Nevada. Now, you're seeing what it's like to have your cake and eat it, too. Isn't it good?" Candace asked. "And don't forget you had that little fantasy in St. Maarten with beach boy." Candace laughed.

"Yeah, I hear you, but I really think, especially at this age, I'm a one-guy-kinda-girl."

"And ain't nothing wrong with that," Nevada interjected.

Candace continued to make her point. "Well, you know how I roll."

"Dangerously...and I hope you learned from those crazy twins," Nevada reprimanded.

"Definitely. That was a scare." She turned to Trista. "Right?"

"*Scare* wasn't the word. More like a *horror flick*." She sighed. "Glad we didn't know the truth until we got back here. If they even thought we realized what was up, we might have ended up on the side of the road."

"Thank God, we're back safe and in one piece."

"Yes, He was on our side."

MONDAYS WERE INTERESTING: EITHER YOU ARRIVED AT THE OFFICE chipper and refreshed from the weekend; or you were blue and not prepared to enter a new work week. Sometimes they reminded Tai of the Annie Lee painting "Blue Monday," depicting a woman drooped on the side of her bed, head hung low with curlers in her hair, as if she were saying, "I am exhausted and I can't get up from this bed."

After Saturday's escapade with the alleged bank robbers and fearing for Trista's and Candace's lives, Tai had experienced more excitement than she had bargained for. Her mood was truly blue on this Monday; her night had been restless and she'd only managed a couple hours of sleep. Her edginess was reflected when she arose to crumpled sheets and tossed pillows. She'd had trouble putting her mind at-ease with the looming break-off with Hasan. Her mind had started to play games about whether she should keep the lines of communication open; her "secure" relationship with Marco might someday fall through. After her two-hour, non-peaceful rest, she awoke with determination that her late-night trysts with Hasan were history.

Tai soaked up the Monday morning scene through her picture window. The view offered serenity; a calming effect. She closed her eyes and meditated for a few minutes, took a deep breath and pulled out her cell phone to peruse her contact list. She picked up her office line and dialed.

"Hello," a pleasant baritone voice answered.

"Hi, it's me, Tai." She glanced at her closed office door to ensure it was sealed.

"Hey, baby, what's up? I didn't recognize this number." Hasan's ears perked up as he was surprised to hear from Tai. He presumed she had been dodging him lately; he was on point. "I miss you, Tai," he said seductively.

"And I…" Tai paused. "I have something to tell you."

"I know it's all good; you can't wait for our Thursday night workout, right?"

"Wrong, Hasan. Listen, I've given this a lot of thought and we need to go our separate ways. I can't do this anymore. It was cool, I admit, for a while, but I realize I'm in a committed relationship and I truly care for the one I'm with. I'm sorry—"

"So, you really feel this way? Woman, I will turn you inside out, upside down, around, and leave you trembling for more. You know how we do." Hasan was enjoying getting into the rhythm of his phone sex; it was no longer straight talk. "I will make you cum infinitely, forever…"

"Okay, that's enough." Hasan's words were titillating and Tai was resisting temptation to give in. She needed to be firm with the breakup.

"Baby, we can—"

"Look, Hasan, I know you mean well. Hey, I'm finding it hard to say no. But I've gotta call it quits." Tai thought to show a softer side. "I apologize, though; I'm glad we didn't let it get out of hand."

"It sounds like you've made up your mind. I'm not in this to beg, but if you ever have a change of heart, you'll know where to find me." Disappointed he couldn't manipulate Tai with his charms, Hasan quickly hung up before Tai could say goodbye.

When Tai placed the phone on the cradle, she reclined in her chair and turned to face the window—her source of comfort. Her mind swirled with the gym memories: the wild sexcapades, the risky and risqué encounters. It had all been thrilling. Now, her focus would be on Marco, the man of her dreams. Lately, she'd been playing cat-and-mouse but now, she would give in and be captured. Cloudy skies brightened her thoughts; it was indisputable: She and Marco were soul mates.

27

Slam, dunk...and party

Candace lounged around her condo in her silk pajamas. She relished the sunlight that streamed through her tangerine sheers. Spring was approaching and it was her favorite time of year to visit New York on her buying missions. After the disappointing encounter with the twins, she actually wasn't eager to go there anytime soon. It would be a solid reminder of the hazardous situation she had experienced. Saturdays were a day of cooling out, dating or hanging with the girlfriends. Everyone was occupied today. There were always the friends who were not in the core group. It was good to touch base on occasion.

She hadn't seen or talked to Sierra in a while. She never knew when Sierra would be in town or at a destination as a flight attendant. Ladies nights were the coveted get-together as Sierra looked forward to letting her hair down. Her position required her to be professional and on her p's and q's. Tai was the premier hostess, always opening her place for the ladies to unwind.

Candace dialed Sierra's cell phone. *She could be in L.A. or Brazil or Paris. Maybe she's in town and we can get together for a drink.*

Sierra picked up on the third ring. "Hello."

"Hey, girl, what you doin'? You in town?"

"Yep, got back last night. I'm here but only for a minute. Girl, I'm getting ready to go to the CIAA next week."

"What's the C-I-double-A?"

"The annual college basketball tournament. It's in Charlotte." Sierra was relaxing in bed catching up on her TV shows that she'd missed during the week. She recorded them to ensure she would keep up with the episodes.

"You like basketball?"

"It's okay, especially if one of my teams is playing. But girl, I don't go for the games; I go for the parties."

"I heard my cousins talk about some party they give down there during a tournament. Maybe that's the one."

"When I say parties, I mean *parties*. Day parties, night parties, you name it. It's one big African-American reunion. You would have a blast."

"I don't know—"

"'Til you go. You've gotta go. It's hard to describe it until you experience it."

"That's exactly what my cousins told me. They give a day party and they say that it's one o'clock in the afternoon and it feels like one at night," Candace recalled. "Well, you know me, and I like to party, so why not? I'm sure you're flying. Maybe I can get someone to ride down with me; help me drive."

"Girl, no worries; I'll hook you up with a buddy pass. You can fly with me."

"Thanks. Tell me when and where and I'll be there."

"Leaving from BWI on Thursday. It's a noon flight. Pack your bag. You can wear jeans to the Saturday day party. Bring something dressier for Thursday and Friday night."

"Cool. You made my day. I was going to ask you if you wanted to go for a drink today, but this sounds even better." Candace started looking in her closet for outfits. "I'll let my cousins know I'm finally coming down and to save me some tickets for their party. I hear you can hardly get any. They're in demand. Last year, they had to turn down people at the door."

"I'm not sure if it's the same party I usually go to, but yes, please get us some tickets. It might be a squeeze to get them," Sierra suggested. "I can pick you up as I'm leaving my car at the airport."

"Where are we staying? You have a hotel booked?"

"Those are hard to find, too. Everything's showing a sell-out. But I'll figure out something and get us a place. Don't worry," Sierra assured. "Be ready at nine-thirty."

"Girl, I'm getting ready *now*." Candace was appreciative that she had a light schedule this week. It wouldn't be difficult to take a few days off. She was telecommuting and didn't have to stop at the office or at any store locations. The trip to Charlotte would be what she needed to pick up her mood. The ordeal with Jansen and Jarrod was still fresh on her mind and she wanted to erase it forever.

It was morning and Candace and Sierra prepared for the upcoming party in their hotel suite. Sierra had told Candace how the parties were warm so Candace decided on a sleeveless black top and a dark pair of 7 for All Mankind jeans. Her black leather boots with a shorter heel and large gold hoop earrings topped off the ensemble. Sierra wore jeans, boots and a spaghetti-strap bronze shirt. It was noon on Saturday and they were ready for the big party. This was Sierra's first time going to this specific day party; she had been to several others.

Candace had discovered that the party was one started by her cousins. It had started small in a hotel room in Richmond, Virginia, where the CIAA was once held. Then it moved to North Carolina and graduated to a hotel suite in Winston-Salem, then Raleigh-Durham. By the time the CIAA reached Charlotte, it was expanded by vast numbers and was held in larger venues. This specific event was credited as being the original day party for the CIAA; now as Candace was informed, a lot of day parties had cropped up following their example.

"Time to go party." Sierra grabbed her purse. "Deja and Evette, you all ready? I'll drive."

"Yeah, we're ready." Deja looked in the mirror. "I'm glad we got our tickets. They pre-sold most of them and I hear they're selling some at the door this year."

"Right. Last year's party was over the top," Evette advised. "They'll have even more people trying to get in this year since they heard about it."

"My cousins said the tickets were tighter than ever," Candace chimed in. "They've been talking about this party for years."

SIERRA PULLED INTO A PARKING LOT WHERE A STREAM OF PEOPLE stood outside of a building. She then realized it was the wrong venue; their day party was across the street.

"Wow. I've never in my life…" Candace was stunned. "Seen this many folks trying to get into a day party."

"I told you, girl." Sierra turned into the lot and scrambled to find a parking space. It was only 12:30; the party didn't start until a half-hour later and the lot was already packed. A long line had snaked along and around Coyote Joe's, a white wooden structure that was devoted to country-western, but not on this day.

"This is amazing. No wonder my cousins and other people keep raving about this party. Damn!"

"Luckily, thanks to you, we have our tickets, so we don't have to stand in that line. Those are folks who have to buy theirs at the door."

After parking, the four women walked through the back door of the establishment. They held on to their tickets like diamonds as they were definitely the prized possession of the day. Any time that many hopeful partygoers were standing in a long line during the early afternoon, it meant that this party must be the happening place to be.

Sierra led the way through the door after all of their hands were stamped for re-entry. They headed straight to the bar where they ordered cocktails. To the right was a mechanical bull where one woman was riding like she was a rodeo contestant.

"That looks like fun. You go, girl." Candace grinned as she thought she might try the ride later.

They walked toward the dance floor; in awe, they stopped in their footsteps to scope out the scene. The cavernous room had transformed into an African-American party paradise. It was now 1 p.m. and the place was packed. Candace found out from her cousins that 3,000 party animals were ready to turn the club out. DJ Sid graced the stage and played back-to-back hits.

Seats were scarce but that was fine with the crowd. Most were anxious to dance the day away. There was new school, old school and older school. There were all types of flavors in any complexion, size, style and dress; from the hoochie skirts to jeans; from hip-hop to dressy casual; one could definitely find someone in the matchmaker haven.

"This is a black man's paradise," one guy said to Candace.

"And a black woman's paradise," Candace responded. *Hmmm, lots of fine brothas up in here.* Her mind started thinking of Nelly's "Hot in Herre."

As they sipped on their bar drinks, they eventually split and disappeared into the humongous crowd. It was definitely possible to get lost in the spacious club, but that was a good thing. The deejay was spinning the sounds and creating a packed dance floor.

Candace was pumped being in heaven, surrounded by plentiful

prospects. She sized up each man who whisked or strolled past her. Some pulled her into the horde of dancers where she moved seductively, at times doing lap dance moves. When "The Wobble" blared through the speakers, Candace immediately realized it was a new line dance. She inspected the moves and soon had the hang of the Wobble. It was Sierra's family from North Carolina that had shown her how to do the Cupid Shuffle when Sierra's family reunion was in D.C. She wondered if the latest dances always originated in the South and moved up the East Coast. After dancing to several hits, she needed a break so she went to stand by the stage. Better yet, she noticed an outdoor terrace where she headed for a reprieve.

The body heat was working overtime and she was drenched on her forehead and her chest. There were others who had taken a break from the sweat-filled room. However, it didn't faze the partygoers; it was like an old-fashioned house party where you partied hard despite the sizzling temps. As she unwound on the terrace, back-to-back men approached her requesting either a dance or her digits. She was savoring all the attention and played it off like she was some movie star being mobbed. Of course, she enjoyed being a major attraction; especially in a sea of hunks.

She'd forgotten about Sierra and imagined she was equally being wooed. Sierra could hold her own. Her personality was similar to Candace's and she also was forever on the hunt. She was sure that Deja and Evette were having a blast. Her head continued to spin as she was mesmerized by the sensation of the oversized party. It was definitely worth the trip to Charlotte and she would put the event on her annual calendar.

Three o'clock and the party was geared up. Some folks were dancing nonstop and Candace was amazed at the stamina. She re-entered the main area of the club and started rolling through to see if she spotted Sierra. There was no need in calling Sierra's cell phone as the music was piercing. After a half-hour of walking through the club and checking out the excitement, Candace gave up trying to locate Sierra.

A spokesman took the mike and thanked the thousands who offered annual support. He explained the origin of the party that had grown into the hottest ticket in town during the CIAA Weekend. A group of ladies, mostly alumni of North Carolina Central University in Durham, had established the scholarship fundraiser in honor of a deceased friend who had suffered from an illness. Tickets to the event were coveted from New York to Atlanta to D.C. Many in the crowd discovered familiar faces from their hometowns. Some ran into those they hadn't seen in twenty to thirty years. It was like an enormous reunion.

The festive atmosphere included one woman who pranced through the crowd blowing a whistle and fanning herself to keep cool. She reminded everyone that it was an old-school affair. *Life is too short*, Candace thought. *A lot of these folks realize it. When I leave this earth, this is how I wanna go.* It was impressive to see the grown 'n' sexy enjoying the thrills on a Saturday afternoon with the feel of a nighttime throwdown.

WHEN THE FINALE BOOMED FROM THE SPEAKERS, MUCH TO THE chagrin of the humongous crowd, folks were either exhausted or ready for the next party. Charlotte offered a choice of late-night events and Candace was eager for round two—after she took a break. She spotted Sierra after most of the crowd had cleared out. She plopped down on a chair adjacent to the dance floor. Sierra followed suit. The chairs were like finding a hidden treasure after strutting, standing and shimmying in heels for hours.

"Whoa, girl, that was a blast." Candace wiped her forehead. "Now, that's what I call a *party*."

"I told you it was hard to describe…unless you experienced it." Sierra sipped a bottle of water. "I heard about some night parties. You game?"

"All I need is a nap and I'll be good to go."

"Let's find Deja and Evette. I didn't see them the whole time."

"Neither did I." Candace crossed her legs and fanned herself. "I see why you make it a point every year. This party was off the hook."

Deja and Evette walked up, looking like they had been drained in a sink; all energy had been zapped.

"What ya'll think of the party?" Sierra asked, knowing what the response would be.

They shook their heads.

"I'm worn out, but that's a good thing," Deja stated. "There were some brothas up in *hairrr*. We had a blast and didn't see each other until now."

Evette laughed. "And that was fine by me. I must've lost ten pounds."

The four headed to the exit where they walked past the bull again.

"I'll have to try to ride that the next time." Candace was aware it would have to be prior to her hitting the dance floor. She would be too fatigued to attempt it afterward.

A neatly dressed man near the door wiped his forehead and looked at Candace. "Baby, I've been baptized today. This was heaven."

"On earth." Candace smiled.

THE FAMISHED AND EXHAUSTED LADIES EAGERLY SET OFF FOR THE hotel. Sierra invited Deja and Evette to her suite to enjoy home-made treats that awaited their arrival. Sierra's aunt who lived locally had prepared and dropped off a salad smorgasbord earlier in the day: chicken salad, shrimp pasta salad, and fruit and nut salad. Sierra had packed the fridge and chilled several bottles of wine. A fresh batch of homemade peanut butter cookies and slices of lemon pound cake topped off their spread.

The ladies needed to wind down from the hype. Sierra knew just the right medicine to mellow out. She inserted her favorite Kem CD in the player and turned it on. The R&B crooner would offer a mental massage; his lyrics were always on point.

"One thing for sure, I've added to my digits collection." Candace pulled business cards and pieces of paper from her purse and waved them. "Honey, I'm outgrowing my little black book."

Sierra agreed, "I bet you are."

"Hey, I didn't do too bad myself. There was plenty variety," Deja noted.

"Actually, I didn't see one guy in there who I'd want to hook up with," Evette stated with certainty.

"You've *got* to be kidding me..." Sierra found the statement unbelievable; not with all the men that filled the space. "You're not serious."

"Well—" Evette started.

"You need to get your eyes checked." Candace laughed.

"Three thousand people and not one? You must've had on blinders, girl." Sierra was amazed.

"Yeah, I don't know what you were looking at," Deja agreed. "Something for everyone. All kinds of shades and spices."

"I'm entitled to my opinion, and that's what I thought," Evette refuted. *I guess I am a little picky these days.* "Anyway, Sierra, thanks for sharing the food. It was delicious. Please tell your aunt. That was really sweet of her."

"I'll tell her. She always fixes a bunch of food. She knows how we do. Come here and be on the run, and not take time out to eat."

DEJA AND EVETTE CHOSE TO CALL IT A NIGHT AND HEADED DOWN-stairs to their own suite. A short night was in their future.

Candace transferred from jeans to her little black Chanel dress. Sierra changed into a sheer low-cut black blouse and black skinny jeans. They cruised the downtown streets of Charlotte in search of festivities. Two hotel parties proved to be winners. Hotels were having a field day and parties were plentiful. Various celebrities were spotted and swarmed for autographs and photos. It was a vivacious evening of networking and adventure. Men, men and more men graced their presence; wining and dining them to their satisfaction. It was a girls' night out of teasing and tantalizing—without any attachments.

SUNDAY ROLLED AROUND AND SIERRA AND CANDACE REGRETTED the culmination of an amazing nonstop affair. Candace was overjoyed that she had decided to join Sierra. Now, it was back to the real world. En route to drop off the rental car, they could see the snail-pace stream of traffic on I-85 North. It was jam-packed with vehicles lined up to return home from a whirlwind weekend.

After returning the car, they caught the shuttle to the departure entrance at Charlotte/Douglas International Airport. A group of three women piled out of a luxury sedan and pulled out their luggage from the trunk.

The female driver, wearing shades and snazzily dressed, gave each woman a goodbye hug. "Remember, what goes on in Charlotte *stays* in Charlotte," she stated firmly. She smiled, hopped back in her car and cruised away.

Overhearing the comment, which was a take on the popular Vegas saying, Sierra thought it summed up the weekend. It had been a getaway with private moments; not all details would be shared back home.

28

Return to roots

Springtime had arrived and Tai had the feverish thing going on. Marco's schedule was now bustling and his social life had diminished. Tai had become restless and desired to break away. She welcomed the serenity that blooming flowers and trees brought along with warm temperatures. Washington, D.C. was simply gorgeous in the spring; famous for its cherry blossoms, National Zoo and Potomac River. All were reminiscent of the season.

Tai had resided in D.C. for almost thirty years and while she adored the city, she'd always had a burning desire to return to her roots someday. She was well-traveled but had never looked back to the place where she was born, raised and trained until her twelfth birthday. She thought that she would erase the tragic experience of her parents' murder-suicide, and had done so for three decades. Now, she yearned to experience what life was like in her hometown of Salisbury, N.C.

Candace's and Sierra's account of their fantastic CIAA Weekend in Charlotte and all its hoopla had sparked a renewed interest in her hometown. She had simply passed through the state during road trips en route to either Atlanta or Florida. In fact, I-85 rolled directly through Salisbury. Tai recalled the small town of Salisbury had landed its place on a map in 1973, when singer Stevie Wonder was a passenger in a car crash and suffered a severe head injury. According to local newspaper reports, the celebrity, whose *Innervisions* album had just released days earlier, was unknown to both the driver of the other vehicle and the attending physician at the local hospital. *Can you imagine someone not knowing Stevie Wonder?* Tai thought when she'd heard about the incident years later.

Ever since Trista had arrived in D.C., Tai was even more intrigued about visiting her hometown. Tai had recently created a bucket list, and a trip to Salisbury to visit her parents' gravesites and revisit her roots was in the top ten. When she'd traveled along I-85, an eerie feeling would overcome her and she'd avoided taking the exit ramps in her hometown. She'd continue full speed ahead toward Hotlanta.

Tai decided she needed private time and sharing her plans with Trista, Marco, Candace or Nevada was unnecessary. She longed for peace and felt it was best to keep the trip to North Carolina under wraps. She would simply alert them that she was taking a solo journey to a secluded location; perhaps a spa retreat. This would be believable. She would suggest if it was an emergency or mandatory that she be contacted, to call her cell phone. Otherwise, her location was private. Tai didn't want any tag-alongs or anyone to discourage her from her road trip. She was about to scratch off one goal on her bucket list.

Tai booted her laptop and checked the ten-day weather forecast; if it looked promising she would hit the highway next week. It showed high sixties to low seventies for the upcoming dates. Driving would be heavenly and peaceful. She looked forward to her journey home.

29

The road ahead

Tai and Marco had dined at Carolina Kitchen in the Maryland suburbs and enjoyed a meal of smothered chicken, collard greens, candied yams and cornbread; a traditional Southern spread. It was quite appropriate as she was headed to Carolina the next morning. Marco had made the suggestion as he had gone there for lunch while working in the area. He'd decided to treat Tai to a down-home dining experience. Little did he know that Tai was set for Carolina in the morning. Tai frequented more of the D.C. restaurants; especially with her girlfriends. He loved to introduce her to new dining adventures. She had become such a gourmet aficionado and he thought soul food would be a good choice.

When Marco dropped Tai off at home, she was tempted to invite him in but quickly thought otherwise. She was determined to get an early start the next morning.

Trista had worked late and arrived home exhausted. She wasn't in the mood for chatting the night away and hoped that Tai wasn't, either.

She climbed the stairs softly and approached Tai's room. An upbeat tune on the iPod infiltrated the room. "Well, have a good trip." Trista stood in the doorway, elevating her voice over the music.

Tai was startled as she turned around to see Trista. "Oh, I

didn't hear you come in." Tai pulled a dress off a hanger and folded it neatly before placing it in her suitcase.

"Maybe someday we can go back to that spa you took me to."

"Oh, uh, sure; we'll have to make it a point," Tai agreed. A feeling of guilt overcame Tai; she grasped that Trista's comment was linked to her belief that Tai was going to a spa in West Virginia for the long weekend. That was all the information she had shared—and then it wasn't truthful. Tai didn't know how Trista would've reacted if she had told her that she was going to N.C. Trista had spent the early part of her adult life there; now, it was time for Tai to revisit her youth.

Tai ceased her packing briefly and walked across the room. She embraced Trista. "Thanks, Sis, for understanding that I didn't invite you. I feel like I need to get in tune with my mind and body; and this time around, it's better alone. You take care. It's weird but I guess this is the first time, other than New York—and we want to forget that ordeal—that we've ever been apart…since you got here."

Trista adjusted her shoulder bag and hugged her in return. "No problem. I'm not sure they would've let me off work. So enjoy. I'll be knocked out by the time you leave. They kept me on my feet steady today and I'm wiped out."

"Have a good night."

"You, too, and a safe trip."

Tai eagerly packed her bags and hoisted them into the trunk of her Jeep. She would leave her Beemer parked at home. The sun glistened through the windshield as she drove the scenic route out of the city and picked up I-95 South. Chrisette Michele and Maze, followed by Erykah Badu were in the changer and kept her company past Richmond before she exited onto I-85. After breaking in South Hill, Virginia, Tai continued to cruise toward Durham and Greensboro. The fragrance from the two-lane, pine tree-lined highway was captivating. The highway expanded to more lanes and Tai pushed the pedal.

The six-hour trip was smooth and without a hitch. Taking the Salisbury exit, Tai, for once, felt at-ease. She was *home*. Before checking into the Holiday Inn near the highway, there was one essential must-have. She craved a Krispy Kreme doughnut. Just the thought made the imaginary cake creation melt in her mouth. She'd already searched online to find the closest location and her GPS navigated her directly to Krispy Kreme. *Hmm-mmm*, she thought.

After fulfilling her sugar needs, Tai headed for the hotel where she checked in for the night. She was ready to relax and get an early start in the morning. She stepped into the shower and welcomed the hot water cascading down her body. She dried off and prepared for bed. Entering the bedroom, she flicked on the TV and snuggled under the cover. She texted Trista and Marco to inform them she had made it to her destination safely, hoping that they would think she'd been settled for a while. West Virginia was a much shorter drive. It wasn't long before she was peacefully asleep.

30

The awakening

The rural road curved and twined past the brick elementary school, now the home of a recreation center. Open fields and homes with gravel driveways infiltrated the scene. It was déjà vu when Tai passed an entrance with a long dirt road leading to a large wooden house on a hill. It reminded her of hot summer afternoons when she and Trista would visit Miss Paula, one of their mother's friends. The driveway was lined with apple trees and the air always promised a pleasant scent of fresh fruit. Despite the blistering heat, the old house on the hill was a respite as the shade of the country acreage managed to cool the farmland.

She remembered sitting on the big porch swing and drinking water from a pump. Those were special times; she hadn't given much thought to her childhood until now. The area was in stark contrast to the sights and sounds of the city. It was so quiet that you could hear each distinctive sound.

Despite following her navigational system, she cruised along with some familiarity. She recalled the old drive-inn movie theater, now a town landmark; the bowling alley and flea market. When she reached her former community, a somber feeling overtook her. This was the site of her home place and once she approached, the memories were pleasant with good times yet the flashbacks were gruesome. Residents had kept the murder-suicide low-key, but news traveled swiftly and Tai and Trista had discovered the truth.

Tai slowed her pace as she crept up to her former home and stopped. The house wasn't dilapidated as she had expected; it appeared to be occupied. Parked cars and a manicured lawn were signs of residents. She accelerated once a man entered the yard from a front door. She was in no mood for conversation or questions. *Wonder if he knows what happened here?* It reminded her of movies where a new family moved into a haunted house unknowingly.

Tai continued to the end of the road and turned right at the stop sign. After a mile and a half, she had reached her destination: Pilgrim AME Church. The small brick and mortar structure beckoned. The tidy landscaping and new stone walkway showed the grounds were attended. Tai drove to the back of the church where she spotted the cemetery. She parked and took a deep breath. Haunting flashbacks of the day of her parents' double funeral permeated her mind.

She recalled hearing buzz about an "affair," and at the time, the word meant little to her youthful and innocent mind. Trista was even younger so it meant even less to her. Tai was able to sense that her father had done something terribly wrong. He'd been called "evil" and "wicked" and "sinful"; those had been biting descriptions of the dad who'd taught her how to ride a bike, taken her on Sunday afternoon rides and helped her with school projects. She didn't comprehend that the church and community folk were bitter about his "immoral" act. She'd heard the words muttered under their breath; not loud or sharp.

It was a heartrending day in Salisbury when her mom and dad were placed six feet under. She remembered the repast at the church and the outpouring of love and support showered upon her and Trista. Despite the sadness, there was an uplifting spirit that blanketed the tone of the farewell; a genuine concern for the siblings' welfare.

Stepping out of her car, wearing her crisp, pinstriped cotton button-down blouse, jeans and flats, she pulled out a bouquet. She had stopped by the local florist to pick up the spring arrangement. She started walking to the cemetery and wandered throughout; it was as deserted as the church parking lot. She entered the grassy area and strolled until she found the headstone: *John and Diana Wilson*. She found it ironic that they'd been buried side by side despite the murder-suicide.

Tai stood before her parents' grave and prayed:

Dear Lord, please forgive me for decades for not returning to visit my parents' resting place. I truly miss them and wish they could have been in my life during my teenage years and adulthood. However, I know there is a place for them above. I'm sure there are people who say my father didn't deserve a spot behind the gates. He committed the ultimate sin. I understand we can be forgiven for our sins. Please continue to watch over them as I watch over Trista, my only sibling, who is now under my guidance. Thank You for leading her to me. I've come far to revisit my roots and to place these flowers here. They are a symbol of my unconditional love. Regardless of the final tragic outcome, Mama and Dad were the best parents a child could ever desire. May they rest in peace.

Tai reached inside her small purse and pulled out a tissue. She wiped the tears that trickled down her face. She was proud that she'd come this far to touch base with her past. They say everyone has skeletons in their closet and this was one of hers: She had never discussed the cause of her parents' death with anyone but Grandma and Trista. Her friends and associates up North were unaware of the tragedy she had experienced. For now, she would continue to keep this unpleasant part of her past tucked away. Tai realized that she had reached out for comfort and had found it among headstones. She was at peace. She started humming in her head the old hymn that once was a favorite inside the small brick church, now guarding her parents: "Amazing Grace."

THE FORK AND SPOON DINER WAS NESTLED DEEPER OFF THE HIGH-way and in between a Laundromat and a bait-and-tackle store. The white brick café featured shades partially drawn and a red neon sign displaying "Open." The wooden door creaked as Tai entered when suddenly all eyes zeroed in on her. She accepted the look that read, *Who is this stranger?* The customers were likely regulars who were unaccustomed to new faces. They figured that she was either lost or had stumbled across the place; it wasn't a destination. Tai felt slightly uncomfortable as she was never greeted with whimsical looks when she entered restaurants. How-ever, tight-knit communities where everyone was either related or acquainted might produce such a reaction. *It's all good. All I want to do is eat. This place was highly recommended when I asked at the gas station.*

"Good afternoon, ma'am." A woman in a white uniform and apron approached her. Her worn shoes indicated she'd spent hours on her feet. Her cocoa-complexioned face showed fine lines and its distinct bone structure spoke volumes that she was likely a town beauty queen from yesteryear. Her gray silky hair was pulled neatly in a bun.

"Good afternoon."

"Feel free to seat yourself. I'll grab you a menu."

Tai sat in a booth by the window. "I hear your food is the best around."

"My name's Ginger. Can I start you with something to drink?"

"A glass of water."

Ginger returned and set the glass on the table.

"What do you recommend? I'm from D.C. and I get Southern cooking every now and then. I'm in the kitchen all the time, so I'll be your harshest critic." She smiled playfully.

Ginger laughed. "We won't have to worry about that. Everyone loves our food. You tell me something you eat here isn't good, and *I'll* pay for your meal."

"Well, since you don't have any recommendations—"

"Oh, I do. The country fried chicken is a secret recipe. It's from my family. My dad, rest in peace, opened this diner back in the seventies."

"And you've been working here ever since?"

"Not totally. I went off to school for a couple of years, then he took ill so I came back here to help." Ginger looked at the chef who was swiftly preparing plates and setting them on the counter. "I'd suggest our mac 'n' cheese, too. We cook to order so I'd better place it now."

"Mac 'n' cheese is great. I'll take a side of that," Tai looked at the menu, "and the baked sweet potato."

"Good choice. And save room for the peach cobbler."

"Hmmm…that's a bet. I make those also; it's a family recipe. My grandmother taught me how to make them."

GINGER BROUGHT TAI'S MEAL AND REFILLED HER GLASS WITH water. "Enjoy."

Tai relished every morsel as she devoured her Southern meal and was too full to eat dessert but took her cobbler to go. Throughout the lunch, she marveled at how she had stayed away for decades. She reflected on the gravesite and her drive through key stops along her childhood memory train.

Ginger returned with the check. "How was it?"

"Delicious. I'm stuffed and ready to go take a nap." Tai laughed. "Kidding."

"Right…they always joke that black folks wanna sleep after they eat." Ginger wiped her hands on her apron. "You just passing through? To or from D.C.?"

"Well, I came down to visit."

"Oh, who you related to?" Ginger's curiosity was piqued.

"My parents are deceased….the Wilsons from Apple Lane." Tai's countenance was now saddened. "I lived here until I was twelve—"

"You're John and Diana's baby. School vice principal. Mom was a teacher," she recalled. Ginger looked at her watch. "It's a little slow right now. Taking a break." She sat in the booth opposite Tai. "Listen, honey, that was such a sad, sad situation. You were young, so I'm sure you only knew what old folks wanted you to know."

"You're right. They kept it under wraps and only shared with me certain facts, and I guess some untruths. Once I moved to D.C. with my grandma, and became a teenager, she told me the whole story."

"Yeah, I heard you'd moved up North and your sis, Trista, stayed here. In fact, she used to work here," Ginger revealed.

"Really? She told me she worked as a waitress several places, but she didn't tell me the names and I never bothered to ask."

"So, you've seen her lately?"

"Yes, she lives with me. It's been about eight months."

Ginger shook her head. "So that's where that cra—" She put her hand over her mouth. "She shoulda gone wit' ya." Ginger paused. "Oh, sorry, I didn't mean—"

"What *did* you mean?" Tai raised her eyebrows. "Well, you

likely heard that my grandma couldn't care for both of us. We had bonded and since I was the oldest, she decided to take me. Trista ended up in the foster care system after Miss Laine passed away."

"Yes, Miss Laine was a jewel. She deserves a lot of credit for taking care of *that* child." Ginger was getting heated up to play her role of one of the town's gossipmongers. "Your sister…never mind."

Now, wait a minute. I know Miss Ginger ain't getting ready to talk badly about my family. She doesn't know me like that.

A couple walked through the door. Ginger immediately jumped up to cater to them as if she was getting ready to take the witness stand and was relieved that court was out of session. "Hello, table for two?" She led them to a table nearby and took their order.

Tai had appreciated the down-to-the-earth attitudes of the few residents she had encountered. But maybe Ginger was a little too much in her comfort zone. *Then again, maybe I should let her talk; I might find out more about Trista's psyche. Her sudden bursts of crying; her guarded conversations; her mood swings.*

Trista, while the two had finally peaked with their sisterly bond, especially after the menacing world of the twins, still maintained an invisible shield. Tai always believed that there was a missing piece; maybe Ginger would be the key to unraveling the mystery.

She paid her bill and left Ginger a tip. It was time to move on. She wouldn't bother to hang around, despite Ginger's hint that something was amiss with Trista.

Tai had noticed the lone man at a window booth near the back. He wore a black baseball cap and salt-and-pepper beard. He appeared to have been engrossed with a pen and pad; perhaps it was a crossword puzzle. Ginger had managed to pique her curiosity about Trista and she was willing to hang around—even if it meant waiting until Ginger was off work—to learn more about her long-lost sister. Tai was keen on picking up a person's vibes. She sensed Ginger was like a 4-1-1 operator stocked with information. But suddenly she had become tight-lipped about Trista.

As she passed by the man's booth, he looked up and made eye contact, then dropped his head.

"Hello, young lady," he spoke without raising his head.

"Hello," Tai responded pleasantly. She stopped in her tracks and waited to see if he would meet her eyes. "I see you enjoy crosswords." She offered friendly conversation.

"Yep, I work them as much as possible." He spoke each word deliberately with a Southern twang. He placed his hand on his forehead as if he were stumped by one of the clues. "They say it helps your brain, when ya start getting' my age, young lady."

"Thanks for the compliment." *Young lady at forty-one? I like that. They say forty is the new twenty.*

"No problem. I heard you talking over there to Ginger." He continued to review the puzzle without looking up.

"Yes, I enjoyed the food—"

"She tell you what you want to know? My ears perked up when I heard 'Wilson.'" He finally looked up and into her eyes. "You related to them?"

"Yes, they were my parents…" Tai reflected sadly. "Why, did you know them, too?"

"Who didn't know the Wilsons? Great people…just a sad ending." He returned his attention to his puzzle.

"Excuse me, sir, I didn't get your name—"

"Paul…Paul Taylor, former deputy sheriff." He looked up at Tai. "Please, have a seat." He motioned for her to join him in the booth.

Tai turned around to see Ginger leaving out the door; her shift was over for the day. With her absence, Tai felt more comfortable to accept Paul's offer.

"And you are?"

"Tai Wilson. I'm visiting from D.C."

"I heard about you. Your grandmother…took you up North after your parents died. Bless their souls."

"Everybody knows everything."

"Especially us old-timers. We've lived through and seen it all."

Tai adjusted nervously in her seat. "Ginger made some comments about my sister, Trista. Do you know what she was referring to?"

Paul sipped his sweet iced tea. "Well, young lady, your little sis gained quite a reputation in these parts." He cleared his throat. "She was a small-time hustler; got involved in an elaborate scheme with this fella…I can't recall his name—"

Tai recalled Trista's story when they'd dined at the revolving restaurant. It had been the first time that Trista had opened up about anyone she had dated.

"That no-good son-of-a-bitch…not your sister, of course." Paul peered into Tai's eyes. "He ran an operation where he dwindled money from his job. Glad his ass is locked up.

"She seemed to have such a hard time here," he continued. "After he was jailed up in that prison, she liketa went crazy…lost her mind or sumpin'."

"Why do you say that?"

"She had a nervous breakdown, or so I heard. She had to be strapped in one of those so-called straitjackets and carried off to the looney bin. Pardon the expression." Paul shook his head in distaste. He hadn't noticed that Tai's eyes were now bulging. She tried to remain calm and show no emotion or surprise at his revelation. *Breakdown? Looney bin? Maybe that's why she comes out of a strange bag at times.* She continued to listen intently.

"So, she must've been pretty close to the guy, huh? You say that's why she had a breakdown?" Tai fished for confirmation and she remembered that the boyfriend was named Dorian.

"Now don't quote me. I said that's what I *heard*. Sometimes you can't believe everything you hear around this place. The news can start out with someone stole a dollar, then by the time it gets up the street it's ten, then when it reaches the back road, it's a thousand. You never can tell the truth 'cuz it gets stretched.

"After all those years I was in law enforcement, I've seen it all. Don't nothin' surprise me, young lady. And I saw it firsthand.

"You know, whatever your bizness is it gets put in the local paper: writing a bad check, driving without a license; it don't matter. It goes in the *black* and *white*." Paul chuckled.

"I've heard about that actually." Tai was acquiring an earful. She would view Trista in a new light. However, as Paul suggested, the rumor mill ran rampant in a small town and some of what he shared may not be truthful.

"Well, do you know what may have happened to Trista?" Tai played innocence. "She's an adult so I doubt she'd still be staying with a foster family. I'd love to reach out to her. Let her know that she has family who cares."

"All I know is that thug she was dealing with had threatened to hurt her if he ever got out. He figures she got away; and he got stuck."

"It sounds like she may have been an accomplice. Is that your opinion?"

"I helped serve the warrant. She was an accomplice but pleaded guilty to a lesser charge. She didn't have to serve any time; only ended up in a different kind of prison...one for the mind."

Tai swallowed; it was a bitter pill. Her sister's mood swings and erratic behavior may have been the result of her "other life." At least Paul's shocking leads offered some explanation.

"Are you okay? I mean, I hope I didn't get you too worked up here." Paul genuinely was concerned after he had presented eye-opening testimony.

"Oh, I'm fine. Just surprised I'd never heard any of this. Grandma has been deceased for a while and I really don't have any connection here."

"You never said why you were here in the first place."

"I wanted to make peace with my parents...I left here at age twelve and never looked back. But now there was a connection I needed to feel. I went to their gravesite today." Tai felt herself on the verge of tears again, as she had experienced at the church cemetery. "I feel so much better, though."

"That was special and I'm sure they," Paul looked upward, "are proud of you, Tai."

"Thanks...I just left D.C. yesterday and drove down here. Didn't tell a soul where I was going. Actually I said I was going away to a spa, by myself. Didn't want anybody tagging along, either. It needed to be a trip with me, myself and I. Sometimes you have to do those. Get in tune with yourself."

"You bet." Paul adjusted his baseball cap.

"She was a pretty girl, too. Looks a little like you," Paul complimented. "She bounced around from home to home."

"Yes, Grandma had told me that she was in foster care homes after Miss Laine passed."

"I'm wit' Ginger. Don't see how poor Laine survived. That girl put her through so much stress and discomfort."

"You seem to know a lot about Trista. Was her business that well known around here?"

"Depends on the kind of business." Paul smirked.

"Do you have any idea where my sister could be? We lost contact." Tai lied and fished for more of Paul's knowledge. "During my teens, Grandma kept saying she would bring me back here, but she never did. I think the memories were too painful to bear; my parents and the tragic loss."

"That's enough to keep anyone away." He paused. "No, I dunno. She could be in the state but doubt she's around here. I'm sure Ginger told you she used to work in this café."

"She did but didn't say much more."

"She and Ginger butted heads. That's probably why. And Ginger's the Queen Bee; she's been at this diner for forty-some years. They never got along. Not sure why 'cuz Ginger's sweet as pie. I think your sister had serious mood problems. You never knew what to expect from day to day. Then getting involved with that knucklehead seemed to make it worse." Paul shook his head. "I know Ginger was mighty glad when Trista disappeared. Or rather, had a…" Paul cleared his throat. "Career change." He chuckled to himself.

"Excuse me?"

"Young lady, it's time for me leave." Paul looked at his watch. "Wife's fixin' an early supper for me tonight." He read Tai's expression. "Right, I'm here at the diner, but not to eat. I come for late breakfast. Just sumthin' to do while I work my puzzles." He looked at his book. "Still can't figure out that clue. Ummph."

"Well, it's been great talking to you. The conversation has been…enlightening."

"Likewise." Paul closed his crossword puzzle book and placed his pen in his pale blue shirt pocket.

"I'd love to reconnect with my sister. It's been a long time," Tai lied. "It looks like I came to the right place to find out about my family. Whoever would have thought a diner would be a wealth of information?"

Paul smiled. "Young lady, if you haven't gotten enough, follow the road," he pointed out of the window, "and when you get to that lavender-colored building—ugh, I hate that color—go inside. See if anyone there knows Trista's whereabouts."

Tai contemplated his suggestion. "Okay. Will do." *Why not? I'm finding out more and more. All this will help me decipher what Trista is all about. I sure can't figure it out on my own. If she wasn't so close-minded, tight-fisted, whatever you want to call it, maybe I'd gain some ground.*

Paul was correct in his color judgment; lavender on a cinder-block building looked tacky. Tai pulled her Jeep into the rocky lot and parked. There were at least a dozen cars surrounding the building. The structure was nestled in a secluded area flanked by tall pine trees. There was no sign on the building, but Tai was sure this was the place where Paul had directed her if she were inquisitive about Trista. He hadn't provided a name. She had learned that usually residents gave directions without street names; only miles, or right and left turns.

So far, she'd discovered that she allegedly—she thought *allegedly* as Nevada always told her that events were alleged until proven factual—Trista had been a cohort in white collar criminal activity, followed by a nervous breakdown, and had spent some time in a mental facility. All were revelations from a small down-home diner. She cringed at the thought of what to expect next.

Tai looked into the lighted mirror, freshened her foundation and lip gloss, then checked her hair. She jumped out of the Jeep and closed the door. It was tranquil in the isolated area. She climbed the few steps onto the cement landing and opened the front door. Music almost blasted her back outside. *This must be a great acoustics system; I couldn't hear a thing out front.*

"Hi, you here to audition?" A tall, dark-skinned, muscularly built man with a large cubic zirconia stud earring greeted her at the entrance.

"No, I don't even know where I am, let alone an audition."

"Well, check it out." He directed her to an open room behind the partition.

Tai was stunned. A petite woman with smooth mocha-colored skin was topless and wearing a black thong as she graced a stage. She gyrated and swirled around a pole, wrapping her legs with efficiency and lowering her head down the pole. She lifted her body and swung around the pole before releasing her arms and standing in place. She moved along the edge of the stage, shaking her hips to show onlookers her booty as they stuffed dollar bills in her G-string. She lowered herself to the floor and lay on her back, then crossed her legs in scissor fashion. The catcalls, hoots and applause almost outdid the booming speakers.

Tai decided to take a seat; she perused the room to see that she was the sole female in the group…besides the dancer. After the dancer completed her routine, Tai arose and followed her toward the dressing room.

Another tall, burly man, obviously a security guard or bouncer, stopped her. "And you are?" He rubbed his bald head.

"I'm Trista."

"Say what?" He peered at Tai closely. "You don't look like her, but then again, you resemble her a little bit. But I know Trista." He showed that he could play the game, too.

"Hmm, say handsome, why don't we meet up after this set?" Tai licked her lips. "You sure look dee-licious. We can get busy this afternoon."

The man's mouth watered and he envisioned a knock-out, throwdown booty call with the gorgeous stranger. He was familiar with seeing women without clothing, and could only imagine what Tai was working with under the conservative blouse and jeans. He often liked leaving something to the imagination. Here, women left nothing for the mind; they showed it all upfront.

"I was kidding you. What's your name?" Tai teased.

I know you were, baby. "Stanton…but they call me Stan."

"Cool, Stan, I'm Trista's sister."

"On the real?" Stan drooled with the thought of Trista. "Where's my baby girl? I haven't seen her in at least a year. She was doing the damn thing here and then she disappeared. Lloyd's been looking for her. He's out now but he'd love to talk to you."

"Who the hell is Lloyd?" Tai was annoyed.

"Oh, he's the owner."

"What's the name of this damn place anyway? No signs out front."

"That's intentional. But everyone around here knows it's Juicy."

"Oh, Juicy? What a cute name for a strip joint." Tai faked her delight.

"Well, getting back to sis, that's why I'm here. I was looking for her. We got separated as kids, so I'm back visiting my roots. Trying to connect." Tai twirled her hair teasingly. "What you know about Trista? You say it's been about a year?"

"Sumthin' like that. Girlfriend had her pockets lined. She was the most requested dancer. All the fellas loved her. That bangin' body; oh sorry, sure you don't want me talkin' 'bout your sis like that." Stan made an attempt to speak politely. "Let me rephrase that. Sis was looking good from head to toe. She had the wildest routine, too. She went by the name Kat."

"Kat, huh?" Tai looked onstage as another dancer began her routine to Cameo's "Candy." She couldn't resist moving to the beat; it reminded her of the '70s parties she liked to throw.

"I see you get down, too. Like sister, like sister. You interested?"

"Hell no. I'm not from around here, either. And if I was, you wouldn't catch me up in this joint."

"Why not? These girls make big tips."

"No thanks. I can do my own thing." Tai inquired eagerly, "So, my sister's a stripper with fans and more fans, huh?"

"Yep, at least she *was* a stripper. Like I said, she's been away for awhile now. Just up and disappeared. Lloyd was some kinda pissed, too, 'cuz she pulled in a lot of dough for Juicy. Nah what I mean?"

Yeah, I know and I'm glad she's where she is now, sucker.

Onstage, the woman with a deep-chocolate complexion and a short haircut, worked her body to the "Candy" beat. Her body looked like she practically slept at the gym; Tai was aware of how much time she must've invested to form the hourglass figure.

"The chick there is a masterpiece. That body blows me away." Stan was mesmerized as he was glued to the performance.

Okay, enough of this body and booty stuff. It's cool but it's not me. Everyone's got to make a living, and if you've got it, why not work it? I'm glad to have found out, though, that this is what Trista was into; from waitress to stripper. Well, she does love *to dance. I can see how she was the top performer. She has an audience even when she's not collecting dollar bills; I can only imagine how much she was bringing home. At least she was doing something she loved.*

"I was going to see if you'd let me follow the ladies backstage. But there's no need, Stan. Thanks anyway. You've given me all I need."

"If you say so…you still owe me…I didn't get your name." Stan eyed her curiously, hoping she would fulfill his offer someday.

"Tequila." She winked and strutted across the room and out of the front door.

"Looking forward to it, *Tequila,*" he said to himself.

TAI HEADED BACK TO THE HOLIDAY INN. SHE WAS BRIMMING with satisfaction. Her stay in Salisbury had been fruitful. She'd found serenity with her parents and now she was equipped with a gold mine about Trista. The road trip back home in the morning would be complete.

T
ai basked in the sunlight and popped Jill Scott into her CD player; one of many soothing sounds to keep her company on the six-hour drive to D.C. She cruised out of the Krispy Kreme parking lot and couldn't wait to satisfy her sugar fix.

Tai toyed about whether to head directly home or stop at Marco's for the night. Her weekend of reflections was so focused on family that he'd seldom infiltrated her thoughts. Now, she was heading up the highway with a strong desire to snuggle with Marco. She truly had missed him. Wondering how Trista had held the fort down, Tai was tempted to call her. Armed with all the revelations, Tai believed she needed to cool out and relax for the night; she didn't want to deal with anything too heavy on the mind. She would gauge how and when she would approach Trista about her past. She decided to call Marco. She hoped he wouldn't be too sour about her tale that she had gone to a spa for the weekend. Waiting to inform him in person would be the best option.

She turned down the volume and put in her earpiece. She pulled up Marco's name and dialed.

"Hey, baby, I was just thinking about you."

Marco was delighted to hear her voice. "Hi, sweetie. I'm thinking about you, too."

"You on your way back? Hope you had a peaceful weekend; especially since you wanted to be alone."

Tai hesitated. "Oh, it was great. Missed you, though."

Marco smiled. "So, what you gonna do about it?"

"I'm heading *your* way...nonstop to Silver Spring. But it'll be awhile. I may make a few stops." Tai wanted to appear that her six-hour drive was two hours, so she thought to indicate it wouldn't be a direct drive.

"Be safe. I'll be waiting. Bye."

"Bye, sweetie."

AFTER EATING LEFTOVER TURKEY SPAGHETTI, TOSSED SALAD AND toasted garlic bread, Marco and Tai showered and lay in bed. Tai opened up and admitted the truth: She had gone to North Carolina to visit her roots and her parents' grave. Marco was aware that she had not returned since their death; Tai had never shared the truth about the cause. *Maybe someday*, she thought.

Marco appeared to take the news with ease. Despite being disturbed that Tai had not been truthful, he wore a blank expression to fake that it actually bothered him. *Why couldn't she have been straight up with me? I guess she doesn't feel as close a bond to me as I thought we shared. I would've supported her; even traveled with her.*

Tai avoided discussing the reality of Trista's background; she only mentioned to Marco that she'd had some interesting encounters in her hometown. Despite her bond with Marco, Tai held some personal aspects of her life at arm's length.

Enough thinking about family now. I need to show this man how much I really missed him.

Tai turned to face Marco. The glare from the low TV emitted enough lighting to create a mood. She caressed his face, closed her eyes and nibbled on his lips. She slipped her tongue into his mouth and explored. She reached under the cover and stroked his member while kissing him deeply. Their passion ignited and a blaze of sensuality overcame Tai. She whispered intimate thoughts in Marco's ear and shifted her body, mounting on top of him seductively. Tai kissed his neck delicately and gently placed his member inside her wetbox, stroking his adorable physique until she was breathless.

Talk of the town

32

Tai had called for an emergency staff meeting at Next Phase of Life. In addition to Noni and Felicia, her ten-employee office included two administrative assistants and five recruiting specialists. She had especially prepared her own catered meal as a thoughtful gesture; besides Felicia, none of her staff had experienced her creative dishes.

Felicia and Noni were the only two who knew why Tai had requested the gathering. Staff members' minds swirled with guesses. If it was an emergency, why did Tai prepare food? Was the company headed for closing? Was someone being laid off? Or did someone have a surprise announcement?

Tai stood proudly at the head of the conference room table. Dressed in a cream suit, she exuded confidence.

"Good afternoon, staff. I know you are wondering what brings us here today. First, let me thank you for joining me on this gorgeous day. I'm sure some of you were planning to go out to lunch. I'll make this short. We have a reason to celebrate.

"Next Phase of Life has been praised for being the fastest-growing, African-American start-up company in Washington, D.C. *The Washington Post* has interviewed me for an upcoming article. *Ebony* magazine has scheduled an interview and *Black Enterprise* will do a four-page spread.

"I would like to thank each of you for contribution to our success. And a special thanks to Felicia for her knowledge, support and management savvy."

Applause filled the room as staffers hugged or gave each other a hi-five.

"To celebrate, we will have a party in the next month where we'll invite the movers and shakers of the city. Maybe some celebrities.

"Now, so not to delay, let's dig in. Help yourself to the buffet. And thanks, Noni, for helping me to set it up, and for keeping the announcement as a surprise."

33

Toast to success

Trista secretly had been the target of Tai's observation. Ever since her return from North Carolina, Tai had not approached her sister about her findings or her behavior that was as unstable as a roller coaster. She had watched her every movement closely and had listened to every word intently. A person's mental state and past life could be sensitive subjects, and for now, Tai steered away.

Tai had decided to wait until after the office event to bring up her North Carolina visit. Then she planned to whisk Trista away to some tranquil location where if she became ruffled, it would be easy to calm the situation.

Candace had completed Tai's hair and makeup; it reminded Tai of going to senior prom when her best friend dolled her up like a princess. Candace perfected her own look. Trista lacked interest in attending the party and Candace encouraged her to join the celebration.

Once the three ladies were glammed up in their little black dresses and stilettos for the red carpet event, they piled into a limo awaiting them in front of Tai's home.

Limos were lined up to escort the employees from the office to downtown's W Hotel.

Tai had planned a soiree fit for the president and after having recently returned to North Carolina, she had contracted a local caterer with down-home roots. Southern food and hospitality would be representative of the down-to-earth image she attempted to project in her personal and professional life.

Politicians to local entrepreneurs to school system administrators to teachers to police officers graced the ballroom. Attendees represented all walks of the community. The speech was presented by the president of the National Urban League. A dance routine was performed by students of Howard University and a slide show featuring the company history and each staffer was presented.

Next Phase of Life business awards were given to staff members.

During the program, waiters in tuxedoes dispersed throughout the grand ballroom and served hors d'oeuvres on large silver platters. These were only a drumroll to the finale of Southern food to be served later. After participants were sufficiently satisfied with the culinary delights, the local band Secret Society geared up to rock the party. Candace had suggested the R&B band after hearing them one weekend in the Maryland suburbs. The band had a large fan base that supported their weekly appearances.

Tai and Marco launched the dancing routine, hitting the floor with the first number. Soon the dance floor was crowded and moved to the beat of the awesome sax player. The band's crooner smoothly switched from singing R&B to hip-hop to ballads. The floor resembled an old-school throwdown where anyone who sat was considered a party pooper. Some women kicked off their heels to make an extra effort to party hearty.

Trista finally broke her sour disposition and playfully joined the scene on the dance floor. Tai noticed that her sister had been like Jekyll and Hyde; sulking at the table and then excitedly springing to action on the dance floor.

Candace had been disappointed that she was unable to find an available date. She always liked being on point with a handsome eye-catcher connected to her arm. Tonight, she had decided not to fret about being dateless; after all, she liked to change up once a month. After everyone started loosening up, Candace felt the pulse was ready for her to scout the crowd. *Okay, you fine hunks, here I am.* She charged the floor and swayed to the beat of Jamie Foxx's "Blame It on the Alcohol." Two men approached and with her in the middle, they created a sandwich effect. Candace loved being in the center of attention.

A LITTLE WHILE LATER, TAI, TRISTA AND CANDACE RESTED LIKE they were completely zapped of any energy. Sierra joined them at the table.

"This is such a lovely affair," Sierra complimented Tai.

"Thank you. It has turned out nice, hasn't it?"

"Definitely," Candace chimed in. "Now you know if Trista and I had to take a break...we can dance the night away." Candace slipped off her Jimmy Choos and rubbed her feet together. Always the fashionista, she would never release her pain by taking them off on the dance floor.

Sierra nudged Candace. "Listen, can I borrow you for a minute?"

"Sure, what's up?" Candace regrettably had to slip her shoes back on just as quick as she'd parted with them.

Sierra stood, followed by Candace. "I have someone I want you to meet," she whispered.

"You mean of the male persuasion? If so, I'd better make a beeline to the ladies room." Candace turned in the direction to head that way.

Sierra stopped her, pulling her arm. "No, you look fine. I wouldn't tell you otherwise."

"Well, hold, up," Candace reached into her tiny, black-beaded shoulder bag, "at least let me paint these lips." She held up her mini lighted lipstick holder and reapplied her lipstick. "You sure my hair looks okay? I don't look like Grizelda? I've been dancing hard."

"Trust me; you know I wouldn't steer you wrong."

"Okay now. I like surprises but I sure don't wanna look like I left home without some mirror time."

"Girl, please." Sierra, dressed in a tea-length knit dress with a deep cutout back, led the way across the ballroom. When she arrived at a table in the corner, she stood before a handsome gentleman in a black tux. His entrancing eyes glistened in the dim light. He stood to greet her and kissed her hand instead of shaking it.

Ooh, I like him already. Candace smiled seductively, giving him the best dental image possible.

"Candace, this is Don. Don, this is Candace." Sierra made the introduction, then disappeared like a ghost in the night.

Don pulled out a seat next to his. "Please, take a seat."

"Thanks." *He is the epitome of Godiva chocolate; gotta have more than one.* "So, are you a guest of Next Phase's or Sierra's?"

"Sierra."

"Oh, I see. How are you two acquainted?" Candace effortless spoke in a proper manner.

"We work together. I'm a pilot." Don smiled. "Can I offer you a drink?"

"Sure, thanks. A Cosmo is fine."

THE NEARBY BAR STATION WAS BUBBLING WITH GUESTS LINED UP for a drink to continue their fun-filled evening. Candace watched Don in admiration. She'd almost choked when he'd announced he was a pilot. He was just her type; she figured he was a thrill-seeker. All of her friends were aware that she got a rush from the adventurous. Don returned as she was fantasized about the two of them sharing a cockpit; her as a co-pilot and working his knob as he worked the controls. *Naughty me.* She laughed to herself and her twisted thoughts.

"Here you are." Don broke her from her dreamy idea.

"Thanks, Don." She sipped her cocktail. "So, how long have you been flying?"

"About twenty years. I trained in the Air Force. I was stationed here at Andrews."

I love a well-seasoned man. "Oh, wow, where have you been all my life?"

"Excuse me?"

"Never mind." *Watch that lip of yours. Don't be too anxious and overbearing. Gotta make a man think that you* may *be available; not instantly available. That's easier said than done. I'm always ready to leap into action. Seems like I can't control myself.*

"And what about you? What do you do for a living?"

"I'm in the fashion industry. I'm a buyer; call myself a fashionista. I just love it."

"I can see that. You look lovely."

"Thanks." She smiled demurely; she was relishing the compliments.

"To be honest, I saw you months ago; when you and Sierra flew to Charlotte," Don alerted. "She told me you two were going to the CIAA. I heard that it was one big citywide party. I had to fly out the next morning so I didn't participate."

"Oh, so you were checking me out?" *Oops, did I say the wrong thing again? Hey, I'd better be me and not put on pretentions.* "You spotted me then?"

Don chuckled and sipped his Merlot. "Lady, I was all up in your business."

Candace giggled. "Oh, were you now? I'm gonna get Sierra for not speaking up sooner." *I didn't know I had a pilot sweating me. Honey, we can fly the friendly skies together. I'm definitely feeling you and I sense the feeling's mutual.*

Candace and Don continued their conversation, oblivious to the partygoers surrounding them. Leave it to Candace, and she was convinced she'd met her heavenly match. *I'm at an all-time high. Good looking out, Sierra.*

THE PARTY EMCEE ANNOUNCED THAT THE LAST CALL WOULD BE in ten minutes. It was close to midnight. Tai reached the stage and congratulated her staffers again. Then she thanked the 300-plus guests. She asked for the band to lighten their sound and for the light technician to spotlight a special person at her table.

"I'd like to give a special thanks to a wonderful person in my life, my significant other, Mr. Marco Moore. Please stand."

Embarrassed, Marco was forced to grin and bear it before the large crowd. He blew a kiss toward Tai. He basked with the acknowledgment that he had been placed on a pedestal in Tai's world. Their love had grown resilient, and there was no rock capable of shattering their bond.

34

Sisters in harmony

"How you think the party turned out?" Tai snipped the stems of the dozen yellow roses that Marco had given her before placing them in a vase.

"It was a blast. I had a good time." Trista suddenly changed expressions and looked down at the kitchen table. "I'm sorry that I acted like I didn't want to go. I hope that wasn't too embarrassing for you in front of your friends."

"I understand, Trista. You've had a lot of adjusting to do since you moved here. I didn't want to force you to go, and couldn't if I'd tried. So glad that you decided on your own and a little persuasion from Candace. I definitely didn't want to leave you out. I didn't announce you at the party because I know you don't enjoy the limelight so much…unless it's dancing, of course." Tai laughed and filled her pitcher at the sink to water her plants.

"Now that I don't mind."

"Then you're on the shy side sometimes, so I didn't want to put you in the spotlight, either."

"No problem. I'm glad you didn't." Tai looked at the clock. "Well, guess it's time for me to head to work. Hope it's not too busy and glad I don't have to work this weekend. That party actually helped, too, because I have been working back-to-back days."

"Remember I've got another sisters day planned for us tomorrow. This time we'll be heading out about eleven. Okay? You packed your overnight bag, right?"

"Right. I'll be getting off early tonight. Told them I can't do any overtime 'cause I've got weekend plans."

"Okay, cool. See you tonight."

Trista grabbed her purse and headed out of the front door.

"You want a ride to Metro?"

"No, thanks. I need to walk off some of these pounds I've been putting on lately."

Tai pulled a bottle of water out of the fridge. *I need to be walking, too*, she thought. *It's a shame I stopped going to the gym…but…* She didn't even want to think the name, let alone say it to herself. *I won't give him or it a second thought. I need to go to Marco's home gym or get some of my own equipment soon. I never intended to stop working out; only the workouts! I need to stay on task as I was doing so well with the routines. And it was starting to show so I can't slack up any longer.*

She reached for her cell phone and dialed.

"Good morning, Mandarin Oriental," a voice answered.

"Hello, would you connect me to the spa, please?"

"Thank you. One moment, please." Tai was transferred.

"The Spa at Mandarin Oriental. May I help you?"

"Yes, it's Tai Wilson. I'm calling to confirm my appointment for two for tomorrow. "

"Yes, ma'am, we have you for eleven a.m. for you and your sister, Trista. We will see you then and thank you for calling."

Tai hung up the phone. She couldn't wait to be deluged with the soothing treatment. Trista had enjoyed their other spa experience in the suburbs; now they would share one in the city at the luxurious hotel overlooking the Tidal Basin.

"Welcome." Tai and Trista were graciously greeted at the spa. The ambience was as soft as the white robes they slipped into. The blend of bronze and oak offered comfort. The Cherry Blossom ritual—Tai thought this was apropos since the Cherry Blossoms were in season and the legendary festival was in session—would last approximately two hours.

The sisters sat side by side as they tuned into the tranquil sounds piping through the system. Their feet were caressed and made them feel like they would forever walk on air; the light touch was gentle. A cherry scrub followed and the essence of the fragrance offered bliss leading up to the aromatherapy massage. This featured hot stones on the back and rewarded them with maximum tension release.

Tai and Trista sipped on cherry tea from dainty white cups. Heading to the dressing area, they felt light on their toes. Tai envisioned they looked like two snails creeping to the spa's exit and through the lobby to the elevators. The experience was so restful that their dreamlike quality was like floating on air.

"This was wonderful." Trista's mind was in another space.

"Yes, it was *divine*. I can't wait to stretch out. Our bags should be in our suite."

A brief nap invigorated the sisters who slept like angels in the middle of the day. They were surrounded by comfort in their Asian-inspired suite. It was peaceful not to have the TV blaring but the light jazz from the iPod. Tai didn't leave home without it.

Tai had brought along a couple bottles of Yellowtail Tree Free Chardonnay and cheese and crackers. She emptied the small fridge, set up the table, then sat down. "When you're up to it, we can go eat. Maybe try one of the new restaurants or eat downstairs."

"Sounds good." Trista arose to join Tai at the table where she poured the wine in glasses.

"That was the best massage; I really needed that. And the cherry scent. I'll need to get some oil for the house." Tai rose and crossed the room. "Actually I think this would be more comfortable." She stretched on a cocoa chaise lounge with an Oriental pattern. "Maybe you should try that one." Tai pointed to an overstuffed mandarin-colored chair.

Trista took her advice, grabbed her wineglass and switched seats.

Tai's mind zipped through various options on how to bring up her North Carolina visit. Finally, she was here…alone…with Trista and was unsure of the most sensitive way to broach the topic. She'd made special efforts to find the ideal day and the best scenario to approach it. She didn't want to appear like a detective who was interrogating a criminal; only a sister who was sharing her discoveries. Tai refused to be confrontational, either. She simply wanted Trista to be straight up, no chaser.

"Trista, you've been here now…nine months?" Tai crossed her legs and sipped her wine. "I'd say we have bonded…however, I feel that you have been holding back a little." Tai paused. "Is there something you need to tell me?"

Trista frowned. "Why would you say that?"

Tai decided to spill the news freely; no more sugarcoating. "Well, remember the other weekend when I said I needed peace of mind and was going away alone?"

"Yes. And you didn't bother to tell Marco or me where—only that it was a spa." Trista scolded as if she were Tai's mother.

"No, I didn't…I'm not sure how to tell you this," Tai rested her head on the chair pillow, closed and then reopened her eyes, "but I didn't go to a spa."

Trista's eyes perked and her eyebrows rose.

"Trista, I went to North Carolina…in search of peace."

"Where? Salisbury?"

"Yes."

"Why didn't you tell me?"

"I wanted to go alone. I figured you might want to go with me."

Trista shook her head. "No, you don't have to worry. I don't want to go back; especially not to live and…barely to visit."

"Didn't Salisbury treat you good?"

"No, it did me wrong." Trista looked bewildered. "Some unpleasant memories down South."

"Trista, I went because I wanted to physically and mentally connect with Mama and Dad. I didn't want anybody asking me questions or trying to go with me.

"I visited the church and the graves. Took some flowers there. All kinds of flashbacks rolled in my head. It had been a longggg time."

Trista envisioned Tai in the cemetery, flowers in hand, and placing them on the graves. "That was good. I always wanted to go but couldn't make myself."

"A calm came over me; it was hard to describe, but I know they're okay."

"So, did you see anyone from the old days? Of course, you wouldn't remember too many folks since you were so young when you left," Trista recalled. "Not like me, anyway, since I'd been there forever. My memories, though, are more bad than good." Trista shook her leg nervously. "Miss Laine was the best thing going there and now she's gone."

"Yes, God rest her soul…along with Mama and Dad." Tai arose for another glass of wine and then returned to her chair. "Let me break this to you gently, Trista. While I was in Salisbury, I ended up at this diner. Turns out it was where you worked."

"Don't tell me you met Ginger."

"I did. And she's a talker."

"Too much."

"But this time she said little. She seemed tempted to talk about you."

"I'm sure; she's gotta big mouth. Don't ever let me hear—"

"I know you aren't making any threats."

Trista caught herself. "Oh, no, not at all."

"Anyway, it wasn't Ginger who let open the floodgates. It was the sheriff, or ex-sheriff, Paul," Tai explained. "Now, he knows everything *and* everyone in that town."

"TMI, too much information."

"Trista, I heard about your experience at—"

Trista gasped. "No he didn't."

"Yes, he told me you'd had a breakdown or something after Dorian went to jail. He couldn't remember his name, but I knew it. You had shared that with me; that he'd gone to jail."

Trista weighed her head in her hand and rubbed her temple. *I can't believe this. Now, she'll really think I'm a nutcase. Of all people in Salisbury, she runs into him at that friggin' diner. Of all eating spots, she ends up where I worked.* "I'm sure you're thinking I need help."

"Well, if you need help, to speak to someone, I have a good friend who's a therapist. She'll be glad to talk to you."

Trista stood and started pacing back and forth. "I never wanted you to know about my past. Tai, I was passed around from foster home to foster home and I was fine. It wasn't until I got involved with Dorian and when he went to jail; that threw me overboard.

"I was so stressed and worried about him. I didn't think I could go on without him. One day I lost it. I trashed everything in my foster parents' home; broke windows, threw furniture. I went berserk and they called the police. I threatened to kill myself. Then after they observed me and tested me at the station, they determined that I needed a psychiatric evaluation.

"The state put me in that institution. That was ninety days in hell. They put me on medication and I later managed to wean myself off of it."

I wonder if she still needs medicine. Her mood swings are serious. Maybe I'll suggest she get back on meds…but not now.

"I never wanted to share this with you 'cause I figured you wouldn't understand, that you'd hold it against me. Think I wasn't stable enough to hold down a job or function."

"No, I'd never make that assumption. You can always feel free to be open with me…about everything. You'll always be my little sis and I'll always be here to support you. Who am I to judge you?" Tai assured in a gentle manner.

"Thanks." Trista sat back in the chair and poured another glass of wine. "Sometimes I still have nightmares about being in that place. Also I worry about Dorian and how he's surviving. I try to remain calm, but then I get tense and shaky."

Tai sipped her wine and made eye contact. "Why didn't you tell me about Juicy?"

Trista initially looked like she had been shocked by a lightning bolt. Then embarrassment permeated her face. "Oh, you heard about that, too?"

"Not only heard about it, but went there…"

"I'm sure it was that sheriff and his big mouth again," Trista responded disgustedly.

"He was trying to look out for me…and you. He found out I was in town to reconnect with my roots. Decided he'd share what he could about my sis. And I appreciated it. By the way, I didn't let him or Ginger know anything about you. For all they know, we still haven't been in touch."

"So, what did you find out at Juicy?"

"That you were the best dancer in the joint. And that wasn't a surprise."

"Yeah, guess I didn't want you to find out about that, either. My ex-stripper life."

"You could've told me. I wouldn't have held it against you. At least you had a good reputation."

"Now that I do miss sometimes; that's why I try to dance as much as possible. It was fun. On the flip side, I used to have regular customers who tipped me well. I was pulling in good dough."

"I understand, *Kat*," Tai teased. "Stan was the nine-one-one at that joint. Told me you were the best."

"Yeah, I had that reputation." Trista contemplated her past. "But, Sis, I never turned any tricks there, just to let you know."

"Oh, I do believe you on that. I'm glad you kept it clean and classy."

"Not to say I didn't have any johns try to lead me in that direction," Trista noted. "It was hard at first 'cause it meant mo' money. But living in a rural area, I was making more than enough, so there was no need to be greedy."

"Trista, I was worried about how I was going to break this all down for you. I'm glad you accepted it well."

"You found out a lot in a short amount of time. I guess that's what happens when you're from a small town. Here it would take months, years maybe, to find out the truth about someone."

"Just know, Sis, that I'm not here to judge you. I appreciate you being my sibling, and I have accepted you as you are. My main concern is you, your health and your mental state.

"You could have told me everything that I found out in Carolina.

There was no need to keep it undercover. I'm not a prude or think I'm all that. We do have different lifestyles, but that doesn't mean for one moment, that I don't care about you or that I don't want to be a true sister to you." Tai arose and crossed the room. She reached down and gave Trista a bear hug full of sincerity and compassion.

"I'm your big sister and when you're ready, feel free to talk to me about anything." Tai felt an outburst of emotion and spoke quickly to avoid tearing up. "Let's go eat." She grabbed her purse and grabbed Trista's arm.

35

Flyin' high

Candace and Don had been inseparable like two schoolchildren sharing their first kiss. The night of the Next Phase of Life party had proven to be a match. And Sierra proudly announced that she had been the matchmaker. Don was a pilot friend who was such a nice guy that Sierra was determined that someone from her cadre of friends needed to hook up with him. She herself would've made a move but thought otherwise because she didn't like mixing intimacy with business.

After meeting, it wasn't a week before Don was back in D.C., inviting Candace on a date. He recognized that her adventurous side would warrant more than a restaurant date or cooking dinner at home; he would think of a unique idea.

Don realized he was overthinking his date, so he decided to go for the simple and not the fancy. He checked the weather on his iPhone and saw that Friday would be a gorgeous spring day. He'd pick up some sandwiches, chips, fruit and wine and they'd go for an old-fashioned picnic, with blanket of course.

Don surprised Candace who was unaware of their date plans. He'd only suggested she wear comfortable clothes. This wasn't an easy task considering Candace always liked to rock her designer attire; asking her to put on casual clothes still meant a dressy skirt, top and heels. He finally had to request she wear jeans and tennis shoes.

Candace initially frowned upon the suggestion as she liked to dress to impress. Then she realized that her first impression was actually the party when she'd shown up in her elegant wear. *That had been enough to hook him*, she thought.

To add to the excitement, Don blindfolded her when he picked her up. When they arrived at Hains Point overlooking the airport, he then took off the blindfold.

They'd spent the afternoon lying on a huge soft blanket and eating what Don had selected.

Oddly, Don enjoyed the take-offs and landings at the airport across the Potomac River. This was an area where he frequented when springtime arrived and the surrounding Cherry Blossoms were in full bloom.

He'd decided to start slow with Candace and then pick up full speed. When he dropped her at home, he was already plotting their next adventure.

TWO WEEKS LATER, DON ASKED CANDACE TO PACK A WEEKEND bag. He planned to whisk her away to a surprise destination. Once again, he blindfolded Candace and took a long drive. Candace relished the idea of surprises; she didn't want to know what fate awaited her. She was truly a woman who knew how to "go with the flow."

Don had picked her up from her Northwest condo and driven her to the Maryland suburbs. He pulled into the lot of a small airpark. He parked and removed Candace's blindfold.

"Where are we?" Candace looked to see a hangar and a few small aircraft. "Don't tell me—"

"Yes, I have my own private plane. We're going up."

Tai was so exhilarated that she almost passed out. She'd always desired to ride in a private plane. "Wow, I can't believe it. Did you know this was one of the things I've always wanted to do?"

"No, sweetie, I didn't have a clue. I'm glad we're on the same page and that you don't mind flying."

"Which one is yours?"

Don pointed to a sleek airplane parked in the distance.

"That's cool…" Candace was in awe. "I guess since you like surprises, you're not hardly going to tell me where we're headed."

"Right. But I promise you, you'll love it. We will have to make a fuel stop on the route."

Candace smiled and touched his hand lightly. "You are full of surprises, aren't you?" She pecked him on the lips. "Thank you, Don."

He gazed at her admiringly. "All for you, sweetie." He popped the trunk to retrieve their bags. "Let's board."

CANDACE WAS THRILLED WITH THE RIDE THAT FELT LIKE SHE WAS soaring on some amusement park ride. They continued in silence as she watched Don meticulously guide the plane with ease. After re-fueling and hours later, she noted that they started to descend. She felt like a scout lost in the woods without her compass. She had no idea of her location. Don was not going to share their destination, so she figured she'd play the waiting game. Wherever they were headed, she considered she was a lucky woman in store for adventure.

THE SIGHT OF BRIGHT BLUE WATER AND PALM TREES INDICATED they must be someplace in the South. The only place in the U.S. with water as brilliant was the Gulf Coast near Clearwater and

St. Petersburg or the Miami coastline. *This is sooo exciting,* she thought. *I've been to Florida many times, but never with a fine man, my own private chauffeur, at the wheel.*

Don finally informed Candace that Miami was their destination. They would be making the final approach to a small airport.

CANDACE REALIZED THAT THIS SCENARIO WAS WHAT DREAMS WERE made of. A private driver awaited their arrival at the airport hangar. En route to the wealthy Fisher Island, they passed by picturesque mansions and rows of palm trees standing like statues. Don explained that one of his millionaire associates spent a lot of time in the Bahamas and had offered his Fisher Island condo for the weekend. He'd also offered his chef, Juanita, to prepare a special meal on their arrival night.

The posh, two-level, two-bedroom condo beckoned. The brightly colored furniture was in contrast to pearl white walls. A sixty-inch flat-screen TV graced the living room wall. Huge pieces of colorful abstract art gave the aura of Tropicana. The master suite had a two-foot-high Jacuzzi, double-sink granite vanity and a glass-block shower.

An enthralled Candace was floating on cloud nine. *Wait 'til I tell my girls about this date; it's like no other.*

WHEN THEY'D ARRIVED, JUANITA WAS ALREADY AT THE HELM IN the kitchen. She lit tall candlesticks at the grand mahogany dining table. She poured glasses of water followed by wine. The three-course meal included salad, honey-baked salmon, rice pilaf and creamed spinach.

"I'm speechless." Candace batted her eyelashes. "This is paradise. It was sweet of you to go to all this trouble—"

"No trouble. I knew you would love the experience."

"That's an understatement. The plane ride...I thought we were going on the road and of course, I had no idea we'd be in Miami. This is surreal. I get in a car blindfolded, end up at the airport and land in the tropics. This is truly the best and most exciting time ever. I love it."

Don arose and walked around to sit closer to Candace. He raised his glass for a toast and she did the same. "Cheers to what will be a fantastic weekend."

"Cheers." Candace sipped her wine.

"That was delicious. I must commend Juanita. Enrique bragged about her cooking." He gazed in her eyes. "What would you like to do? Let's head to the front."

They walked down a long corridor to the living room space. The dining area and kitchen were in the rear of the condo. Candace admired the interior design elements of soft and bold colors; clean architectural lines; the vaulted ceiling and floor-to-ceiling windows with plenty of light.

Don led Candace by the hand to a huge, plush, L-shaped sofa. They set their glasses on coasters on a unique-shaped glass coffee table. Don grabbed the remote and clicked on the massive flat-screen TV, then wrapped his arm around Candace.

"You deserve to be treated like a queen. I like to go all out for someone like you. You're special, you have class, spunk, a lot of character. I've enjoyed the time we've shared so far." He held her cheek and pulled her to his lips. After a lengthy kiss, Candace lost control. Her passion for Don catapulted and she started caressing him so that his member became rock hard.

The sun was setting and the once bright room dimmed. Don grabbed Candace and lifted her.

Oh, wow, how romantic. Candace was cherishing every moment.

Don carried her steadily up the stairs to the second level to an expansive loft. He continued to a king-sized, low California-style bed with a black comforter and zebra-print throw pillows.

Candace attempted to resist as she had preferred to take a quick shower. But Don was aggressive and irresistible. She let it all release.

SOUTH BEACH WAS THE SCENE OF THE NEXT DAY'S ADVENTURE. She had no trouble shopping—her favorite pastime—and found a stylish two-piece bathing suit. Candace and Don lounged lazily on the beach and soaked up the sunshine and dipped their feet in the breathtaking water while taking a stroll. Their evening ended with a private dinner in a VIP suite at an upscale ocean-front restaurant.

CANDACE WAS STILL FLOATING ON A CLOUD WHEN SHE RETURNED to D.C. It was hard for her to readjust to work on Monday. The return flight was smooth and enlightening; Don explained some of the mechanics of flying, so it was an educational experience. Candace realized she had reached her zenith of the dating world with the Miami trip; it had surpassed all of her expectations. And she was eager to share their heavenly weekend with the ladies.

Friends are forever

"**O**kay, ladies, sorry I'm late. Thanks for coming. You're in for a treat." Candace joined Tai, Nevada and Sierra at a table at the Half-Note Lounge in Bowie. Candace had encouraged the group to stray from their usual restaurant meetings. Tonight, they would hear the live music of Secret Society, the local R&B band that she'd recommended for the Next Phase of Life anniversary and awards party. Candace was aware that Tai was a live music enthusiast. She'd already praised the band's performance at her own event. Now she would have the opportunity to experience it at another venue.

The lounge was packed on the weekends and Candace had reserved a table to celebrate her fortieth birthday weekend.

She had caught up age-wise with Tai, who had been dropped like a bomb once she reached the mark where many women thought it was the end of their road. This group was determined to break that stereotype; "forty is the new twenty" was their motto. Full of liveliness and excitement, the quartet would take forty to new heights. They had refused to let age be an indication of getting "old"; acting or dressing grandmommish. Giving up dating or sexcapades or entertainment wasn't necessary. Forty was whatever you made it. And in their eyes, it meant a new beginning, a new phase of life. They'd refused to feel washed-up or unappealing. They were in their own little world and didn't care what anyone thought of their vivacity.

The dynamics of many African-American women mirrored their lifestyle: youthful, unmarried and childless. But they didn't view this reality as a hindrance.

Physicians had informed them that the fertility rate normally drops in their early forties. They accepted the notion that they may never personally fulfill the role of a mother. And they were fine with it. Motherhood was not designated for every woman; sometimes it was not in the cards. They were satisfied being "mothers" of nieces and nephews or godchildren.

Tonight, they celebrated friendship; they always looked for a reason to celebrate life. They never took it for granted. Hell, simply being alive was something to appreciate. Unfortunately, some of their friends had gone to meet their Maker at an early age. Their thought was to carry on the tradition of friendship and fun times.

Awaiting Candace's arrival, the ladies had munched on Buffalo wings and French fries before the band started.

"You know how we do," Candace stated matter-of-factly. "I couldn't wait to tell you about last weekend and I had to do it in person." She commanded their attention. "You will *never* guess where I ended up with Don...or how I got there."

"Tell us," Nevada stated.

"Of course, he's a pilot, but I had no idea that he had his own plane." Candace was ecstatic. "Girl, we flew on his *private* plane."

"Now, don't tell me you were trying to sex it up on that plane," Tai teased.

"No, are you kidding? I value me too much, and him, to have distracted him up in the air." Candace giggled. "The best part is he blindfolded me so I wouldn't know we were headed to the airport."

"Ohhh, that sounds kinky," Sierra interjected.

"It was sexy. Well, once he picked me up, he drove to the airport and flew me...to Miami!"

"Say what?" Nevada asked, excited. "Now that's what I'm talkin' 'bout. That's what I call a first-class date."

Sierra was proud that she had made the introduction. "I realized he was cool but now that's original. All these years I've been a flight attendant, I haven't been invited on a private flight. You had a blast, right?"

"Did I? I can't wait 'til the next adventure. He's full of surprises. After my little romantic picnic...now, when's the last time a brotha took you on a picnic—I didn't know what to expect." Candace smiled. "He puts a lot of extra thought in his plans. I like that."

"I don't think it's possible to top that," Nevada suggested.

"I wouldn't put my life on it. The man is awesome. Can't wait 'til the next go-round." Candace was like a kid who had entered a candy store.

"Yeah, it does say a lot; you got yourself a good one, honey," Sierra complimented. "And let me tell you, a lot of women be checking him out. So hold on."

"And I thank you again for thinking of me. Chances are he would've never met me. I'm glad I flew to Charlotte. I didn't know that trip would be a jackpot."

Secret Society geared up to perform and the crowd ratcheted up a notch. The sax player and band leader announced Candace's birthday, which was followed by applause. Candace stood up and waved her hand excitedly. *Forty, fit and fabulous,* she thought. *And I'm fortunate to be with true friends.*

THE R&B BAND AROUSED THE LOUNGE AND THE MERRIMENT began and continued until closing. Prince's "Purple Rain" completed the last set with the guitarist breezing effortlessly through the famous solo. Rounds of drinks later, the ladies were satisfied with their evening of dancing and conversation. The band had delivered and they promised one another they would return.

Nevada, as designated driver, cruised along 450 to the Beltway and headed north toward Tai's house. It was now after midnight, Tai's official birthday, and they would continue with slices of Tai's chocolate mousse cake and champagne. To top off their ladies night and birthday affair, each of them would read an excerpt from one of the erotic stories in Zane's *Sex Chronicles: Shattering the Myth.*

Don had to work over the weekend. Candace was pleased that she was surrounded by her longtime companions. She would've loved to have spent the milestone birthday with her new love interest. However, her friends were a vital part of her life. A platonic male friend had once told her, "Your girlfriends will be your friends longer than your boyfriends." There was truth to that statement; that men could come and they could go, but true girlfriends are forever. It was like a script based on her life.

Don had promised Candace that he would make up his absence on her birthday. After the Miami trip, Candace could not have imagined what surprise plans he'd conjure up. Her speculation was endless.

"TAI!!!! I'M GOING TO PARIS! DON'S TAKING ME TO PAIREE!" Candace yelled into the phone in her animated tone.

"Great, girl. That's wonderful." Tai was equally excited that Candace finally had met her equal. She had captured the quintessential partner for life. Her manhunt had netted someone who was compatible, compassionate and competitive to the stable of men who had crossed her path. Always the one who believed in "there's more than one egg in a basket" mentality, Candace had thrived on multiple relationships; often simultaneously. Most had been short-lived, but Tai's gut feeling was that Don was a permanent fixture in Candace's world of fashion and adventure.

"How many years have I been saying to plan a ladies trip to Paris?" Candace asked elatedly. "I guess it wasn't meant to be 'cause now it's a romantic interlude with Don…Juan," she joked.

"It'll be heaven for you in the fashion world, *fashionista*."

"You got that right!"

"So when are you going?"

"Two weeks. That gives me plenty of time to get my clothes together."

"Girl, you'll have the plane loaded down with your bags." Tai laughed. "Better leave some space in that luggage. You'll be the queen of shopping."

"Well, let me call Cori. I haven't told her yet. My sister'll be excited, too. See ya."

"Bye." *Paris. Now that's what I'm talking about*, Tai thought.

Candace quickly dialed Cori's cell phone. *Miami. Paris. Where next?* she thought.

37

Change gonna come

Trista wiped down the last table for the night, refilled the napkin holder and salt and pepper shakers. It had been a long evening and she felt like she could sleep for a week. Seacoast had been particularly busy since it was during the Cherry Blossom season and the city was packed with tourists. She slipped into a booth chair and stared ahead, looking outside of the window. There was also a celebrity concert tonight and it had contributed to the horde of street walkers.

"Hey, you okay? You haven't looked yourself tonight." Cynthia sat across from Trista and took a swig of her glass of water. "We were some kind of busy tonight. Always this way during festival times and concerts."

Cynthia was accustomed to the fast pace of a bustling restaurant after her decades of employment. While Trista had entered her eighth month at Seacoast, she was still adjusting to the demands. The cafe paled in comparison to the small diners she once called her second home.

"I'm fine; just exhausted. Thanks for asking." Trista took a deep breath. "I'm glad I usually work the day shift."

"How's that sister of yours, Tai?"

"She's great. Took me to a spa visit not long ago. It was the best."

"Lucky girl to have a sister look out for you." Cynthia sensed that Trista had more on her mind; she was often called psychic.

She eyed her again. "Look, I'm not trying to be nosey, but I still feel like something's buggin' you."

"Nothing's buggin' me," Trista insisted. "It's all good. During the spa visit, Tai and I really connected. We needed that."

"Yeah, my sister and I never got along. It was just the two of us, too. God rest her soul. We were only two years apart, like you two, but we never had that sister thing going. Spats, arguments, you name it. As I got older I realized the importance of sisterhood. By then it was too late."

"Sorry to hear…"

"No problem. Just treasure what you have. I remember you telling me that you'd been separated since your childhood. And that you found her on… what you call it?"

"Facebook. On the Internet."

"Right."

Trista turned around to face the kitchen area and scouted to see if anyone was nearby. "Miss Cynthia, sorry, I mean, Cynth… after my sister and I bonded during the spa day, I have a whole new outlook." She exhaled. "Someday I think I'd like to leave this place. Does that sound bad? I know I just started working here."

"No, not at all. Young lady, nothing says you have to make a forty-year career here like I did. Nowadays there are so many opportunities for young folk like you. The sky's the limit. So I say, if you can break away, let yourself be free."

"Just a thought… and I wanted to share." *I'd love to figure out another way of life. Now that Tai knows about my past, I feel like something could break loose. Open a whole new world for me.*

Trista had a newfound identity and confidence since Tai had delved into her past. Now that the tension was released, she didn't feel like she was living on the edge. Harboring secrets was like being confined in a tiny room where you wanted to explode from claustrophobia. She was relieved that she didn't have to bury her "bad-image" background anymore. Tai had not looked down on her nor considered her shameless. They were in diverse worlds, but had fused as sisters regardless of their differences. Often this was the case with siblings where their lives were unparalleled.

For the first time, Trista grasped the reality that she truly had grown to love Tai as a sister. She regretted that she'd had bursts of uncertain behavior. Tai now realized that it was more than spontaneous conduct; it was deep-rooted. Tai had accepted her hands down, deleting mental institution and stripper club from her resume. And she was proud that her sister valued her like a priceless gem.

38

Cheaper to keep him

Nevada zeroed in on the email history of one of her clients. It was another husband-may-be-cheating-on-his-wife scenario. After appearing in the news as the crucial lead in the capture of the twin bank robbers, her firm had become inundated with calls. It had been remarkable to see how Sleuths On Us had been placed on the map following her five minutes of fame. She had no complaints but started to realize she may need an assistant.

America's Most Wanted had notified her that her reward money was forthcoming, based on the twins having been indicted by a grand jury. They had been extradited to Miami where they were awaiting trial. Yes, those gorgeous twins were on their way to the slammer.

Nevada had toyed with the idea of splitting with Ryan after she received the reward. After much contemplation, she determined that it would be unfair. She'd hung in there with him all these years. Sure, she wanted to get married eventually, but she'd accepted their relationship as cohabitants. With money in her pocket, if she left now, it would appear that she had only remained with Ryan because he was a source of income. This was far from the truth; she loved the ground he walked on.

He'd had her back when she'd first lost her newspaper job and prior to her launching her detective business. Ryan also had invested time in helping her build her entrepreneurship and recommending clients he'd met as a police officer.

She figured there was no rhyme or reason to entertain such thoughts of leaving him—even if she offered him a share of her jackpot. There was always the old saying, *If it ain't broke, don't fix it.*

Nevada was approaching her mid-forties and finding a decent mate was not an everyday occurrence. Plus, Ryan was such a sweetheart. He never pried in her business or complained about her hanging with her girlfriends or spending countless hours on her cases.

Likewise, she accepted his unending addiction to TV sports; he could watch for hours without Nevada interrupting his space. Cooking was not an issue, as the word was banned in their household. Carry-out and delivery were more the norm.

They were compatible and their lifestyles were in sync. As far as Nevada was concerned, there was no need to start over in the relationship game. She was always viewed as the stable one in the pack; being content with monogamy.

Occasionally, she had imaginary visions that she'd link with a stranger, but for now, the eight years she'd invested were like secured funds in a bank account.

39

Dancer's delight

Felicia stretched in her reclining office chair and swiveled to gaze out of the window. Perplexed, her mind raced with lightning speed as she searched for a solution. As a proud mission of Next Phase of Life, the company boasted of the capacity to handle all requests. Her office manager role consisted of appeasing all clients and never turning away potential ones. Her last caller had asked for the unusual: a dancer.

She had scrolled through their pool of prospective employees. There were none who had indicated a dance background. Felicia stood and absorbed the city skyline, then looked to the street level. *How and where can I find a dancer?*

Not ballet, tap or jazz…but hip-hop.

Dre Dyson, a new national recording artist, would be filming a video in a few days. The site was the Mall in the Nation's Capital. The lead female dancer scheduled to appear in the video had fallen that morning and broken her leg. A rehearsal was scheduled that evening at a local hotel. "Kapital Krush," his sophomore single based on the lifestyles of Washington, D.C. and written by Dre Dyson, would feature clips of President Obama's inauguration on the Mall, scenes from local go-go clubs, and for history's sake, the Million Man March.

Felicia poured a cup of coffee, then opened her office door. She headed to the receptionist area to brainstorm with Noni. Sometimes the younger staffers could offer fresh and creative ideas. Felicia had felt ancient when the call had arrived—like she was stuck during the days of a record player versus today's iPod. Noni likely was familiar with Dre Dyson. She'd never heard of the popular hip-hop artist.

Arriving at Noni's desk, she set her coffee cup on her ledge. "How are you this morning?"

"Great. How about you?" Noni was a multi-tasker so after she made eye contact, she returned to typing on her laptop as she engaged in conversation. Not to disrespect her boss, but she had a keen ear.

"I'm baffled by our latest request. You heard of Dre Dyson?"

Noni stopped in midstream and turned quickly toward Felicia. "Definitely. He's tight." She batted her eyelashes teasingly. "You expecting him?"

Felicia smiled. "No. It's too bad, huh?"

"Yeah, I'm just saying, he's the bomb. I'll work on whatever he needs," she stated flirtatiously. "On the real, what's up?"

"The last call you put through was his manager. Dre's set to film his new video here on Friday. Down on the Mall. The main female dancer broke her leg this morning—not sure if she was super excited and lost it; or if she tripped on something. He didn't say."

"Poor thing."

"They need someone who can pick up choreography quickly and also be able to mix well with the personalities." Felicia was perplexed. "We never get dancing requests, but of course, you know I refuse to be stumped too long."

Noni contemplated the issue. "Hmmm, we could contact one of the local dance studios. I've heard of hip-hop classes. Maybe we can recruit from there."

"Great idea. But you have to be at least twenty-one. Now, which studio? He emphasized that it's urgent."

Noni directed her attention back to her laptop. She would save her work and start searching for a hip-hop class. Felicia was tense and Noni picked up her vibe and sense of priority. There was no time for chitchat; they needed to resolve this situation immediately.

"What about Trista?!" Noni suggested suddenly. "I'd heard you talk about how she works it on the dance floor. Then I saw her at the office party."

"Oh, yes, she's all the rage." Felicia agreed by the seconds. "Trista...I'm sure she could handle it." She paused to reflect. "But I guess I'd better go check with Tai; get her opinion." Felicia grabbed her dose of caffeine. She dashed off, talking over her shoulder as she headed for Tai's office. "Thanks. I owe you."

"You're welcome." *Wish I could be in Trista's shoes right about now—literally. Dre Dyson? Anytime.*

FELICIA KNOCKED BRISKLY ON TAI'S DOOR.

"Come in." Tai swiveled her chair to face her. "Good morning. You look excited."

"Tai, we've had an interesting request. I was speaking to Noni about it and she had a great suggestion." Felicia sat in Tai's chair, coffee in hand, and leaned over her desk. "We received a call from the manager of a hip-hop artist, Dre Dyson."

"Never heard of him—"

"Neither had I, but Noni says he's hot. The manager said that they're in town to shoot a video in a few days. The female dancer slipped and broke her ankle this morning. They need a dancer to fill in; someone who can pick up the choreography and be ready for the shoot."

"That is a first for us—"

"Noni thought about Trista." Felicia searched Tai's eyes for approval.

"Why not?" Tai agreed without hesitation. "Give her a call. She's off a couple of days." Tai's thoughts trailed to Trista's strip scene. "You've seen how she grabs attention at parties." *But if you'd only heard how Sis was on the stripper stage.* "I'm sure she'll jump at the opportunity."

"Great. He told me if we didn't have any options, he'd contact Howard U where he knew a lot of dancers had emerged. That there might be a student who could step up to the plate."

TRISTA YAWNED WHILE LYING ON HER BED AND GROGGILY answered her cell phone. She jetted up once Felicia informed her of the request for a dancer. She wasn't familiar with Dre Dyson or his single, but she was elated to try out for the video. It was an honor to be considered and she thanked Felicia repetitiously. She figured she was much older than the typical video dancer; probably at least by a dozen years. However, she was in tiptop condition and felt she could rival the best contenders. A surreal feeling overcame her and she immediately started fishing through her wardrobe for an outfit for that night. Her signature jeans and T-shirt would suffice for an audition. Instead of heels, she'd wear tennis shoes so she could be at her best performance.

Seven p.m. wouldn't arrive soon enough. She'd be a half-hour early. If nothing else, she had learned from Next Phase of Life that punctuality was a must for interviews, let alone an audition like this one.

Wingin' it

A jittery Trista entered the spacious auditorium at Duke Ellington School of the Arts in Georgetown. All eyes zoomed in on her as she slowly strolled to the front area, just below the stage, where everyone was congregated. She attempted to exude confidence as she felt like an outsider who had interrupted a secret powwow. Soon her fears ended when a woman approached her.

"Hi, you must be Trista." Dressed in a white top, tie-dyed bohemian skirt, the woman wearing locs offered a kind spirit. "I'm Jovani, the producer. Thank you for coming to help us out."

"I hope I can," Trista gushed, trying to show assurance and convincing herself in her mind that she was more than capable.

"I'm sure you can." Jovani motioned for her to sit in one of the theater chairs in the third row. "We're getting set up now. Thanks for being early."

"No problem." Trista slunk in her seat, then realized that was bad posture and would show lack of confidence. She straightened up like a pen. I still can't believe I'm here to perform with a hip-hop artist. After Felicia's call, Trista had Googled Dre Dyson to gain some bio knowledge of her soon-to-be cohort. She'd discovered that he was an up-and-coming artist and his first single had been a hit. She envisioned that if she could get in on the ground running, with this second single, perhaps this moment would propel her to reach new heights.

After her humbling experience with Tai—their sisterly bond; her acceptance of her past; simply her outpouring of love and support—she considered that her lifestyle couldn't be surpassed.

The no-nonsense choreographer, Darnell, briefly requested Trista and the two male dancers do warm-ups. He then asked Trista to observe the routine from the sidestage as "Kapital Krush" blared from the house speakers. Trista also had familiarized herself with the tune on the Internet. She didn't want to appear in the cold without any sense of the artist or his music. Darnell had instructed he would provide her with a video of a rehearsal featuring Skylar, the injured dancer. She could have the night and following day to study the solo moves. Meanwhile, she could learn and practice the group routines while in-house.

Trista noticed a youthful man standing along the side of the stage opposite her. He was wearing jeans and a short-sleeved shirt revealing cut arms and a large tattoo on his right arm. *That must be Dre Dyson*, she thought. *Looking so good I wanna slap my face. Focus, girl, focus.* She drew her attention back to the two male dancers. *They are fine, too. Well, at least I'll be surrounded by these killer-looking brothas. That's more than enough reason to make sure I get these moves right. I may get some staying power, plus have some eye candy. I think Candace has rubbed off on me. Maybe for the better*, she amused.

HOURS PASSED AND TRISTA'S STAMINA WAS BEING TESTED. IF THE gig worked out, she would need to make the gym her best friend. Drenched with sweat, she took a break to swig a full bottle of water. Trista had picked up the group routine with ease. Now she would need to review the rehearsal video to grasp the solo routine. She had planned to spend her entire day off tomorrow working on the full choreographed set.

Darnell called Dre Dyson and the dancers back to the stage for a final round, then called it a night. Trista was surrounded by accolades about her speed and capability. She clinched the spot and was asked to return the next evening for rehearsal. The crew offered a limo ride home as they were unsure about Trista on a solo subway trip. She insisted they could simply drop her at the station, but they refused to leave her alone. Trista was thrilled during her first limo experience, and even more thrilled that she was wedged between such hunks. The testosterone and man scent permeated the stretch. Their manager, Jovani, sat on the end, scrolling through her BlackBerry.

Trista awoke Tai from a deep sleep to alert her of her good fortune: she was officially a part of Dre Dyson's backup dancers. Tai sat up in bed and clicked on the light on her end table.

"That's great news. I knew you could do it." She groped for the TV remote and clicked on the "off" button. She encouraged Trista to sit on the edge of her bed.

"Oh, no thanks. I'm whipped. I danced my ass off tonight. You would've been proud. I made Mom and Dad proud."

Tai thought it was interesting for Trista to bring up their names; as if she were looking for approval from them, well beyond her childhood or teen years.

"So, you film on Friday, right? Maybe I can take off the afternoon and check it out." She reached over and picked up her iPhone to view her stored calendar. "Yep, it's looking good—no meetings or appointments."

"That would be great. I'd love to have you there."

"And I'm not going to miss it, either."

Trista walked toward Tai, reached over and hugged her. "Thank you, Sis, for all you've done. I can't thank you enough."

"What'd I tell you about over-thanking me? That's what I'm here for. If I can help other folks, I can certainly help my own blood. I'm glad it worked out."

"Bet." Trista turned to walk out of the bedroom. "Well, have a good night. I've gotta crash."

"Thanks. You, too."

THE WEATHER PROVED IDEAL FOR AN OUTDOOR VIDEO SHOOT. DRE Dyson rocked the mike and displayed a highly charged performance on the Mall. The Reflecting Pool leading to the Washington Monument on one end; and the Capitol on the opposite end offered a little nostalgia. Once the clips of various historical events were infused, the video would showcase textbook moments. The three backup dancers showed precision and finesse as they moved to the lyrics of "Kapital Krush."

Tai stood on the sidelines and observed her talented sister who had handled the dance assignment with assurance. *Dancing paid off at a level she never expected. That one call to the office will be the change of her life, the next phase of life, now at a crossroads.* Tai visualized that Trista would soon shed her Cinderella image and blossom into a picture of confidence. She'd already seen a transition starting to take shape. For the first time since she'd arrived in D.C., Trista glowed like a full moon on a brightly lit night. Tai marveled at how her little sister had captured the video routine that would be viewed throughout the world.

THE SHOOT WAS A SUCCESS AND TRISTA WAS ECSTATIC THAT SHE had connected with Dre Dyson and his crew. He was so enthused about her capability that he'd had invited her to join him on tour, kicking off in L.A. in a few months. She had graciously accepted with enthusiasm. It was still hard to shake the whirlwind truth. Trista had introduced him to Tai and he commended the new asset to his entourage; making Tai feel that she had helped groom her younger sister into a prime candidate. She couldn't take any credit for her dancing skills; however, she had opened doors to a new-found lifestyle.

In only a few days, perhaps Trista had finally discovered her true niche. And she didn't want to fade out of the limelight. She considered it a miracle when duty called and she was able to ace the opportunity. Miss Cynth's philosophy was likely becoming a reality; she would soon kiss the waitress gig a fond farewell.

Men and a meeting of the minds

Candace bubbled with excitement: for her fortieth birthday, she had been blessed with the ultimate gift. She and Don had become joined at the hip. She had turned in her playette card for monogamy. Of course, it didn't mean that she'd wear blinders. Her antennae for eye candy would be a permanent fixture; she would simply look but not seek. It was such an intrinsic part of her flirtatious nature.

Candace walked into Desiree where her friends awaited her usual late arrival. They were halfway into their meals.

"Hey, ladies. Sorry I'm late." A huge grin was plastered on her face as she grabbed a chair.

"Been shopping?" Nevada raised her eyebrows and looked at Candace's tote bag.

"Do you have to ask? Every time I'm downtown, I can't help myself. Just picking up a few bargains." Candace smiled. "It's great to see you, Trista. I hear you're doing some fantastic things." It was Trista's first time joining the ladies' luncheon powwow.

"Thanks. Good seeing you, too."

Trista had turned over a milestone. Her world of menus and meals had transformed into one of music and moves. Miss Cynth had congratulated her and both women vowed to stay in touch. Trista would miss her as she had been more of a mother figure than a co-worker.

"She was just sharing with us about her new gig," Nevada said.

"Congratulations! I'm sure you are having a blast," Candace stated proudly.

"Lovin' it. I've been out to L.A. twice now. Dre treats me like royalty. Limos. Palm trees. Venice Beach. Sunset. Hollywood. I can't get enough and can't wait to go back." Trista was still in a surreal state, despite the reality.

"True. I'll have to get out there again soon." Tai reminisced about her grad school days and subsequent marketing job in California. She was truly an East Coast chick, but never let the West Coast experiences die. "Maybe next time you fly out, I'll join you. It'd be great to see my friends from the old days."

"Except for Vince; I know you don't want to run in to him," Candace teased, reminding Tai of how she'd skipped out on him for a love tryst in St. Maarten.

Tai laughed. "Please don't mention my bad-girl island adventure."

"What happened?" Trista had a quizzical look. "You holding out on me, huh?"

"Sis, I'll tell you about it one of these days." Tai had bonded with Trista and didn't mind pulling any of her skeletons from the closet.

"Okay, I'm gonna hold you to that." Trista had a newfound confidence that was etched on her face; an easel portraying her attitude, body language and even her attire. She had expanded her wardrobe beyond the jeans look.

"We're getting ready for our twelve-city tour," she continued. "I never dreamed I'd ever be a part of something like this."

"Guess it doesn't compare to the restaurant biz," Candace interjected.

"No, I get to dance and travel; who wouldn't want that? I keep in shape with all the rehearsals. I'm meeting a lot of interesting people."

"Plus, you starred in one video here and now you're going to be onstage and tour the country." Tai beamed proudly.

"What are the cities?" Candace inquired.

Trista contemplated the list. "I don't remember them all but Oakland, Chicago, Atlanta, Detroit, Philly, New York, Raleigh and of course, D.C."

"That is exciting. I love to jet-set around the country, too."

"And the world," Nevada added.

"How was Paris?" Trista had missed Candace's rave reviews upon her return. "It was right up your alley, I'm sure, with the fashions."

"Fabulous, simply fabulous. That was sweet of him to take me as a belated birthday gift." Candace glowed with enthusiasm.

"Honey, let me tell you, Don and I are christening each city." Candace leaned in to whisper. "We are breaking beds in every hotel." She laughed. "Just kidding, but we're making sure we leave a love trail everywhere we go."

The two had ventured from the French Quarter in New Orleans to the Colorado Rockies. Joined at the hip, they were truly a vision of companionship. Their personalities had synched along with their bodies. Don had managed to captivate Candace's attention solely. Tai and Nevada never thought a man would be capable of such a feat, tying down the Queen of the Manhunt.

"Guess the next stop," Candace suggested. "One of those places you always hear about, but never know anyone personally going there."

"Where?" Tai asked.

"He's taking me to *Tahiti*..."

"Girl, all these exotic places. I'm envious." Nevada poked her mouth out like a spoiled toddler.

"Wow, that is different. The name alone sounds romantic." Tai imagined a tropical oasis. Maybe she would add the location to her bucket list.

"Hey, take me in your suitcase," Nevada teased, then looked at Trista nosily. "We hear you have some other news…besides the tour."

Trista blushed. "Say what?"

"You've got a love interest?"

Trista looked at Tai. "You—"

"Of course, I told Nevada," Tai admitted. "I hadn't caught up long enough for Candace. This is how we do; we share the good stuff."

"Well, I'm seeing one of the dancers now. They call him Kwik."

"Interesting name…I'm sure he's quick on other moves, too." Candace smiled.

"You could say that," Trista responded shyly. "I felt his vibe the first time I saw him at the video rehearsal here. He and I tried to play it off. Then I think Kwik picked up on the chemistry. After I went to L.A. the first time, it was a done deal.

"Hmmm, that tight body of his. When we'd gotten hot and sweaty during rehearsal, he pulled off his shirt. That's when I fell in love." Trista laughed. "With his body. No, he's good people, too." Her candid conversation confirmed that she had slowly emerged from her shell.

"Reminds me of my girl here." Nevada eyed Tai. "She fell in love with Marco when he took off his shirt in that blistering sun in her backyard. Must be something 'bout you sisters and those chests that make men irresistible."

Tai agreed. "You couldn't have said it better. Mmm-hmm."

"Trista, you deserve it. So, tell me more." Candace expressed her usual inquisitiveness; especially when it came to men.

"Well, Kwik's real name is Darren; he's from Philly. Years ago, he won some type of citywide competition for hip-hop dance. Let's see, he's been with Dre Dyson since the beginning, which has only been a year. What can I say; he's a good dude. And what I like most is he keeps it real."

"Sounds like a winner." Candace added with raised eyebrows, "And I'm sure he knows how to handle his biz."

"Oh, you mean the dickster?" she responded for shock value. "Oh, yeah, he's on point in that department." *Especially since I've been celibate for all these damn months. A sistah was needing some lovin', but the wait allowed me to tune into myself for a change. Gave me some me time.*

"I know that's right." Candace turned to Tai.

"And, like Sis, he's a young'un. Like eight years younger."

"Ooo-wee, you Wilson sisters are working the younger men, ain't ya?" Candace teased and looked at Tai. "And how's Marco?"

"Oh, he's fine. Body and soul. And you *know* this." Tai was obsessed with the love of her life. "Things are going well with his business, too. He picked up more clients. He has to really compete with the larger landscaping firms, though." Tai looked at her watch. "Actually, I'll be going to his place tonight. Another one of his romantic invitations for a dinner date. Girl, he's making it so special that he sent me an invite in the mail. Can you believe?"

"Now, that sounds like my kinda man." Candace relished the idea.

"I guess I'm next so I might as well tell you before you ask." Nevada had to offer her own update in the relationship arena. "I had given it some thought about splitting with Ryan; maybe I was simply complacent and in my comfort zone. But, hey, I seriously realized that I do care for him. We'll probably never get married. He's not into it, or up to it, so with no kids on the horizon, I figured I may as well stay. Sometimes a longtime relationship is meant to be just that, a relationship."

"I understand," Tai stated. "Felicia always says she has so many friends whose relationships might have worked out and not have ended in divorce, if they had only remained as friends; and not have married. I think there's some truth in that. Some men decide to get brand-new once you're wearing that ring. And I must say, it's not always the men, either. Women can start tripping, too. Dating can go smooth and then when it comes to the piece of paper, things can go downhill from there."

"I'm surprised at you, talking like this. You, the one who's always appreciated the sanctity of marriage," Nevada countered.

"Oh, don't get me wrong. I still do. I'm only saying that marriage isn't for everyone," Tai advised. "In these days and times with the digital age, you can best believe you'd better keep on the up and up. Cell phones, email, texting, social networking sites; they can all ruin your relationship, if you're not careful. So, you need to make sure it's tight before you tie the knot. And if you're not, please be sure there are many ways to track a cheating spouse."

"Amen to that...and that's one thing that helps keep me in business," Nevada added. "Cheating spouses."

"And I say if the shoe doesn't fit, don't force it," Candace added.

"Well, after what happened with Austin, I don't take it for granted anymore. We had a solid relationship for five years and it simply fell by the wayside. I believe he got cold feet." Tai shrugged her shoulders.

Don't know why she's even bringing up that bastard's name, Candace thought.

At the time, I should have trailed him to see what he what he was up to, Nevada reflected. *But I figured what I didn't know wouldn't hurt me. It could have hurt my girl and that would have been a no-no.*

"It's like magic with Marco and me," Tai continued, "but I learned not to have high expectations. So…I have *no* expectations. I go with the flow. Our favorite expression."

Candace chirped in, "I hear ya."

"I used to work for this older guy who always told me to simply get yourself together, make yourself the best you can be in all aspects," Tai recalled. "Then when the time was right, a man would come along, so don't be searching. He said, don't focus on finding anyone, a Mister Right; work on yourself.

"I see he gave me good advice. I wasn't hardly looking at Marco in any way but business."

The waitress approached with their bill in hand. "Dessert anyone?"

"No, thanks. I'm too—" Nevada felt weighted down like an over-stuffed potato. She also was on her perpetual diet.

"No she's not," Tai interrupted in a forceful tone, then responded to the waitress.

"We'll have bread pudding for all." She leaned in and looked at Nevada, Candace and Trista as if she were sharing a secret. "We have to indulge sometimes, ladies."

42

Special delivery

The light rain splattered on the living room window, offering a soothing melody with the rhythm of lightning and thunder. The early summertime orchestra was noisy but yet peaceful. Nevada and Ryan were set to relax throughout the day and watch DVDs. Nevada was craving pizza and would throw her diet out the window once again. Her willpower was running on empty. They snuggled on the sofa during the lazy afternoon and *Shawshank Redemption* had captivated their attention for at least the eighth time. Their collection was filled with crime dramas and thrillers and this was one of their favorites.

They had dozed off lightly—not due to boredom; they practically knew the script and the scenes by memory. The doorbell rang and startled them. Nevada jumped up abruptly. *Who in the world?* They rarely had outside guests and, except for a few neighbors on their floor occasionally stopping in, they kept a low profile.

Ryan stirred and looked toward the door as Nevada walked to open it.

"Hello, Ms. Washington." It was their postal worker.

Whew. No company. I can go back to my snooze, then keep with my pizza plan, Nevada thought.

"Hi, Carol." The carrier handed her a certified letter and a pen to sign the return receipt. "That was some storm." Nevada signed the form and handed it to Carol.

"Thanks. Yep, and I'd love to be where you are now. It won't be long; just a couple more hours. Well, enjoy the rest of your Saturday."

"You, too, and be safe."

Nevada reviewed the large brown envelope as she strolled back to the sofa and sat beside Ryan. The return address was a P.O. box in D.C. She tore open the envelope and inside was another smaller envelope.

"Special delivery, huh?"

"Yeah, let's see what this is." Nevada ripped open the letter. Her eyes popped and mouth dropped like she'd had a frightful encounter. "Oh, my…"

"Wow," Ryan said, looking at her letter. "Say what?"

The mystery mail, delivered in an envelope within another envelope, was a check made payable to *Nevada Washington* for $50,000.

"It's my check for the *America's Most Wanted* capture of the twins. I'm speechless."

"Baby, you deserve it; you do great police work."

"Thank you. This was a pleasant surprise. I had no idea if it was coming or when it was coming." Nevada hugged Ryan. "You know what; let's forget about that pizza. We need to step up our game tonight. Someplace we've never been." Her mind raced to drum up a restaurant with a cozy and intimate ambience. "We've gotta celebrate."

"But not before we celebrate at home." Ryan pulled her closer for a passionate kiss.

43

The love connection

"Those were the best crab cakes. You did your thing. I may have to close my kitchen and have you open yours," Tai teased. It was Marco's second major dinner that he'd prepared for the love of his life.

"Thanks, glad you liked them. But no, I don't think you'd better close it yet. I'm still getting the hang of this cooking thing." Marco was a well-known patron of Silver Spring's restaurant row; the wait staff members knew him by first name.

After their meal that Tai compared to any upscale seafood restaurant, the two made their way upstairs in his home. When they reached the landing, Tai followed a trail of roses—red, white, pink, yellow and orange; each symbolically represented a specific emotion. She was impressed that he had methodically placed the flowers for the special occasion. The floral path led to the Jacuzzi tub where Tai and Marco undressed and tossed their clothes to the floor.

Marco ran a warm and soothing bath that oozed of orange and vanilla oils to create an aphrodisiac. Mini candles surrounded the ledge of the tub and provided sensual lighting effects for their romantic rubdown. They glided slowly into the water. They sponged each other with loofahs, then pampered each other with back and foot massages. They playfully kissed and licked each other like candy; her chocolate mounds and his lollypop. Tai and

Marco became fervently enticed and cut their playtime short. They rose up slowly, lips and bodies locked. Marco reached for the towels and handed one to Tai. They both stepped out of the tub simultaneously and dried each other off, then fluidly sauntered out of the bathroom and into the bedroom. Marco's king-sized bed awaited.

Marco gently laid Tai on her back onto the bed. He kissed her passionately as he deftly placed on a condom while not losing eye or lip contact. Marco entered her with ease and their rhythm became one. Tai locked her legs around his back as his thrusts became powerful. She matched his momentum, focusing on the melding of their heated bodies. As Marco increased his pace, Tai swelled and wanted to hold back so they could release in harmony. Suddenly, Marco reached his peak fervently and Tai bit her lip so not to scream with ecstasy. Marco collapsed seductively atop her and then rolled over to be by her side.

"Baby, I love you," he panted raspily.

"I love you, too." Tai smiled and pecked his lips.

TAI HUMMED WHILE SHE WAS IN THE BATHROOM WHERE SHE freshened up. She slipped into her latest Vickies purchase and posed in the mirror. They'd already had their dessert; maybe it was time for icing on the cake. Even if it was time to simply sleep, Tai ensured she never went to bed without a sensual image. This was how she wanted her man to see her at night and how she wanted him to see her in the morning: like a sex goddess. She sprayed on a dash of Taj Sunset.

She opened the door and seductively strolled into the bedroom. Marco patiently awaited her return as he lay on the bed, bare-chested and in his boxers. He had lit a lavender candle to create a relaxing aroma.

"You are a fox, babe. You are so sexy. What you trying to do to me? Make me go for another one?" Marco asked smoothly.

"No," she teased. "Unless you want to…"

Tai joined him on top of the bed and relaxed her back on the pillow. "Thank you for such a wonderful evening."

"No problem. Likewise." Marco arose and walked toward his dresser. He turned around and walked back to the side of the bed where Tai was stretched. She had thought about their first anniversary approaching in two weeks. She would reciprocate and prepare a special meal for Marco. He reached for her and pulled her forward to place her legs over the side of the bed. He bent on his right knee and gently moved her left hand toward him. Inside his left palm, he revealed a diamond solitaire and placed it on her finger.

"Will you marry me, *Miss* Tai Wilson?" He gazed at her with hope and admiration in his eyes that penetrated her soul.

Tai bubbled over with joy. "Yes, Mr. Marco Moore. I will marry you."

Marco beamed, rose up and planted a powerful kiss as he rolled her onto her back.

44
Island magic

Eight months later

The tropical sun glistened on their pool-drenched bodies. The trio—Tai, Candace, and Nevada—along with Trista and Sierra, now honorary members of the ladies club, chilled on chaise lounges and sipped on Yellow Bird cocktails. Their home for the weekend was the luxurious Atlantis hotel in Paradise Island, compliments of Nevada.

Her reward check had funded the quintessential bachelorette event for Tai, who for years had offered the comforts of her home for their ladies nights. Now Nevada showed her appreciation of their camaraderie by treating all to the gorgeous Bahamas destination. She was a ride-or-die chick and would forever be indebted to her girls for their friendship. Despite their island spree, Nevada had generously given Ryan $10,000 to splurge on his own desires. He'd shown dedication and support throughout the years.

THE PRESIDENTIAL SUITE WAS DECORATED WITH AN ARRAY OF tropical colors to create a Caribbean ambience. The ladies had eaten in the dining room area and had savored a dinner of red snapper, conch fritters, peas and rice, and Johnny cakes. Nevada had hired a cook to prepare the Bahamian menu in the suite's kitchen.

After dinner, they congregated in the living room area. Nevada prepared glasses of champagne to toast to Tai, who radiated with excitement. Of all the club members, she was the one who had been determined to meet "Mr. Right," if such a person existed. To her, Marco was a Prince Charming who had brought her fantasy to fruition. They would all wish her a lifetime of happiness—and definitely future ladies nights.

Each woman picked up a glass of champagne for Candace to present a toast.

"I'll keep this short and sweet. Cheers, ladies, to Tai and Marco! They deserve the best! Lots of happiness and great sex!" The group burst into laughter and clinked their glasses. "Cheers" was said multiple times.

Suddenly, the doorbell rang to the suite. Nevada feigned surprise and walked to the door and opened it. A man slipped something into her hand, then walked toward the living room.

"Hello, Bahama Mamas." A chocolate hunk with a deep voice entered as he carried a tray of cocktails in fancy glasses. He placed the treats on the coffee table. "Brought you some delights," he announced in a heavy accent. All thanked him.

While the women picked up their Bahama Mama drinks, Nevada moved across the room, placed a CD in the stereo system and turned it on. Wreckx-N-Effect's "Rump Shaker" blasted through the speakers. The women looked at each other in amazement, then at Nevada, who beamed about her smoothly planned surprise.

They would be delighted all right, with their own private show. After settling into seats, the room soon filled with shrills and screams as Rump Shaker, who used the same stage name as his theme song, stripped from his colorful palm-tree-patterned shirt and his jeans. His G-string revealed a rump that was the finest they could ever imagine. His bulging thighs and body-builder chest glistened with oil. All eyes zeroed in on the entertainer.

Tai displayed a wide, permanent smile as he scooped her up and thrust her on top of his thighs. It was only the beginning of a long and lustful evening in paradise.

ABOUT THE AUTHOR

Charmaine R. Parker started writing fiction during early childhood. It included poetry, skits and short stories. She has a bachelor's of fine arts in theater from Howard University and a master's in print journalism from the University of Southern California. Born in North Carolina, she was raised in Washington, D.C. She is a former journalist who worked as a reporter, copy editor, production editor and managing editor. You may email the author at charmainerparker@gmail.com. Visit the author at www.facebook.com/charmainerobertsparker.

AUTHOR'S NOTE

I have finally completed my debut novel after years of contemplating writing one. I started writing fiction as a child (my mom tells me it was in kindergarten; I remember poems I wrote at age seven.) In addition to poems (based on my travels), I wrote skits (one was performed during elementary class) and short stories. I recall having a vivid imagination and creating characters and storylines.

My parents were both educators; my father was a university professor and my mother was an elementary schoolteacher. They stressed to my three siblings and me the importance of a good education. We traveled frequently throughout the United States from coast to coast. These experiences were rewarding as a young child and greatly influenced our thoughts. They opened our eyes to the world. My parents also ensured that we read books, enrolled us in children's book clubs and maintained a vast home library. Mysteries were my favorite.

During my high school years, I explored drama and appeared in several plays. I envisioned acting was my forte and while enrolled at Howard University, I performed in various musicals (loved the dancing routines). During this time, I also created a play.

After relocating to California one summer after visiting for the season, I decided to enroll in graduate school at the University of Southern California. I majored in print journalism and received my master's degree. Previously I had taken graduate journalism courses at American University in Washington, D.C. prior to my move to the West Coast. It seemed that journalism would be at the center of my journey. Once I returned to D.C., I worked in the newspaper industry. As a metropolitan reporter, it was a challenging experience as I worked the police beat, courts and education beats, and general assignment. Later I moved on to copy editing and for years worked on the sports and features desks. I worked extensively as a copy editor, layout editor and production editor. The industry offered the opportunity to be involved in the entertainment world. I met and interviewed Vanessa Williams (my first celebrity interview); Marla Gibbs, Philip Michael Thomas, After 7, Oleta Adams, Angela Winbush, Vesta, Dru Hill, Blackstreet and Tony! Toni! Toné! among others. Phone interviews included Babyface, Janet Jackson, Al Jarreau and Deion Sanders. From a Q&A with Rev. Martin Luther King, Sr. to the local community activist to the entrepreneur, I connected with interesting personalities and through my writing, I showcased their lives.

Writing is in our family and I inherited the creativity as both of my parents are writers. My youngest sister, Zane, the national *New York Times* bestselling author, also started writing as a child. I always thought she would end up writing mysteries. In 1997 during a holiday party in Charlotte, N.C. (she was then living in N.C.) she shared with my other sister, Carlita, and me that she had started writing erotic stories and selling them on the Internet. With a grass-roots beginning and an underground following, it was a brief time before she became extremely popular writing under the pen name, Zane. After relocating back to the D.C. area, she self-published her first book, an anthology of short erotica stories. Her growing fan base encouraged her to compile her short stories into a book. Her two novels followed. She had delivered *Addicted* to me to edit (I still have the manuscript on paper.) It reached No. 1 on the *Essence* magazine list and remained there for several years. She later self-published her second novel, *Shame on It All*, which is dedicated to Carlita and me. I will never forget seeing an *Essence* issue where her first three books were in the top five on the list. I knew then that my sister had truly risen to success as this unknown identity. Now more than twenty-five novels, anthologies and a nonfiction book later, she has found her niche in the publishing world as an author and a publisher.

I joined her in the publishing business in 2001 shortly after she launched Strebor Books, which was formed to publish her own titles. The company grew steadily and we became an imprint of Atria Books/Simon & Schuster in 2005. Zane started publishing other authors and opened doors for many writers whose works had been constantly rejected.

It has been an amazing journey and sometimes things come full circle. I started out with an interest in creative writing, switched to journalism and nonfiction, and now I'm back to writing fiction.

As publishing director I oversee all aspects of producing a book from the manuscript submission to editing to its printing. I also assist in reviewing submissions and acquiring titles. It's been a decade of nonstop editing and producing books for other authors. I'd been encouraged by my family for years to write my own book. "You're always working on someone else's book," they'd say. They were right. I finally took the step and put the project in motion. Now my debut novel has come to fruition.

After growing up as an avid reader and appreciating literature, I compiled a large book collection. It has been incredible to see the expansion of African-American titles. Besides my own children's book collection, I recall the only books I discovered during my teen years were ones that I happened upon in my dad's library; classics to urban literature. The boom in African-American literature has encouraged our youth to value literacy.

My debut novel, *The Next Phase of Life*, was a labor of love (the late-night hours became my best friend.) Like the characters featured in the book, I am blessed to have a true circle of tight friendships. The novel evolves around women who share this type of bond and celebrate life; it is crucial. Women's lives are often stressed with multiple roles of wife or significant other, mother and career woman. The journey can be challenging and rewarding. We also need to take "me" time. Treasure your life, and be prepared for the next phase.

In the novel, I also show sisters who are opposite in their lifestyles but connect despite their differences. Sisterhood is to be celebrated; among both friends and siblings.

Keep moving forward and keep your thoughts positive.

And remember that "forty" can be viewed as the new "twenty."

I hope that you enjoyed this novel as much as I did creating it.

Peace,

Charmaine R. Parker
April 2011

READER DISCUSSION GUIDE

1. Does Tai reflect the views of many women when it comes to their interest in a loving and longtime relationship? What are the challenges and possible solutions?

2. Do you have close friends whom you consider confidantes? Tai did not tell her friends about Trista's past. Would you have shared?

3. If you discovered a long-lost sibling, would you accept him or her into your home as immediately as Tai accepted Trista?

4. What types of activities do you share with friends to release stress and have fun?

5. Do you feel that once you turn age forty, that you are considered "middle age?"

6. If you are forty or older, do you feel that forty is the new twenty; or that it is time for you to "slow down?" Do you embrace your age? Why or why not? Do you feel that you have experienced everything that you would like to, or is there more to explore?

7. Would you consider dating a man ten years younger or more? Would you consider dating a man who has a different career background, or an income level lower than yours? Why or why not?

8. When Tai discovered Trista's past after her visit to North Carolina, do you agree she should have informed Trista or kept her knowledge secret?

9. What are the messages portrayed in the book?

10. Which character do you relate to the most and why?

11. Do you think Tai was right not to tell Marco about her "gym nights" with Hasan after she ended the private trysts? Would you have admitted cheating?

12. Trista and Tai have contrasting lifestyles. Can you relate or do you know of siblings with a similar relationship?

13. Did Candace seem too desperate to get a man or do you think she was simply living life to its fullest? Have you ever thrown caution to the wind when it comes to your dating practices?

14. Why do you think that Trista had a mental breakdown? Was it because of a failed relationship or because of being separated from her sister, who was chosen over her by their grandmother?

15. Do you think it is okay to start dating someone that you deal with professionally? Was Tai in the wrong for flirting with, and later dating, her landscaper?

16. Do you believe that most people discover their true calling later on in life, like Trista did with her dancing? Do you think that Trista was too old to be in music videos?

Curtis Bunn and I both grew up in Washington, D.C. We eventually teamed up when we both worked in the sports department of *The Washington Times*. I was a copy editor and he was a phenomenal writer. He later wrote *Baggage Check*, which became No. 1 on the *Essence* bestseller list. Zane personally suggested I read it, not realizing that the author and I were former co-workers. I truly enjoyed his debut novel.

Now Curtis Bunn has joined the Strebor Books team with his novel, *A Cold Piece of Work*, which also was released in the same month as *The Next Phase of Life*.

Curtis Bunn is the founder of the annual National Book Club Conference in Atlanta.

Following is an excerpt from *A Cold Piece of Work*, a virtual tour inside the mind, heart and soul of a man whose troubling experiences with women turn him cold, ruthless and afraid of commitment. I'm sure you will enjoy it.

—C.R.P.

A
COLD
PIECE
OF
WORK

A NOVEL

CURTIS BUNN

Available from Strebor Books

CHAPTER 1
LOVE TO
LOVE YOU

The force of his thrusts pushed her to the edge of the four-poster bed. She was lathered as much in satisfaction as she was in sweat, exhilarated and weary—and unable to hold herself atop the mattress against his unrelenting strikes. A different kind of man would have postponed the passion; at least long enough to pull up her naked, vulnerable body.

But Solomon Singletary was hardly one to subscribe to conventional thinking or deeds. He always had a point to prove and always was committed to proving it—with actions, not words.

And so, Solomon thrust on…and on, until they, as one, careened onto the carpet together, she cushioning his fall from beneath him. So paralyzed in pleasure was she that she never felt the impact of the tumble. Rather, she found humor that they made love clean across the bed and onto the floor, and she found delight that the fall did not disengage them.

Solomon lost neither his connection to her nor his cadence, and stroked her on the carpet just as he had on the sheets—purposefully, unrelentingly, deeply.

"What are you trying to do?" she asked. "Make love to me? Or make me love you?"

Solomon did not answer—not with words. He continued to speak the language of passion, rotating his hips forward, as one would a hula-hoop. Her shapely, chocolate legs were airborne and his knees were carpet-burned raw, but hardly did he temper his pace.

His answer: Both.

She finally spoke the words that slowed Solomon. "Okay, okay," she said. "Okay." She gave in, and that pleased Solomon. She would have said the words earlier—before they tumbled off the bed—but he never allowed her to catch her breath. All she could make were indecipherable sounds.

"I mean, damn," she said, panting. "We're good together… Damn."

Solomon kissed her on her left shoulder and rolled off her and onto the floor, on his wide, strong back. He looked up toward the dark ceiling illuminated by the single candle on the night-stand, so pleased with himself that a smile formed on his face.

Then he dozed off right there on the floor. She didn't bother to wake him. Instead, she reached up and pulled the comforter off the bed and over both of them. She nestled her head on his hairy chest, smiled to herself and drifted off to sleep with him, right there on the floor.

That was the last time she saw Solomon Singletary. And he only saw her a few times, but only in dreams that did not make much sense.

"I wish I knew what the hell it meant," he said to his closest friend, Raymond. He and Ray became tight five years earlier, when they got paired together during a round of golf at Mystery Valley in Lithonia, just east of Atlanta. They had a good time, exchanged numbers and ended up becoming not only golf buddies, but also great friends.

Ray was very much the opposite of Solomon. He was not as tall but just as handsome, and he was charismatic and likeable, in a different way. Solomon was sort of regal to some, arrogant to others. Ray was more every man. He had a wife of seven years, Cynthia, and a six-year-old son, Ray-Ray. He was stable.

Solomon knew a lot of people, but only liked some and trusted only a few. He really only tolerated most; especially the various women who ran in and out of his life like some nagging virus. "In the end," he told Ray, "the one person you can trust is yourself. And even with that, how many times have you lied to yourself?"

Ray figured there was something deep inside Solomon that would bring him to such feelings, and he figured if Solomon wanted him to know, he would have told him. So he never asked. Ray and Solomon coveted each other's friendship and had a certain trust. And they shared most everything with each other.

Ray's way was to provide levity when possible, which, for him, was practically all the time. His upbeat disposition seldom changed. If the Falcons lost a football game, he'd show disgust and disappointment for a while, but he'd let it go.

Solomon Singletary was not that way. He could be solemn at times, even-tempered at others and occasionally aggressive. Above all, he was quite adept at pulling people close to him. He had a unique ability to be open but remain private. He could be disinterested but still engaging. And those unique qualities made people open up to him; especially women.

"You're so interesting," Michele told him that last night together. "We've dated for six months. You try to act like you don't love me, but you do; I can tell by how we make love. Why won't you say you love me?"

"Come here." Michele came over to him, to the edge of her bed. "Don't get caught up on what I say to you or don't say," he said. "Worry about what I do to you; how I make you feel."

"Is everything about sex with you?"

"See, I wasn't even talking about sex. I was talking about how you feel inside, when we're together, when you think of me," Solomon said. "That's more important than what I say. Right?"

Before she could answer, he leaned over and kissed her on the lips softly and lovingly. "What does that kiss say?"

"It says you want to make love," Michele said sarcastically. "Some things can get lost in translation. That's why you should say it. Plus, sometimes it's just good to hear."

"Hear this." Solomon kissed Michele again. This time, it was not a peck, but a sustained coming together of lips and tongue and saliva. He leaned her back on the bed, and she watched as he pulled his tank top over his head, revealing his expansive chest and broad shoulders.

He smiled at her and she smiled back and the talk of saying "I love you" ceased.

"Whatever happened to that girl?" Ray asked Solomon. "You regret not having her now?"

"Regret? What's that? You make a decision and you stick to it. No looking back. But a few years ago, I saw a woman briefly who reminded me of her, and it made me think about calling her."

"You thought about it? Why didn't you call her?" Ray wanted to know.

"Hard to say. Young, dumb. Silly," Solomon answered. "What would've been the point? I got a job here with Coke and wasn't about to do the long distance thing. So what was the point?"

"Well, did you at least breakup on good terms?" Ray asked.

"The last time I saw her, she was on the floor next to her bed, sleeping. I got up and put on my clothes and left. The next day, the movers came and I drove here, to Atlanta."

"Wait," Ray said, standing up. "She didn't know you were moving out of town?"

"Nah," Solomon said, looking off. "Nah."

"How can you just roll out on the girl like that?"